The FARIS Affair

Gillian Jones

Berberis Books

Berberis Books
ISBN 0-9543768-2-X

Berberis Books brings you excitement and suspense
with an ecological edge

www.gillianjones.net

Cover design by Ben Gilchrist
Photo: Shutterstock, copyright *esinel*
Author photo: Ruth Pearman

For Hugh and Nick

CONTENTS

PROLOGUE

I - Palm Gardens

It's the middle of the day and along the white path leading to the palm gardens the air is vibrating in the heat. White heat ricochets off the rocks, off the mountainside and off the ochre walls of the mud-built washing chamber where women have long since finished the daily wash and the clothes, laid out to dry in the sun, have been folded and taken away. The water, as it flows from the washing chamber along the channel towards its next appointment downstream, is scalding hot from the unremitting heat of the sun. It is on its way to the palm gardens where the trees, drooping dustily in the heat, are thirsting for their turn in the regulated cycle, a timetable of hours, days and weeks, when they receive their own life-sustaining ration of water.

The heat and the air tremble and the stifling sawing of the cicadas is silent. Nothing moves until, almost invisible in a corner of deep shade, the Arif gets to his feet. He spits, adjusts his robe and his round cap, and squints first towards the sun and then to the stick which stands vertical, at the height of a goat, stuck in the ground next to the channel of water at the point where the white, beaten path forks. After examining the stick and, more particularly, the shadow that it casts, he glances at his watch and, apparently satisfied on both accounts, makes his way down the track that borders the water and leads to the palm gardens. In his walk he disturbs some small green frogs from the side of the runnel; they leap out of his way and into the water with a refreshing plop. He pays no attention. He is the Arif, in charge of the sharing of the water in the village's falaj system and he takes no notice of small frogs leaping out of his way.

The Arif continues his way along the main channel of the falaj and, at some fifty metres into the network of shade of the palm gardens, an observer would see him pause at a point where channels branch off into the gardens. He bends down and, with one hand, lifts a slate lying at the side of the branching channel. He holds it over the centre of the left-hand channel where the water is running, ready to lower it into the water. With his right hand he lifts another slate, which is holding the water back from the channel that runs at right angles. With a practised movement he lifts the one and drops the other into its appointed slot and now the water, prevented from flowing ahead, diverts to the left. It flows in a steady trickle, dampening the dusty soil of the dry channel and making its way to the craters around each palm tree where hands have mounded up the orange-coloured soil to capture a ration of water for each tree. This small task done the Arif makes his way back to the main falaj and to the next set of gardens. After three more of these operations his work is finished for the next two hours and he returns to his place in the shade, next to the time-keeping stick.

As he makes his way slowly, figures appear among the trees and the alfalfa that grows in their shade in the gardens where water is newly flowing. They guide the water to the trees; scrape a way for it in the dusty earth, heap up the protective mounds forming the bowls around each tree.
"*Salaam aleikum!*"
"*Aleikum wa salaam!*" They salute each other.

Greetings are exchanged and the figures watch the retreating back of the Arif whom they respect and trust although he carries no book of rules. He knows by heart the shares allotted to each garden and member of the village and, when changes take place – as happens when landowners fall on good or bad times and shares of water are bought or sold or mortgaged – the Arif writes them in the book, where each landowner has a page recording his portion of the shares in the village's water and where changes are noted.

These days there is pressure on the shares and their price is rising at the yearly auctions; inflationary pressures are at work and shareholdings are becoming consolidated. The reason is known to all: the water is not flowing as it used to do.

II - The World In An Ice Cube

Cruising low, at a height of 7,000 feet, the pilot of the Learjet blinked his eyes in disbelief at the sight below. It looked like a giant ice-cube towed behind an oil-tanker, but surely that couldn't be the case?

Dan Bradwell glanced at his co-pilot.

"Do you see what I think I see, Si?"

Simon shook his head signalling his equal disbelief.

"If that isn't the most....... So is that what they wanted us to fly low to get a look at? Are you going any lower?"

Normally on a flight from London to Dubai, and at this stage of the journey, they would be flying at 30,000 feet or more – too high to make out individual vessels on the sea below, but today his passengers, a Sheikh returning to Dubai with his guest, Alastair Singleton, the chief executive of a UK-based plc, had specifically required him to drop down to 7,000 feet and had given him the co-ordinates where this descent was to be made.

"Lower? What for?" Dan asked. " Do you really think if I go down a bit, we might see a polar bear on the top?" We just might! Remember those Polar Mints you used to get? The wrappers had an iceberg with a polar bear on the top!"

"D'you reckon it's a stunt they're pulling?"

"Can't be anything else. Must be planning to tow it to the Palm Island and moor up alongside".

It took a lot to surprise the two seasoned pilots and not even the sight of an iceberg hitched to an oil-tanker could draw from them more than a jocular form of speculation.

The door from the main cabin opened and their stewardess looked in.

"Hi guys! Can I interest you in lunch?"

She had brought them a tray with smoked trout sandwiches, which she placed on the flat surface between the two seats.

"What's the conversation back there, Kelly"

"Couldn't really say Dan, except that they are both peering out the window and sounding excited. In fact they've asked for champagne so I'd best be getting along!"

"Hang on a sec: do you want to see what the excitement is about?" Simon asked.

She nodded.

"Take a look down there".

The pilot indicated to the stewardess where to look.

"Oh wow! That's extraordinary! Is that why they asked you to take us down so low?"

"That must be why. You'd better get along with the champagne –I imagine they have asked for it on ice! And, Kelly….!"

"Sir?"

"Tell His Excellency that I'll be taking the aircraft up again to 30,000, in five minutes time if that's fine by him."

"Will do!" and Kelly disappeared into the main cabin again.

A boardroom in Dubai is furnished and decorated on the lavish side. The table itself is of engraved crystal and the supports are fountains whose water is laced with powdered gold- leaf that catches the light and shimmers. Gold and white brocaded chairs and settees line the walls and rose water perfumes the air.

His Excellency, having recovered from the six-hour flight and feeling refreshed, welcomes his flight companion to a place at the table and makes the introductions. Looking around the table he addresses them in Arabic:

"*Salaam aleikum*" and turning to his guest from London, "*Ahlan wa sahlan!*"

"Welcome! Welcome to the head offices of Al Zuwaidi Enterprises. It is a pleasure and we wish you a happy stay and a good and fortunate outcome for both our enterprises!"

Alastair Singleton nodded and smiled his appreciation of the greeting and accepted the thimble-sized cup of coffee and the sweetmeats that were passed with ceremony by a servant in crisp white dishdash, his head-dress in the livery of the company he served.

And for the time-being that was all. The ceremonial would be lengthy. It was clear to the guest that nothing was to be hurried and propriety was to be observed. He sipped his coffee and ate the almond-encrusted pastries. The people he had come to meet, six or seven of them, did the same and exchanged small talk, mostly in Arabic.

Were they asking about each other's families? Or the state of the market? business news, from the Emirate and the other Gulf States? Having nothing of the language beyond the formalities of greeting, the guest could not tell.

Fifteen minutes passed, after which the servant cleared the coffee cups and sweetmeat plates from the table and the host, the chairman, sitting back in his upholstered chair, prepared to address the meeting in near-perfect English.

"Gentlemen: it is pleasure for me to present to you our guest Mr Alastair Singleton   from Pure Spring Akwa of the United Kingdom"

Starting from Singleton's right he made the introductions around the table.

"Shaikh Abdul Karim al Zuwaidi; Director of al Zuwaidi Enterprises – Mr Alastair Singleton." Both parties greeted with nods and murmured politeness.

"His Excellency Said al Zubair al Thiwani; Minister of Commercial Affairs", more nods and greetings.

"His Excellency Shaikh Rashid al Bayid al Buraidi, Minister in charge of Water Resources and Distribution....."

The introductions continued until Alastair had mentally ticked off all the names on the list he had been memorising during the flight.

The meeting got down to business. Alastair Singleton had prepared meticulously. To say he was nervous would be an exaggeration. Nervousness was not in his make-up but he was not one to under-estimate the risks involved in striking a deal and preferred not to leave anything to chance. Watching his audience closely for their reaction he outlined the services that his company could offer and the expertise and experience that made up their track record over the past twenty-five years.

"Our business is to carry out tests and to advise on the exploitability or otherwise of underground water supplies which might literally be the source of a new bottled water and mineral water extraction industry here in your country. We have a staff of geologists, chemists and economists who would be at your disposal to carry out feasibility studies. We can advise on matters including factory sites, construction, equipment and bottling and distribution systems. Should you commission us we would, as a matter of course, investigate the state of the market and existing competition."

As he spoke he let his eye move around the table making contact with individuals as he emphasised his various points of interest. They presented an array of expressions which, he admitted, he found difficult to read. He continued.

"It is well known that the market for bottled water is…er buoyant" any pun that might have been appreciated by an audience in London passed un-noticed. Alastair sighed inwardly: shame about that; he had thought some of them might get it.

"First, take the young," he continued. "Bottled water for young people is not just a matter of thirst, nor indeed merely an acknowledgement of a healthy life-style; it is a statement of fashion and of style. Indeed some young people seem to be unable to function without the comfort of regular sips of water, often flavoured with limes or orange flowers or other exotic additions. Here in the Gulf States you have an abundance of limes and other citrus fruits as well as spices; you need only take a stroll around your souks to savour the variety on offer to provide the flavours and the perfumes!"

The audience smiled.

"But young people are just part of the market and you know better than I do that bottled water, in packs of six or twelve, are a regular item on the family shopping list," although, he reflected, looking around at them, these men in the Gulf were not likely to do the weekly shop.

"Now, most of your bottled water is imported and the names on the shelves of the supermarkets here are ones that I recognise from the UK. Over there however a niche market is enjoyed by small and local sources: sources like Kentish Hills and Chiltern Spring Water produce relatively small quantities and sell locally at a premium price and I envisage that here, in the Gulf States, this trend would find favour, especially among the huge number of visitors who search for authenticity, for locally produced goods, and a change from the global brands which they can get everywhere."

"Extraction costs would be high and the premium would have to reflect that" the Minister for Commercial Affairs commented.

"Intelligent marketing will be required to justify the extra margin; as I hinted before, subtle flavourings – the range of spices and fruits which have never been used in this way – the presentation, a variety of value-adding marketing devices will make the brand attractive."

"This is for the marketing department to put forward. At the moment we will commission the study and make a decision. The important question is sustainability – sustainability of supply. The geologists will need to work with our university departments which have mapped the aquifers"

"I believe that your policy is to reserve ground supplies for government approved projects?" Singleton queried.

"That is so. Much of the water used in our cities comes from desalination. And, naturally, grey water is used for the amenities, the greening of our environment."

"So the water we plan to use will come from the deep reserves?"

"That is so. Exploitation for this project will in fact involve drawing supplies from extremely deep aquifers"

"I might add," the minister continued, "that the aquifers are not respectful of national boundaries: it is something that can cause friction with our neighbours, but that is our concern and not anything that you need to take into account. Spring water, please remember this, is becoming a scarcity and a luxury."

"And there, precisely, lies our marketing opportunity" Singleton responded elegantly.

The meeting broke up with agreement reached that the studies would go ahead with a view to production starting in eight months from the day. It would be a challenging target and Alistair Singleton needed to get to his hotel to set the action in motion. His host escorted him down to the foyer where a car drew up and His Excellency's personal assistant stood ready to escort him to his hotel.

"It has been several years since you last visited, Mr Alistair, and before returning to your hotel you must see the development that has taken place and in particular the islands we are so proud of. Zaid will be your guide."

"Thank you! I was hoping for this opportunity".

The car drove them to the creek where a private launch was waiting. Ten minutes was all the time it took to wend a way down to the mouth of the creek and another ten minutes at full throttle with the launch's bow battering against the incoming waves out into the bay.

"Our destination is New Zealand" Zaid shouted, against the buzz of the engine and the slapping of the waves. "Please, take some food."

It was two in the afternoon and the fish pastries were welcome.

The driver throttled back and the bow of the launch settled in the water. They put-putted towards a jetty protected by a sea-wall but still under construction, surmounted by cranes and grabs where they had to shout over a cacophony of pile-drivers and heavy-lifting machines

From the marina where they tied up Zaid proposed a tour of the island, which Alistair was keen to see. Construction ashore seemed to be almost complete: new-built villas stood in newly planted gardens where work was still going on. As they walked around Alistair could see that gardens were still being put in place: *instant gardens* he thought – *the way they do it at Chelsea* - and watched as a fully-grown palm tree was hoisted into a hole in the sand with crates of Irish peat moss lined up to bed in around it. He could see the irrigation system, black hose piping encircling the area, with drip-feeders spaced at two or three foot intervals.

Zaid was leading and as they walked he indicated a villa and garden where the trees and plants seemed well established.

"This garden is the leader" he explained. "Your garden expert…" it was a name that Alistair recognised, "She designs this one for us four years ago. Two years ago she come and supervise. Trees are planted, flowers for patios, small bushes, water bowls for fishes, nice fountain and lights for night time to make beautiful this garden."

It was delightful and Alistair took time to wander around, deep in thought but mindful to record the scene with photographs.

"This is beautiful. But I have work to do and a plane to catch and I know His Excellency won't want me to cause a delay. A quick look inside one of the completed villas – then back to base please, Zaid. And thank you for the tour. I've enjoyed it a lot."

As the launch transported them, flat out, back across the bay, Alistair had a final question for his guide.

"Do you have any islands near to the Antarctic?"

His guide looked puzzled. Alastair tried to clarify.

"The Antarctic, where they have icebergs and penguins!"

The guide shook his head.

"Maybe here. New Zealand I think have snow and ice…"

"Mmm. Not icebergs though" Alistair muttered to himself.

An hour later the small plane had taken off. It circled over the bay giving a fine view of the islands that Alastair had visited. Three palm trees like emerald jewels in gold settings were laid out below him in a sapphire surround that glinted with the white crests of waves. And coming up ahead of them now, the outline of The World, which he had recently visited.

New Zealand was below them – he could almost make out the gardens he had seen and Africa next with the Americas coming up ahead. As the islands receded and the sky began to darken, the plane gained height and Alastair caught site of a tug-boat. He had seen it before with its tow-load, that giant cube, refracting now the last rays of the sun.

Alistair declined the champagne and sat back with a whisky and his thoughts. The meeting had gone well – as well as he had hoped. And if the project could be signed and sealed and work start eight months from today he would be well satisfied. He would also feel that he had made his mark at Akwa UK in the short time since he had been invited onto the board. He stretched his full six foot two out on the reclining chair, shrugged off his jacket and, running his hand through his only-slightly greying, rich brown hair, allowed his mind to dwell on the Palm Island villa. It seemed to offer the ideal set-down pad between time zones which he urgently needed as his other concerns gathered speed and he felt sure that, with a little persuasion Jessica would take to it with enthusiasm.

The sun sank into a horizon of orange and indigo cloud. Alastair was ready to shut down for the night and the bedroom cabin looked inviting. Six hours of sleep would be good.
"Wake me at 5 am - UK time" he told the attendant.
He would need time before they landed to prepare his address to the company's board, not to mention to work out how he would put his plans to Jessica in the evening.

PART 1

Chapter 1

The City of London

The City of London is an area in central London, England. In the medieval period it constituted most of London, but the conurbation has grown far beyond it. It is often referred to as the City (often written on maps as "City") or the Square Mile, as it is just over one square mile (1.12 sq mi/2.90 km2) in area. These terms are also often used as metonyms for the United Kingdom's financial services industry, which continues a notable history of being based in the City.
From Wikipedia, the free encyclopedia

I have always taken a keen interest in the doings of my only grandchild, Anisha. When she was little we were very close as my daughter Jessica was an unreliable mother in several ways. Impetuous and prone to do things on a whim, Jessica appeared to base her decisions more on her star signs than on rationality. Besides, being on her own Jessica was obliged to work, and a willing grandparent who would step in at a moment's notice came in very useful. Anisha treated me as her special friend, told me her secrets when she was little and continued to confide in me as she grew up. Now that she was in her first job, communication was less frequent but we would get together periodically and have catch-up sessions

Anisha is a spirited girl and, once she has got her teeth into something will not let go or be put off by obstacles in her way. In fact the name, Anisha, an Indian name chosen by her mother for reasons which will become clear, apparently means 'unobstructed', though whether that referred to the manner of her birth – which was an easy one – or to a wish for her future, I have never been sure. While she was a student she was proud to call herself an eco-warrior, going on protests and supporting campaigns, so I was surprised when she informed me, on leaving university, that she had been offered and accepted a job with an investment firm in the City of London.

Getting to work in the morning from her flat south of the river was no problem for Anisha if she could overcome the initial obstacle of getting the bicycle out of the flat and down three flights of stairs, and solve the question of where to store it once she arrived at work. She decided that a folding model would be the answer as she could keep it in the office's cleaning cupboard during the day and in her flat, where it would not take up much space, at night and at weekends.

Another question was how to dress suitably for cycling to work and for being at work. For the office she liked to dress cool: her preferred style was short black skirt, dark tights and boots and to set this off, she bought a series of long, floaty, trailing scarves in a variety of bright colours which wrapped round her neck and hung down in loose folds. This wasn't a practical outfit for cycling so over it she pulled a pair of baggy pants, tied below the knee in order not to catch in the chain, and an all-enveloping sweater on the top which stopped the floaty scarves from streaming back in the wind. A small backpack carried her essentials for the day – purse, smartphone, bottle of water. The cyclist's helmet was streamlined and sunglasses protected her eyes from smoke and flying specks of debris from the pounding traffic of the South London streets. Some days, when the weather was bad, she wore a nose-mask as well.

On one particular morning, on the pavement outside the flat, she had unfolded her machine and was ready to go. At the end of the street a dustcart with its team of bin-men blocked the street; they dashed to and fro' dragging black bins to be hauled up to the back of the lorry and emptied of contents. As Anisha gathered speed on her bicycle a man with a full bin on one side of the road and another with an empty on the other side were poised to cross in front of her and a headlong collision with the approaching bike was imminent. Anisha continued to pedal and true to her name to defy all obstacles.

"Coming through guys!" Her shout alerted them and they paused on either side to let her by. She thought they knew her by now, but you could never be sure if it was the same team each week.

Having negotiated this first hazard Anisha threaded her way through the labyrinth of the back streets of Southwark and down to the riverside. She paused there to lean on the stone parapet and drink in the view of the Thames and then on she went. It was a gentle cycle ride now – no traffic permitted along this stretch – to Bankside where she had to dismount to cross the great river by the gleaming Millennium footbridge. After that it was head down and all her wits about her in the traffic of Upper Thames Street, left into Gracechurch Street and Bishopsgate. Only when she had passed Liverpool Street and its station, from which a sea of commuters was streaming towards their offices, could she dive into another maze of small streets and alleyways, threading her way through Bell Lane, Crispin Street, Old Spitalfields Market, where grand office blocks towered incongruously above tiny, ancient churches and modernistic steel and glass buildings fitted neatly into a pattern of old lanes and alleys. Now Anisha had to keep a sharp look out for pedestrians. This was rush hour with everyone heading for work, their minds fixed in one way or another on the day ahead and not on the lookout for speeding cyclists. She cycled slowly and allowed herself time to cool off before arriving at her place of work in one of the more modern, sleekly-designed buildings, on the corner where Blossom Street meets Fleur de Lis Street.

Taking off her cycle helmet in the Ladies Room, Anisha shook her head from side to side to free her dark hair and let it fall in springy waves on her shoulders. The rest of the cycling gear she bagged and left with the bike in the concierge's glory-hole. She was ready for the office.

A lift took her to the second floor where a water feature bubbled soothingly among greenery, the glass walls on three sides looked into a central court and low tables held the Wall Street Journal and Financial Times, to occupy any visitors who needed to wait there. Beyond these, visible through a glass wall and entered by a wide glass door, was the main office; a light and airy room the size of two tennis courts. On one side windows gave onto a central court and on the other to the exterior and the narrow City lane below.

The room was laid out with an aisle down the middle and off it rows of desks in the style of a dealing room, adjoining each other, each with its computer monitor and freedom to see and communicate with its immediate neighbours.

Making her way along the aisle and some eight rows into the room Anisha turned right to where six desks were grouped together and a reference library of books was stacked in the available space around. This was base for the Green Team, of which Anisha was the newest member.

Good! Empty desks; she was the first in.

Anisha slipped into her place, stood her bottle of spring water on the desk and switched the mobile phone in her pocket to silent mode.

Actually she wasn't first in; Rob Underwood, the fund manager, had seen her and was coming over. As she saw him approach Anisha reflected how much she liked Rob. In his late forties, and with a figure on the rotund side, he was unlikely to be cycling to work. His homely manner belied his qualities of judgement and experience and the high expectations he had of those who worked for him and as she got to know him Anisha realised how much she respected and appreciated him. Rob managed more than one team but the Green Team was his special baby which he had nurtured since its beginnings. And he looked after his staff. It was he who had told the buildings manager not to be so stuffy and to find a place for Anisha's bike.

"How was your ride?" he asked her.

"Great! You should try it some time," she suggested.

"Be careful; if you convert too many of us there won't be room to store all the bikes."

"Maybe they ought to make room; perhaps in the basement somewhere?"

"You can worry about that when it happens. What are you working on at the moment?"

Anisha pointed to a pile of books on her desk and was about to open up her computer.

"It's the energy portfolio: aluminium-foil technology for solar-powered generation. You said you were thinking of buying into it. I'm checking out the company in Germany and I've found one company in China which is planning a start-up."

"There may be others." Rob told her. "Look in India; I'd like a complete list. It's the kind of technology our clients expect us to hold funds in."

'Ethicals' were only a small proportion of the funds which the company offered but they attracted a fair number of clients whose social and environmental concerns influenced their investment decisions, organisations like cooperatives and private investors who declined to invest in arms or tobacco or others industries that might have a negative effect on the environment – the list was quite long. Anisha found herself learning about clean coal, carbon-capture and other technologies, some of which were viable, others less so.

Researchers for the Green Team came and went and Rob made sure while they were with him that they gained experience and insights into the ethicals field.

"You can learn a lot if you take the trouble Anisha," Rob told her that morning as she settled to her work.

"Your predecessors in the Team have all gone on to good jobs," he went on. "Some of them are fund managers themselves right now. How does that sound to you?"

Anisha paused, uncertainly.

"Well, it's early days. Not sure that I'm ready for a real City career just yet."

"Certainly not yet," Rob agreed "You've a lot to learn and I shall be relying on you and the research you do."

Anisha nodded seriously.

"If the trust fails to live up to standards," Rob went on "You can be sure our investors will be the first to let us know. And of course the board of Trustees keeps a close watch on things."

Anisha took this in with the utmost seriousness.

"Keep on with the solar-power and see what you find." She nodded and prepared to get to work.

"Can you handle another assignment alongside this one?" Rob put to her.

"Of course!" Anisha was up for as many assignments as he wanted to give her.

"It's about our holding in Akwa."

Anisha didn't recognise the name.

"It's an international company producing bottled water in a number of countries. Some clients have raised concerns."

"What kind of concerns?"

"Some of the water sources may be unsustainable, or may be working against local interests; at least that's what's being suggested."

"Where should I start?"

"I suggest you look first at the countries where they have plants and where they have granted licences. Look at recent developments and see if there is anything we might have overlooked. If there is then we'll have to contact the company and clarify any issues."

"And is that enough to bring about a change? I mean is the company likely to change what they do to keep us on board?"

"If there is anything to worry us I can meet with the management and put it to them. In many cases, labour relations, environmental issues or whatever, they look at it and make changes. Corporate Social Responsibility is a big PR issue and if something bad in CSR hits the headlines the damage to the company can be huge."

"So if we hold funds in a company it's like a kind of guarantee of respectability in that way?"

"Which is why we have to be scrupulous in our monitoring. That's what you'll be doing with the Akwa holding. OK?"

"Fine" Anisha nodded happily, pleased to have a new range of products to investigate

"Good. I'll see how you are getting on in a day or two but if you come up with anything first, please let me know."

Anisha spent the best part of that day and the following on Akwa, researching on the web and with the help of directories and a large atlas. She felt as snug and safe as in her old university library; sitting here at her desk within its rampart of books, where the rest of the company that occupied the rows of desks beyond might not have existed. She also made a point of taking her full hour at lunchtime to buy something to eat and explore the city. One or two friends from university were working around here and they would meet up for lunch or after work. Somewhere in the area her stepfather had his office but she couldn't remember the name of the street and wasn't planning to look for it anyway.

After several days of research Anisha was able to show Rob details of three small companies, which Akwa had acquired in the past year and two more which were operating under licence, effectively using the Akwa expertise and name as a guarantee of purity of their product. She had also learnt that plans were going ahead for two more under the same type of licensing agreement. When she showed them to him Rob seemed pleased with her work.

"Do you think you'll be taking any of this up with the company?" she asked him.

"Certainly. That's my job and Akwa will be on my itinerary next week. I've got meetings in Rome and Ljubljana and I can fit in Paris on the way back. While I'm away, see if you can get more facts about the companies that are planning to operate under licence."

Anisha got down to work. By 5pm that day she was able to report that two were in Eastern Europe – one in Romania and one in Bulgaria – and one more projected in one of the Gulf States. When she passed these new details on to Rob he raised his eyebrows as well.

"Hmm; I didn't realise they produced their own spring water in that part of the world…. Didn't think they had much water to spare!"

"Do you want me to look further into it?"

"Well, I'll be away from the office for a couple of days but, yes, I'd like you to dig a bit deeper. You did geography didn't you? It should be right up your street."

"Definitely! Do you want me to email you while you're on your travels?"

"Email me if there's anything relevant. If there's sustainability or an environmental problem I'll raise it with Akwa and give them time to take steps. They need to know if we are thinking of disinvesting; that's only fair. It's the way we always do it."

Anisha wished him a good trip, shut her system down and packed up for the weekend.

Downstairs in the Ladies' Room next to Reception, she changed into her cycling gear and retrieved her bike. The concierge on duty watched her; the bicycle folded up so small there was no problem carrying it through the revolving doors.

"You should mind how you go out there; the traffic's a killer; coming at you from all sides; so fast you wouldn't know what hit you."

"Thanks for the warning!" It wasn't the first Anisha had received; nonetheless she appreciated the fact that he bothered; it was the first friendly word he had given her. The job was working out OK; two interesting assignments to research, a helpful manager to work to and a friendly concierge as well. Life was fine and she left with a light heart for the weekend.

Chapter 2

The River Thames flows through southern England. It is the longest river entirely in England and the second longest in the United Kingdom. Many Thames islands are called "aits" or "eyots". Aits are usually longer thinner islands that have built up through an accumulation of silt.   From Wikipedia, the free encyclopedia

Half way home Anisha's mobile phone rang.

"Hi Ben, where are you? Oh right! No, not yet, I'm on the way: just crossing the river; it's nice…No, not cycling, not allowed on the bridge; I'm just pushing …."

Ben was a friend from Anisha's schooldays. I remembered meeting him: a nice boy. These days, having a group of friends seems to mean so much to young people and I know they played an important part in Anisha's life. Perhaps it's because the parents and families these days are frequently dysfunctional that the friendship group becomes a substitute family. In any case Anisha had kept in touch with many of her school friends and they were planning to meet up for the weekend, together with some more recent friends from university, one of whom was living in a rented houseboat on the Thames. They would somehow all cram in. It should be a good weekend.

Anisha accepted Ben's offer to pick her up at the flat in a couple of hours.

Once over the bridge Anisha remounted for the ride along the riverside but after only a couple of hundred yards her phone rang again. This time it was her mother.

"Hi Mum, how are you?"

Anisha held her breath slightly; her mother usually had some tale of woe these days. It was the case today.

"Sweetheart, can you come for the weekend?"

"Mmn, not really. Sorry, I've just fixed to meet up with the crowd; we're spending the weekend on a houseboat," she explained. But of course her mother wanted to know more.

"I'm not sure exactly where, somewhere along the Thames, Teddington or somewhere like that. Ben's picking me up."

"Darling, I really need you down here. How about coming just for the evening – or stay the night and join your friends tomorrow?"

"Can't it wait until next weekend?"

"No, it really can't. It's…." she hesitated, "Your father…."

"My step-father Mum. I do wish you wouldn't keep trying to…."

"Oh alright! Your stepfather wants us to move. He wants to sell the house."

Anisha was shocked.

"Why? And where to?"

"I can't explain on the phone. Can you come?"

"I suppose so; I'll have to ring Ben." Anisha grumbled, "He really is a pain – that man!"

"Don't call him 'that man' Anisha. I married him; and anyway he helped you get that job and you should be a bit more grateful!"

"He what….?" This time Anisha was more than shocked. "What do you mean by that? I got the job on my own account!"

But her mother had rung off.

Feeling furious as well as disturbed Anisha rang Ben and explained that she would join them the next day. Ben offered to pick her up at the nearest tube station. Anisha made her way back to the flat, re-packed her bag with things for the weekend and caught the train for the nearest station to her mother's home in Surrey.

The journey only took half an hour but that was time to reflect and wonder what the idea behind selling the house could be. It wasn't a stylish house but Anisha had grown up there and would be sorry. On the other hand perhaps the plan was to stay in the same area, just to buy something bigger and grander. After all her stepfather could afford it; he already had a fine apartment in London and a proper country house would boost his ego no end: not that, in Anisha's opinion, his ego needed any boosting at all. And her mother? How was she going to feel about the idea? Her friends were in Epsom and Anisha felt that Jessica would miss them badly if she moved. Regretfully she felt that her mother was likely to go along with such a plan as, in her daughter's opinion, she was turning into something of a wimp these days, quite unable to stand up for herself. Something that Anisha was unable to comprehend at all was how her mother, feisty, red-headed, flower-power girl as she had apparently been, could have changed so radically over the years.

Anisha hadn't known her own father and knew very little about him beyond the fact that he was from India and played the sitar; however hard she pressed her mother, only the barest details were forthcoming. She knew that Jessica, after two years as a PA in a travel firm, to the dismay of her family in England had set out to travel and see the world for herself: that backpacking through Afghanistan the year before the Soviets invaded she had met her romantic hero and together they had travelled on through Pakistan and spent three months in the Kashmir valley. Anisha imagined that for Jessica it must have been a dream-time. She imagined her mother, in her early twenties, a curly-haired red-head with back-pack and fleecy Afghan coat, meeting along the way her 'Indian prince'. She would have allowed herself, in her fantastical way, to plan a wonderful life together, but as they neared his home her boyfriend's mood had changed. It wouldn't work, he had said: his family would never accept her: she wouldn't adapt to the way of life. They parted in Delhi and Jessica hadn't even discovered there was a baby on the way. She returned to

England and, of course, her father and I helped her out. The baby girl was given the name Anisha but nothing else of an Indian heritage.

Jessica found that motherhood gave her a reason to stay in one place and keep a job. She did well and, with parental help, managed to buy a house for the two of them. She hadn't formed any new relationship but for Anisha, first a toddler then a schoolgirl, life was fine. Looking back, Anisha knew that they had been really happy, just the two of them, with grandparents in the background.

It must have been when Anisha went away to university and her mother found herself alone for long periods that she began to look around her. Good looking, still with that magnificent head of red hair and now financially independent, it was not surprising that Jessica should have been snapped up; perhaps it was only surprising that it hadn't happened before. She was working as secretary to a Surrey golf club, a sociable milieu which brought contact with an affluent range of members and their guests and it was here that she met the man she would go on to marry, in a ceremony which included an elaborate reception at the clubhouse.

Anisha certainly did not grudge her mother her happiness but she confessed to me her puzzlement at how marriage had changed Jessica from the independent, if rather scatty person she knew to someone less sure of herself, preferring to let her new husband take the decisions.

Even so, surely selling the house would be a step too far? Anisha suspected that her mother was really rather unhappy about the idea.

"Well, let's see if she will stand up for herself this time," she thought.

One more stop to go and Anisha remembered with a shock her mother's words before she rang off: "He helped you get that job: you really should be more grateful!"

Anisha stood up to shrug on her back-pack as they drew in to Epsom station. She certainly would not be grateful – not the smallest bit grateful because she had applied for and landed the job entirely on her own merits and in the face of considerable competition. This at least she was ready to make abundantly clear.

She had phoned from the train and Jessica was waiting at the station with the car. It was only five minute's drive but Anisha was glad of the lift at the end of the week. She gave her mother a hug and climbed in.

"What's all this about selling the house Mum? You don't want to, do you?"

"Let's get home first. Would you mind terribly if it was sold?"

"Hmm. Not sure. It depends where you plan to buy, I suppose. And I do feel I have my roots here – even if I don't come down all that often."

The evening was fine and it was warm enough to eat out on the patio. Jessica had cooked salmon fillets and tiny new potatoes with tomatoes which Anisha had been ordered to pick from the greenhouse.

"They really do taste different when they are fresh off the plant. That was delicious!"

Jessica smiled her pleasure. It was good to cook for her daughter.

"Now, no more dodging the issue: what's all this about selling the house and why does he want you to do it?"

The reply came somewhat hesitantly.

"He wants to move to the Gulf."

"To where? What Gulf?"

"You know; the Gulf states – the Persian Gulf I suppose, if you want to be accurate."

"Why ever does he want to do that? I mean isn't his business in London?"

"Oh yes, he'd keep the flat there, but he's convinced it's the place to be; the place to buy property – and have a great life-style."

"You'd be bored out of your mind, wouldn't you?" Anisha demanded. "It would be a totally expatriate existence. What on earth would you do with yourself? You wouldn't be able to work, would you?"

"Well, no but there would be plenty to do making the house nice and the garden...

"Quite a challenge I imagine, making a garden out of sand!"

"And he has in mind that I would help run the business from that end. The company has interests in that part of the world. And entertaining, and all that...."

She tailed off in the face of her daughter's scepticism.

"Well, how much time does he plan to spend there with you? I should think that's the crucial point!"

"It will vary of course, but long weekends as well as the times when he has to be there for business."

"Hmm; don't forget it's something like an eight-hour flight from London," Anisha objected.

"There's a company jet; I'm not sure if you know that...."

"I didn't but it doesn't improve matters; think of the air miles – just for one person? How do they justify that?"

"Darling it's a fabulous place – and you know how I used to love travelling; it will be a chance to lead that kind of life again – well, sort of...."

"But what about me, Mum? I know I don't come down all that often, but it's important to me to know you're nearby, all the same"

Jessica moved around the table to put her arms around her and mother and daughter hugged.

"You can phone me whenever you want....I'll pay the phone bills! And you can come whenever you get the chance. Think how lovely to escape there in the middle of winter!"

"I'm really not happy about the idea. I need to know more about it. And I still don't understand why he wants to do it."

"You can look up the website. The house is part of a development. It's rather stunning. Have a look at it and we'll talk some more tomorrow."

"I want to be off in good time. I'm already missing one evening of the houseboat weekend. But yes, we can talk more before I go."

"Exactly" her mother replied. "And nothing's decided yet."

Anisha thought this might not be strictly true.

The two of them cleared supper away and Anisha settled at the pc to look up the website. She was so absorbed by what she saw that she didn't hear her mother when she went to bed. Anisha slept in her old schoolgirl room, a shelf of animal friends above her head and on the wall opposite and posters of pop idols in every available space. How many more nights would she sleep here? Probably not many more.

At breakfast Anisha confronted her mother.

"You didn't tell me it was that Palm Treeisland, where he wants to buy his property! I find it hard to believe!"

"So you've heard about it before, have you?"

"Of course! It's a kind of developers' folly on an unimaginable scale!"

"Oh I don't think so; in fact it's a charming idea and it's going to be really popular."

"I know exactly the kind of people it's going to be popular with and they have more money than sense – or taste. It's the ultimate in unsustainability."

"I don't want to argue with you dear because I know I could never convince you but the way I see it these countries are looking for ways to give themselves a future and they are using all sorts of clever technologies to do it."

"If he's so determined to buy into it, why does it mean selling up here? I mean, you could hang on to this place, maybe find tenants for it? Why sell?"

"I think your father - your step-father - wants us to go into it together. Isn't that rather sweet? And if we do that we can buy the place outright with no need for an expensive mortgage"

"It's a shock Mum. I have to say it – a shock."

"Darling I know that you will love it! You can bring friends of course! When the weather is too cold for house-boat weekends you can bring them there. Oh and when you fly in it's just amazing; this sort of jewel-like palm tree-shaped island set in blue, blue sea. It's magic!" she enthused.

"So you've been there; you've seen it and looked at the house; and all without saying a word," Anisha reproached her. "It sounds to me very definite indeed."

"No, don't take it like that. I really do need to know you will – well at least promise to think about it….positively…please?"

"I have to go! Ben's expecting me to ring from the train. I'll talk to you in the week. Thanks for supper; I can walk to the station."

Anisha was opening the front door when she remembered.

"By the way, whatever was that you said about being grateful? To him! What do I have to be grateful about? You know I got the job on my own merits?"

"Of course you did! I just happened to know that he put in a good word for you. Probably it made no difference at all!"

"And why, oh why should he do that? It's not as if he has anything to do with the company…"

"Oh but he knows so many people, all around the City. It's not surprising if he has a friend there. And he was just delighted to hear that you were looking at a job in the City and in asset management."

"I know he was dead against me taking any sort of environmental job – reckoned it was a waste of time."

"Well yes, that is rather his point of view. But that's why when he heard you would be in fund management he was pleased. It doesn't surprise me in the least that he put in a word for you. I shouldn't have told you!"

"I wish you hadn't! Anyway, did you tell him that I'm in their Green Team? Researching all the things he thinks are a waste of time? Did you tell him that?"

"Well, I don't think I did – no. Because in fact you only told me after you had been there for a month or more".

"OK, well please don't mention it now. Alright?"

She gave her mother another hug and they parted on reasonable terms.

"Just try to stand up to him a bit more. And if you want to keep this place on – do it! It belongs to you after all. It might even come to me in the long term - had you thought of that? And I'd certainly prefer to inherit a house in Epsom than a villa off the Emirates coast!"

Jessica looked confused and sorry as she waved goodbye to her daughter.

Never one to let unwelcome fears disrupt her immediate plans, as soon as she was on the train Anisha resolved that she would put the whole house-sale thing out of her mind as well as any resentful thoughts about her stepfather whose intrusion into her life had become so unwelcome.

Ben kept his word and picked her up at Teddington, the nearest station to where the houseboat had its mooring. There on the boat she found the familiar crowd plus a selection of everyone's more recent friends from their various universities. Most had spent the night on board but by the time Anisha arrived sleeping bags had been rolled up and put away, both above and below decks, where they had somehow all found a space to sleep. A game of football in the nearby water meadows was the plan, followed by a barbecue on the island opposite.

After the game, which she took part in, Anisha found herself with one of the newcomers. No-one could fail to have noticed Gregory – or 'Grego' as everyone seemed to call him - because of his intense ferocity on the football pitch.

"Do you always put so much into the game?" Anisha asked him as they cooled off. "Anyone would think that you were aiming for the World Cup!"

Grego was edgy, hyped up by the game.

"I don't believe in doing things by halves." he fired back at her. "Do you?"

Anisha was more measured.

"I haven't really thought about it," she replied mildly.

"Well you ought to! You ought to give it some thought. If you believe in doing something you need to give it everything you've got."

"Pardon me but you sound like an advertisement for….not sure what; maybe for joining the army or something."

"No. Not the army, in any case."

"But you train regularly and keep fit, do you? "

"Sure!"

"How?"

"How do I keep fit? I run. And swim and I cycle, among other things."

"Ah, there we have something in common. I cycle too."

He didn't seem interested; instead he stood up,

"I'm off to the island now. Are you coming?"

Anisha looked at the muddy water and the swift current swirling between the shore and the island.

"Thanks; I'll take the easy option."

There was a rowing boat already being put to good use, taking four people at a time.

"I'll join the queue!"

"Suit yourself."

"Someone has to bring the food over; see you there."

Anisha watched him take a running dive into the river and strike out for the distant island. A confident swimmer, obviously, but his manner, she thought, was more than just confident. Good looks like his would account for some of it but there was more; she wondered what gave him that edge of arrogance.

It took several trips with the rowing boat to transfer everything and everyone to the island; first across was the barbecue and a sack of charcoal and the first group to land had the task of getting it going straight away. In the meantime a game of Frisbee kept people occupied and when it landed in the water Gregory had the job of water retriever. After 20 minutes of this he had had enough and waded ashore onto the island.

He came to dry off to where Anisha and Ben were tending the barbecue.

"Have you had enough?" Ben asked.

"More than enough! The water's full of weeds, not great for swimming." Gregory replied, nodding towards the Frisbee players. "They'll just have to throw more accurately."

The barbecue had been set up next to a fallen tree and Ben and Anisha were perched on its trunk. Grego spread his towel on the grass and sat with the sun in his eyes squinting up at them.

"So how long have you two known each other?"

The two of them exchanged a look.

"A long, long time" said Ben and Anisha smiled.

"Same school," she explained. "From Year 11 up until the end. Until Leavers Day saw us torn asunder!"

"How come torn asunder?"

"We went our separate ways; in other words, different unis."

"And now?"

"Part of the crowd, man. Regular get-togethers"

"Right, yeah, well, cool. "

31

"So what do you do? I mean have you got a job or something?" Ben asked.

"I'm a researcher" Grego replied, somewhat evasively Anisha thought. "For the time being. I don't mean to be one for long but yeah, for the time being that's what I do."

"Anything interesting? Your research I mean. Scientific? Where do you do it?"

"In London"

"London's a big place: anything more specific?"

"Westminster.... Specific enough?"

"Oh! – I mean, um....cool"

Ben looked baffled and the conversation came to a temporary standstill.

"What kind of research is it?" Anisha asked. "I mean, is it secret or something?"

"No, of course not; it's not secret. Some of it could be confidential or restricted though. Most MPs have researchers; or at least a share of one. That's what I am, a parliamentary researcher. OK?"

"Well-paid?" Ben had recovered himself and put the obvious question.

"Not particularly. But, I'm doing it for the experience," Gregory replied defensively. "Not for the long-term."

"So are you going to be a politician?"

"Maybe; I don't know yet. I mean I can't tell at this stage." For the first time Anisha sensed a slight crack in the arrogance but Gregory had decided it was time to return fire.

"How about yourself?" his question was directed at Anisha. She looked amused.

"Well, now, wait for it - I happen also to be a researcher!" Grego nodded.

"Alright - I don't think I've seen you around though."

"Not at Westminster! I work for a company in the City. I research stocks and shares."

Gregory nodded

"Cool! Do you like it?"

"Yes, I have fun! I enjoy my work"

"And she's quite well paid too!" added Ben with an innocent air.

Gregory glanced briefly at Ben, as if he had forgotten that he was there, and then turned back to Anisha.

"I actually come to the City sometimes; from time to time, usually at short notice …" There was some electricity here: Ben wasn't sure if it was a two-way current but he knew he wasn't needed. Muttering about going to look for the food he left them:

"Keep an eye on the barbecue; I'll be back with stuff to cook."

Chapter 3

Bottled water is drinking water (e.g., well water, distilled water, or spring water) packaged in plastic or glass water bottles. Bottled water may be carbonated or not. Sizes range from small single serving bottles to large carboys for water coolers. The global rate of consumption more than quadrupled between 1990 and 2005. Spring water and purified tap water are currently the leading global sellers. By one estimate, approximately 50 billion bottles of water are consumed per annum in the U.S. and around 200 billion bottles globally.

The rate of consumption more than quadrupled between 1990 and 2005 Spring water and purified tap water are currently the leading global sellers. By one estimate, approximately 50 billion bottles of water are consumed per annum in the U.S. and around 200 billion bottles globally. From Wikipedia, the free encyclopedia

On Wednesday morning Anisha was at her desk, flushed from the cycle ride, gulping from her bottle of water when Rob arrived. He picked up the bottle and examined the label.

"Ha! An Akwa product. You'll be seeing a lot more of these!"

"That sounds interesting; can you tell me more?"

"Yes; the Fund, as you know, has holdings in the company.'

Anisha nodded, 'I've been researching them – as you asked me to,' she said.

"Good, because clients have raised several more issues raised while I was away and they all have to be followed up. That's what I want you to do. If we can't give the company a clean bill of health we'll have to transfer our holdings."

"You'll have to tell me how I start." Anisha asked. "Do I pick up the phone? Go and see them? And I'll need to know about the queries that have been raised"

"Don't worry; I'll give you all the details."

Later in the day Anisha found herself with two appointments with Akwa in her diary, one at its UK headquarters, in Wiltshire, and the second, a week later, in Southern Spain. She took a train to Swindon and a taxi from the station.

"It's jus' roun' the corner, dear; not sure that you need a taxi!" the driver told her and she realised from his accent that she was now in the West country.

"That's alright, please; you know the way and I don't!" she replied.

"Akwa Corporate, would it be then?" he asked, driving less than 500 yards from the station forecourt. Without waiting for a reply he swung his vehicle through some gates and pulled up in front of a large neo-Georgian office building. "We're there a'ready!"

"I need a receipt for the fare if you don't mind."

"No trouble at all'". The taxi driver received the tip appreciatively. "Straight up the steps – you can't go wrong." He told her.

Shallow stone steps led up to wide glass doors and a spacious reception amphitheatre. She looked around for the reception desk, almost hidden by tubs of Corduline palms.

She gave her name to the receptionist adding "From Focus Asset Management".

After a few minutes' wait Anisha was taken up two floors in a lift, along a palm-lined corridor to a door marked Board Room. Her escort knocked and opened, standing aside for her to enter. A woman, perhaps in her early forties was wearing a soft, fawn outfit with some expensive jewellery pinned to its collar. She rose from her desk and came to greet Anisha.

"Ursula Lemoine. It's good to meet you and thank you for coming all this way!"

Anisha wondered if she heard in the woman's voice a note of amused condescension; she smoothed her hair and drew herself up a little taller. The woman went on:

"I'm in charge of PR for Akwa UK." They shook hands and Ursula Lemoine went on to introduce the man who was rising to his feet. "This is Morris Paxton. Morris is Head of the finance office and he's keen to meet anyone from Focus Asset Management personally."

Lemoine gave Paxton a sideways look, to see how he was taking the arrival of this apparent teenager. Nonetheless the 'teenager' was from one of their important investors and the meeting proceeded along conventional lines.

Anisha, hardly aware of the undercurrents and intent on carrying out her first assignment with credibility, shook hands with Morris Paxton. After a short exchange of pleasantries Ursula Lemoine made the transition to business matters.

"I'm sure you have your own agenda but I would very much like to give you the virtual tour of the business as we handle it from the UK. Akwa's head office, as you know, is in Canada but it is here in the UK that we handle the European part of the business, extending in fact into North Africa and Turkey and expanding all the time."

She turned to a laptop computer and indicated the screen on the further wall.

"I know you will be taking this back to your own head office," she remarked pointedly, "So, to give you an idea of the extent of the company's interests, this map shows where we have plants and subsidiaries in Europe." She indicated sites in France, Belgium, Italy, Austria.

"And developments in Eastern Europe are going ahead."

Anisha was making notes and feeling very much the rookie researcher.

"Could you tell me where expansion is planned?" she asked nervously.

"We are expanding fast in Eastern Europe at present…"

"Is there much of a market there?" Anisha was gaining in confidence.

"The market is growing. The interesting feature of Eastern Europe is their strong tradition of taking curative waters."

Lemoine appeared to have started on an aspect that interested her particularly and Anisha paid close attention whilst making notes.

"This gives us a good base to build the market on." Lemoine continued. "There is also an abundance of exploitable natural resources so that, while we may not market at full strength within these countries, the surplus can be exported to supply our other markets where demand is very high. I hope I am not jumping ahead or going too fast for you?" Lemoine enquired.

She was patronising but at the same time Anisha could see that Lemoine was genuinely anxious to get her message across.

"Not at all. But why is the demand so high in our part of the world? I mean, in Western relative to Eastern Europe?"

Eyebrows raised in incredulity to her colleague signalled Lemoine's disbelief at the naivety of the question but Anisha continued, determined not to let her way be blocked by company PR-speak.

"No really, I mean, I'm sure it's a very obvious question but I would really like to hear what you consider is behind the demand on the one hand and the lack of it on the other."

"In Western Europe" Lemoine explained, "Drinking bottled water is a lifestyle choice." It's linked to a multitude of activities like working out at a gym, taking part in sports and keeping fit. But in Eastern Europe the tradition of taking the waters and using spa waters for therapeutic purposes still exists

- mainly among the older members of society but at the younger end of the market the use of bottled water, linked to a young and healthy lifestyle is still quite undeveloped."

"So a market is there waiting to be developed?" Anisha asked.

"That is correct. Our products are enormously beneficial, as we all know, mainly because our lives here are increasingly sedentary and because our marketing devices link the use of our products to an active lifestyle."

Anisha felt she was beginning to understand.

"You have certainly convinced me of the health-giving effects of using your bottled waters!"

"And I can see that you are one of our customers!" Ursula Lemoine pointed to the small bottle which was visible in Anisha's bag.

"Yes indeed," Anisha replied. "I cycle a lot but also I find being in a dry office space for much of the day is extremely de-hydrating."

The man, who had hardly spoken, smiled.

"We could offer you a place on our marketing team; you are making the points for us!"

The Lemoine woman looked thoughtful and responded to him.

"You could have an idea there!" And, turning back to Anisha, "I wonder – would you be interested? We are planning a marketing campaign featuring different people, their lives and how our products fit in." She was reflective now: "Fund management researcher – cycling to work in the City – busy modern life…"

She looked at Anisha appraisingly, her healthy complexion, shiny, curly black hair and general impression of fitness.

"Would you be interested?"

Anisha was amused.

"Thank you; I'll bear it in mind!"

Checking her notes Anisha remembered that Rob wanted her to find out where new plants were planned. In answer to her enquiries Lemoine and Paxton gave her details of one plant in Turkey and three in North Africa.

"We are looking at the possibility of more expansion in this area and perhaps even further afield into the Middle East. But Turkey and North Africa are where we'll be looking to get things up and flowing first," they told her. Then they discussed the arrangements for Anisha's forthcoming trip to a bottling plant.

"We think you'll find our Andalusian installation most interesting. It combines traditional with the most modern technology."

"I had also hoped to see something of the Eastern European developments." Anisha told them. "Can this be arranged?"

"Certainly. Contact us as soon as you get back from Spain and we will fix a date."

Anisha came away from her meeting in no doubt as to the health-giving effects of the company's products and looking forward to learning about the process of extraction and bottling on her trip to Spain. Whilst the beneficial characteristics of the product was an important criterion for inclusion in Asset Management's Ethical portfolio, she must not miss out on Rob's other criteria, work-force conditions and labour-relations. She thought that there would be an opportunity to discuss them with the Manager of the Spanish plant, a trip that she was greatly looking forward to.

Back in the office Anisha wrote up her notes and gave Rob a brief description of her visit.

"They even wanted me to take part in their marketing campaign; 'Cycling City-girl cools off with sparkling Akwa', that sort of thing"

"You turned them down of course?"

Anisha hesitated.

"Conflict of interest," he reminded her gently. "The last thing you can do is incur any indebtedness to a company that features in our portfolio."

Anisha bit her lip; she could have kicked herself: how could she have been so naïve as to even say she would think about it?

"Yes, of course!" she reassured him. "I wouldn't even dream of it!"

"That's fine. We wouldn't want to score an own goal, would we?"

"Absolutely not!" Anisha agreed.

Chapter 4

Blue water footprint – Volume of surface and groundwater consumed as a result of the production of a good or service.
Sustainability criteria – Sustainability criteria are generally categorized into three major themes: http://www.waterfootprint.org/

The day before she was due to fly to Spain Anisha had a call from Gregory.

"Hi Grego! Nice to hear from you!"

"Hi. Do you want to meet for a drink some time?"

She told him she would be away for a couple of days.

"How about after work on Friday?" she suggested.

"Sounds good. I could come up your way and meet you – where?"

They arranged to meet by the entrance to the tube station on the Circle Line. Gregory wished her a good trip.

The flight to Malaga would take 3 hours. My grand-daughter, always meticulous where details were concerned, had checked out the company's guidelines on travel.

"Don't you think I ought to travel by train?" She asked Rob and she pointed to the page concerned. "It says here that environmental criteria are top priority when making travel arrangements."

"I'm afraid we can't spare you for the length of time that the train would take, or the extra costs."

If Anisha thought he had got his priorities wrong she didn't say so but Rob went on.

"We pay the carbon offsetting, so you needn't feel too bad about it." Anisha nodded.

"You'll need a car at the far end. Ask them to book it at the same time as the flight." She nodded again.

"Your Spanish is okay isn't it?"

"Oh yes; it'll be good to have a chance to use it!" she replied happily.

It was late afternoon when she flew in to Malaga Airport, picked up the car and drove to the hotel where she was to stay the night. Next morning early she set off along the coastal motorway. The sun was just breaking through the morning mist and thin cloud, glinting on the numerous stretches of polythene tunnel which flanked the road. For the first half hour the motorway was crowded with trucks, loaded with produce from the many market gardens. After half an hour the highway divided and, glancing down at her directions, Anisha took the left hand branch which swept inland and up into the hills. The earth and the rocks flanking the route were red and the landscape here was more arid. Another hour's driving and Anisha was looking for her exit. She was glad to have studied the map carefully in advance and had written out directions and route numbers clearly so she could glance at them as she drove. It was hard enough finding your way when you were driving alone, even without the added problem of driving on the unaccustomed side of the road and with unfamiliar road signs.

Spotting her exit in good time it was a relief to be off the motorway and on country roads. Soon she was driving through small towns and villages, where tall and dusty chestnut trees lined villages of stone walls and white-painted houses. It was trickier now to follow her own directions and she needed to go slowly and stop from time to time for a closer look at the map. The town she was aiming for bore the same name as the bottled water which had its plant there so it was not difficult to know when she had arrived. 'Los Cristales' announced itself as the home of pure health and at the entrance to the town there were advertisements for a variety of spa hotels and treatments. In the central square she found somewhere to park the car. She had made good time and, with an hour to spare, she could get something to eat and enjoy the atmosphere and charm of the old spa town. Water was the prevailing theme. From a background of sheer rock cliffs a waterfall cascaded across the road forming an arch of water that the cars had to drive through to continue on their way. It created a pleasant breeze and a rushing noise. She noticed a cafeteria in the square, flanked by eucalyptus trees and curtains of climbing greenery with blue-purple flowers. Here she chose a table and ordered mineral water and an omelette. The waiter brought a dish of olives along with the mineral water which was from the local spring, bottled by the company she was to visit.

An hour later Anisha was being shown around the factory. The first thing she wanted to see was the water extraction and that was where she now stood with the production manager explaining how it worked. He explained clearly in Spanish and Anisha had no trouble in following once she had grown accustomed to the background of rushing and churning water. A glass wall separated them from the rock wall out of which the water gushed to disappear below the platform where they stood and reappear at the other side as a roiling boiling fountain to be captured and led along a canal towards the main plant. The atmosphere was moist, cool and invigorating and she could feel the effect of the negative ions rushing around the space where they stood. Her guide moved on and the words he shouted back to her were snatched away by the maelstrom of air and water.
She followed in his footsteps
"This is where we test the water for its chemical content," he shouted over the maelstrom of rushing water before moving on. "And this is the bottling plant." The explanation was hardly necessary and Anisha watched as bottles moved past, were filled, capped and labelled. Then a thought struck her.

"How much water is used in the process?"

"More than we would like," he replied. "But we're working to reduce it all the time."

Back in the managerial suite, they sipped small cups of black coffee.

"How long has Los Cristales been part of the Akwa Group? Anisha asked.

"Fifteen years. We were one of the first when the industry began to consolidate. Akwa were based in Belgium and were looking to expand inside Europe. They had already acquired a plant in Northern Spain and that gave us confidence. It's been a good move. Our output has increased, we've gained access to new markets and we have benefited from the new technology and the know-how of the parent company."

"And has there been a down side?"

"None at all."

"It sounds almost too good to be true! What about the future? Will the demand hold up?"

"No doubt about that. You know, in this part of Spain we're experiencing an increasing number of shutdowns, when the water supply is cut off during the day. So of course people stock up with bottled water so as not to be left short. And when the supply comes on again it's often cloudy and unappetising. You saw the poly-tunnels as you came along: that's what's behind the water shortages: that and the tourist industry."

"So your product is a regular on the shopping lists of people in this part of Spain"

"That's for sure. But it's the same all over the country. Everyone wants to drink bottled water and to have it in their offices and workplaces. Demand is high. I suppose our only concern for the future would be if Akwa were to continue to expand to such an extent as to lose that individual contact with each of its subsidiaries."

"And do you think there is much likelihood of that?"

He looked thoughtful before replying.

"We know there's to be a big expansion into Eastern Europe and then possibly Turkey, North Africa maybe. I've even heard murmurs of a move further into the Middle East."

"Where in the Middle East?"

"Oh, I couldn't say; it's not properly on the agenda yet and I'm sure we will hear if there are any definite plans"

"I see. It's an interesting thought; I mean there must be a lot of thirsty people in that part of the world. And when you think of the disrupted water supplies, the demand for clean and healthy water must be huge."

Anisha had prepared a questionnaire for the visit and she felt confident of ticking the health sections.

"What other questions can I help you with?" her host and guide asked courteously. "I am sure we want to give your investors as much information as they would like; this company has a high tradition and reputation so, please, tell me your questions."

Anisha consulted her notes and turned to questions on labour relations and terms of employment.

When she felt he had answered her fully and satisfactorily it was time to wind up the interview. As he saw Anisha to her car she put a last question to him as a pleasant form of compliment.

"So the company looks fair to continue into the next generation, and the next after that?" she enquired.

"God willing" he replied with a smile, "God willing and provided that we use the water wisely."

"And in your opinion is it wisely used?"

He shrugged and opened his hands in a gesture to her; "You drove here; you have seen a little of how we use it; our agri-businesses depend on it. If this is wise....? Who knows.... as we say, *Quien sabe?* I hope you have found your visit useful," Anisha shook his hand warmly to signify that indeed she had,

"And I wish you an agreeable and safe journey."

It was growing dark as Anisha left the spa town and headed back towards the motorway. The last of the light faded as she reached its southern end and turned right to drive westward on the coastal route back to Malaga to the hotel where she had stayed the previous night. So on the return journey she saw nothing of the miles of polythene shelters that lined the coast, but instead found herself in the company of large trucks carrying their produce. She reached the hotel at eight thirty, which, by Spanish standards was early for dinner. As she was eating, a text message came through from Gregory; 'Meet you tomorrow at the airport!' Well, if he wanted to come and pick her up that was fine by her.   She didn't have to check in for the plane to London until 10 o'clock the next morning so, after a good meal she worked until after midnight, writing up her notes on the day's visit. She was pleased with the way things had gone on this, her first foreign assignment for Focus Asset Management.

Chapter 5

Aquifer

Definition: a layer of rock, sand,
or earth that contains water or allows water to pass through it
(Definition of aquifer noun from the Cambridge Advanced
Learner's Dictionary & Thesaurus © Cambridge University
Press)

Anisha wrote up her report that evening and the first thing
on her mind next morning, after an early breakfast at the hotel,
was to return the car to the hire company outside the airport.
When that was done, and with the receipted bills tucked into
her holdall, she made her way towards the check-in zone.
There, however, she was brought up short by the unexpected
sight of Gregory, a big smile on his face, looking relaxed in
beach shorts and trainers.

"Grego! What are you doing here?" she exclaimed. "I
thought you said......"

"Surprised?" he asked and took her arm to steer her away
from the check-in.

"Of course! Your text said 'meet you at the airport'..."

"It didn't say which airport though, did it?"

"Correct; so where are you going?"

"No: where are *we* going?" he retorted. "Listen, how
about this for a plan for the weekend?"

"Uh-uh, Grego" she protested, "I'm going on a plane back
to Heathrow."

"Wait: you haven't heard. There's this villa along the coast
which belongs to some friends of my Dad's and there's a group
of us going there, and you can come along and it'll be great!"

"That's ridiculous! I have my ticket here, booked, for
today!

47

"No problem; we can change it. Here, let me see; as long as it's not one of those book in advance non-refundable ones... no, it's alright, we can fix this one easily."

"Hey, Gregory; stop a minute. You haven't thought this through and you're taking a lot for granted; like I might really want to go straight back to London; that I might not want to spend a weekend totally unprepared, with a group of people I don't even know. For all you know I haven't got anything with me except my office clothes."

"I didn't suppose that you would come to Spain, even on business without some swimming things in your luggage – now did you?"

"But that's the only non-office item...."

"And that's all you'll need!"

And so it was that Anisha tacked a weekend onto the end of her working trip.

Now I personally have had my doubts about 'Grego', as they all seemed to call him; I could only go by what Anisha had told me but from her account he seemed both a little wild and more than a little arrogant. However it was an enjoyable weekend with swimming and jet-skiing from the beach-front villa of Gregory's friend's father's villa and since, contrary to Gregory's overly-optimistic assertions, no seat to London was available on Sunday evening, it was not until the Monday morning early that she found herself on a plane out of Malaga bound for Heathrow. And before they parted she and Grego had arranged to meet after their work at the end of the week.

That day, for the first time since starting her new job, Anisha was not the first into the office. In fact she arrived red-faced and out of breath and wishing she had another set of clothes other than those she had been wearing when she had set off for Spain the previous Thursday. Rob's eyebrows rose when he saw her and she made haste to pull the report from her holdall and hand it to her boss.

"I wrote my notes up as soon as I got back to Malaga" she told him, indicating the sheaf of A4. "Everything seems to be fine. I think I asked all the questions …"

She prepared to hand him the report but hesitated. "There's just one thing which I could pick out," She pointed to a paragraph near the end. "I think it could be important, it's about how much water they use in their production process." Rob took the report and read the paragraph.

"But of course this is important Anisha; this is the basis of the industry. The sustainability issue is right at the top of our investors' concerns. Everyone knows that the South of Spain suffers from water shortages. If you had missed this out I would have turned you round and sent you right back to Spain." Adding after a pause, "At your own expense!"

Anisha felt hot and cold as she saw how something she had nearly passed over might actually be the most important item in the report and she had only narrowly avoided a very major omission: on her first foreign assignment with all that it meant for her reputation and her career. It had been a near-thing, she realised, and she was grateful to Rob for not pointing out how close she had come to a really bad mistake.

"While the water industry scores high on all of the health issues and Akwa seems to do everything expected of it in terms of employment conditions and relations, the question of sustainability does need to be addressed."

Anisha furrowed her brows and Rob continued.

"Since you have learnt that they intend expansion into the Middle East I want you to see what you can find about the state of underground water supplies in those geographical areas."

She listened attentively and nodded.

"You've got plenty to work on, my girl, so get going! We'll talk before the end of the week, let's say on Thursday."

49

Anisha returned to her desk. She wasn't sure that she liked being addressed as 'my girl' but understood that, rather than a reprimand, it was to be welcomed. She took a long swig of water from the bottle on her desk and reflected: those flights were so dehydrating!

To begin the search Anisha needed to define its terms and identify the key words; Middle East, Gulf States and water supplies seemed as good as any. After that she tapped in groundwater and aquifers and opened a 'Water Issues' folder where, within a short space of time, she had more than fifty sites saved. That made it time to pause and do some weeding out for she could see that Water Issues included a great range of topics of which bottling spring water for commercial exploitation was just one. She had already lost time following up some topics which turned out to be complete red herrings: a plan to create a conduit for water to pass from the Mediterranean to the Dead Sea to generate electricity. Disappointingly the dateline on the website was at least 15 years old. What had become of that project?

Oh my God! She reflected. Three hours gone by! Where was she on mineral water supply? She moved to another site: North Africa and the Middle East, groundwater systems: maybe here she would find some relevant material. An aquifer, she learnt, had been discovered accidentally in North Africa; this looked more promising.

'British team prospecting for oil in Libya accidentally drills into unknown desert aquifer; the start of the North Africa River Plan.' That sounded exciting. But the next lines were a disappointment: this artificial river plan would water the fields for little more than 50 years and, she continued to read, once exploited, the aquifer would take centuries, no, millennia, to replenish.

She pulled herself up and returned to the subject: drinking water in bottles - that was what she was meant to be researching and she must confine herself to the subject! If a company wanted to extract water to sell in bottles to a fastidious, fashion-conscious and thirsty public in the Gulf States, how much would it amount to in the life of an aquifer? Anisha navigated her way, web-wise, towards the Gulf States, hopping from site to site and noting items of interest.

Searching for clues to this question she was soon once more completely absorbed, exploring the mysteries of an ancient system of underground tunnels and channels which had brought water from Persia to the deserts of Arabia, for the growing of date palms and, in the shade of those trees, the cultivation of green crops. An even more surprising fact, Anisha thought, was that the system was still in use and, as she delved deeper, how village culture had grown up around it. Aware of her manager looking over her shoulder, Anisha looked up.

"You've been at this a long time; how is the report coming along? I'll need you to move on to a new topic soon." Anisha nodded:

"Will Friday be alright for the report? It seems to me that groundwater supplies is something we should look at and I've still got some way to go with the research. There does seem to be a question mark in some of these areas."

"I'll give you until Friday for the report." Rob responded. "Set out the possible problems and I'll put them before the Board of Trustees at the next meeting."

"Fine!" Anisha was glad to have his approval for what she was doing.

Anisha immersed herself happily in her researches which brought her, later that day to the scanned copy of a paper dating from the 1960's on irrigation systems in the Gulf States.

51

Included in it was a list of the official titles of village elders and the functions they carried out in the village hierarchies: different roles revolving around the interwoven institutions of very old water rights and their administration as well as the legal and administrative systems of the village itself, underpinned by Koranic law and by older civilisations which had preceded Islam. Anisha was fascinated to learn that the *bayadir*, were labourers who worked under as well as above ground to keep tunnels and channels clear and functioning: the *basir* or water diviner, was skilled at finding new supplies of water to supplement existing sources: the *arif* had the responsibility of adjusting the sluice gates on the branching channels every few hours to ensure each villager got his allotted ration. Reading further she learnt that the *basir* was kept increasingly busy these days as old water sources began to run dry. Shouldn't that point be put to the Board of Trustees, she wondered, when they met to consider the case of Akwa and its proposals for new bottling plants?

Anisha had spent more time on the topic than she could afford if she wished to keep in Rob's good books. She had two interviews and a stack of notes to write up to complete her report, then she must move on to the next subject; it was hardly likely to be anywhere near as romantic as the oasis villages of Arabia.

Chapter 6

*A logo is a graphic mark or emblem commonly used by commercial
enterprises, organizations and even individuals to aid and promote
instant public recognition. Logos are either purely graphic
(symbols/icons) or are composed of the name of the organization* (a
logotype or wordmark). From Wikipedia, the free encyclopedia

On Friday Anisha arrived early for their date. She and
Gregory had agreed to meet at 8.30 at the Jermyn Street hotel
where he was attending an official reception to do with his
work.

"I'll meet you in the lobby area" he had told her. "And if
my event ends earlier I'll wait for you there – under the potted
palms!"

Now it was only eight o'clock and Anisha sat and looked at
the newspapers that were laid out for guests. After ten minutes
of this she stood up to wander around. Through double doors a
sign with an organisation's logo pointed towards what must be
Grego's reception; a buzz of conversation emanated from
behind another pair of doors. Anisha wandered over to speak
to the girl standing at a table where lapel badges with names
were laid out. She was immediately taken for a guest.

"Can you see your name here? "

Anisha smiled and shook her head, about to explain, but the
girl anticipated her.

"Not to worry, there seem to be a few badges missing,
yours is not the first. I can make you one, it won't take a
second."

Anisha had no objection; it would be amusing to surprise
Grego. In a few minutes she was having her name badge
pinned on and shown in to the Reception. A waiter with a tray
offered her a flute of sparkling wine; the real thing, she
guessed, sipping the champagne and looking around for
Gregory. She spotted him in conversation with a man whose

face was familiar even if she couldn't immediately put a name to it. She decided it would not be the right thing to interrupt. Just then there was a clearing of throats and tapping on a glass; someone, she couldn't see his face from where she stood, was going to speak.

"Just one more word ladies and gentlemen before you leave. I'd like to thank you again, for coming along this evening, and especially our speakers. I know you'll agree that they have left us with plenty to think about and the one thought I would like you to take away from the evening is – as our speaker said – 'IT'S HAPPENING ANYWAY, SO; JOIN US FOR THE YEARS TO COME!'. We'll be repeating the message in the coming weeks to people like yourselves around the world. As they say in business: it's always a good idea to get in on the ground floor. And I would just ask that, if you do decide that we are on to something, that it is the right way forward, in my view the only way forward, make sure that we have your details to contact you just as soon as we are ready to move to the next stage. Thank you!"

The guests began to surge towards the doors and among the crowd Anisha thought she recognised more of the faces. Allowing herself to be carried along, she found herself once more by the desk where she took a seat and, tidying the lapel badge away in her bag, kept a look out for Grego. She spotted him quite soon, shaking hands and saying goodbye to a tall character, silver hair over a surprisingly young face, in grey jacket and relaxed cord trousers. They parted and Gregory turned to look for Anisha.

"Hi, have you been waiting long?"

"Not too long; hey wasn't that Sir Alan Fletcher?" she asked.

He nodded, about to add a comment but Anisha went on:

"Who are all these people? I seem to recognise quite a few."

"It's quite a cross section," Grego replied vaguely. "Hey, let's go!"

Fifteen minutes later in a restaurant in Brewer Street they were ordering appetising choices from the Italian menu.

"So how was your event? And what was it all about?" Anisha asked him.

"Good champagne and interesting speakers," Grego replied.

"And the subject they were speaking about? I mean, from the impression as they came out, there was quite a buzz, and I'm intrigued to know what had caused the stir."

"Just one of these corporate gigs; getting the public enthused and keen to buy into the product."

"And the product?"

"Environment and energy. A research company."

"And will you be buying into it? I mean…" she hesitated, "I didn't realise you were up there in the rich list….?"

"Don't worry; I'm not! I was there for the research; my bosses wanted someone to go along and I drew the short straw."

"Some short straw; judging from the champagne that seemed to be flowing!"

"Sorry you didn't get to try some; it was good!"

"So you made notes, talked to people? I mean what's the angle of interest for your bosses?"

"More of the usual really; there's a hundred and one of these environmental groups, all keen to sign up anyone with half a claim to celebrity status – or just being in the public eye. It's not a big deal." Gregory changed the subject. "What have you been up to? And how's life in the world of asset management? You've never told me what you do there; tell me all about it!"

Despite the weekend in Spain, which had been entirely without romantic interest, Anisha had not so far been able to fathom Grego and she was reluctant to say too much about her own role in the company she worked for. In fact both of them seemed to want to keep the conversation on neutral ground: music, games, mutual friends and life online. The meal was comfortable and they parted an hour later on good terms, planning to meet again – nothing more.

Next morning Anisha parked her bicycle with the concierge in good time. She was on friendly terms with him now and he made sure that Anisha never set out without her crash helmet buckled. After changing from cycling gear to City attire she took her seat at her desk in the Green Team's area well before the main rush of arrivals. As she unpacked her bag in search of a pen, her mind on the day ahead, out fell the lapel badge from the previous evening. The symbol intrigued her and she paused to study the logo more closely - a bubbling spring, or a fountain perhaps, surrounded by a series of letters in a variety of scripts. Anisha could make out, in addition to letters R-S-A-F-I in the Roman alphabet, letters in Arabic, Cyrillic and other scripts, which she failed to identify, but which could have been Hindi or Tamil and Chinese or Japanese. Whatever they were they made a pleasing pattern and she put the badge away carefully to keep as a curiosity. She must remember to ask Gregory about his command of any of these languages; meanwhile, as a brain teaser, she tried to make a word or a sensible acronym from the Roman letters: R-S-A-F-I SAFIR? RASIF? IFARS? Nothing came to mind that made sense. She put the puzzle aside, it was time to get down to work.

Anisha divided the day between the telephone and the internet, making use of the Green Team's pile of business directories as and when she needed them, working on the new topic which Rob had given her relating to the company's holdings in rail transport. By the end of the day she was ready for some relief from railways and the chance to follow up the subject which interested her. She opened the folder of websites which she had created on water topics and looked for the village water systems which had so caught her imagination - even though, as far as the company was concerned, she had done all the research required. First she would check out the names she had found '*bayadir*' the labourer; he worked underground, clearing the channels of debris, maintaining the flow of water. It would terrify her, working underground in channels just high enough for a man to crawl, in order to keep the water flowing. Then there was the water diviner; she tapped in the word, *basir*: as the waters flowed more slowly the demands for his services were becoming more common. Then the man in charge, the administrator of the water system, perhaps the lynchpin of village organisation; she tapped in from memory *faris*, to learn more about the way his tasks were ordered.

The configuration of the website changed unexpectedly. Had she got the word wrong? Here she was looking at a different style of page altogether. She blinked and read 'FARIS – Homepage'. She was about to tap the 'back' arrow when, glancing to her right to the lapel badge on the desk beside her hand, she noticed they were the same letters – stupid! She had been looking for *arif* and had keyed in *faris*; nevertheless an easy mistake. Her hand paused as she took a quick look to find out more about the organisation which had thrown the champagne party. Their web page was not very enlightening: the same intriguing logo followed by a rather uninteresting series of questions:-
Fit and Ambitious?
Ruthless and Intelligent?
If you are a Survivor we'd like to hear from you.

The way the letters were highlighted led easily to the acronym but Anisha was as much in the dark as before as to what exactly FARIS was all about.

Another date with Grego was what she needed. But was she that interested?

She pressed the back button and this time typed in *arif* correctly. The work of this village elder was passed down from generation to the next, often in the same family. Tradition played a strong part, or perhaps it was the long apprenticeship that was required to ensure the true transmission of knowledge and practice. But the traditional system was under threat and it didn't take much insight to realise that if the age-old irrigation system went, the pattern of village life went too. She wondered how the waters were being depleted now: was it simply a matter of population pressure? And would one bottling plant tapping into the ground source really add to the problem? That old system of the desert had caught Anisha's imagination and she hoped that, with Rob's approval she might get to see for herself how it worked. With some annual leave due to her in a few weeks' time, she decided that if she could add some working days to her holiday it would make for a really great and unusual way to escape from twenty-first century city life for a while.

Chapter 7

Whistlejacket is an oil-on-canvas painting from about 1762 by British artist George Stubbs showing the Marquess of Rockingham's racehorse, rearing up against a blank background. The huge canvas, lack of other features, and Stubbs' attention to the minute details of the horse's appearance give the portrait a powerful physical presence.
From Wikipedia, the free encyclopedia

"You know, Alastair is just so delighted that you got the job at Focus Asset Management. And that you seem to be enjoying it." Anisha's mother told her daughter, speaking on Skype from her new home in the Gulf, a few evenings later.

"I know, you said that already! He might not be quite so keen though if he knew I was on the eco-team."

"Listen sweetheart; the fact that you are in the City and working for an investment company is enough for him. He could not be happier about it."

"He probably sees me following in his footsteps. Making a fortune is in his blood! But I get the impression that he doesn't have any time for environmentalists."

"You make him sound completely ruthless!"

"Well, isn't he?"

"Not at all; he's a softie underneath."

Anisha was doubtful. "All the same, don't tell him I'm in the Green Team Mum, promise? And especially don't tell him my views on the Palm Island."

"Yes alright – promise! But you may change your mind after you've seen it. I had my own doubts but it really is a dream. I can't wait to show you!"

"Well you won't have to wait long. I've booked my flight and I'll be with you in two weeks time."

"Sweetheart – that's wonderful. Now, how long can you stay? And there are a few things I'd like you to bring for the house."

"No problem; as long as you pay my excess baggage!"

"Oh it won't be anything enormous; just one or two little finishing touches. I could always go to the mainland and shop there but you can save me the trouble. How long can you stay?"

"Four days is my plan."

"Is that all? Why not longer?"

"I'm going on somewhere after. I've got ten days holiday – only been with the company six months so ten days is not bad."

"So where are you going on to?"

"I'll tell you about it when I see you. Will you be at the airport? Got to go now Mum. See you soon!"

"Love you darling! Bye!"

Anisha put the phone down and felt a ripple of excited nerves. Just two weeks to set up the trip she had set her heart on and she hoped it would be time enough to follow up her research and make the contacts she needed. Before that she had another date with Grego and there was a list of things she wanted to find out from him.

They met after work at the National Gallery.

"What shall we look at? What are your favourites?"

Anisha answered without hesitation,

"Turner. What are yours?"

Grego paused for a moment.

"Probably Velasquez – shall I tell you why?"

"Of course!"

"He's a psychologist. He sees inside the heads of his sitters and you can read their minds. There's one of the Pope; he doesn't flatter the man – and that's quite unusual for a painter of the time. You can read in his face power, experience, weariness."

"Let's have a look." They were at the top of the staircase and had to decide which rooms to take.

"It's not here; I saw it in Madrid." Gregory told her. "There are some Velasquez here but why don't we start with your Turners?"

Anisha led the way and soon they were standing in front of her favourite.

"It's sad; it's meant to be sad. The magnificent ship – look at the sails and the rigging – being towed along by a dirty little tug boat, to be broken up in some ship-breaker's yard. The end of an era!"

"He couldn't help seeing it that way" Gregory commented. "He was old himself when he painted it. He'd fallen prey to the sickness of looking backwards. He'd forgotten how to look to the future. That's no way to live."

"But you can understand that feeling of nostalgia, can't you?"

"It has no appeal for me," Gregory said firmly. "Show me a picture of strength and power – something that I can admire for itself and I'm fine with it, but spare me anything sentimental."

They were passing a painting of a giant racehorse which took up the entire height of the gallery's wall.

"Is that the kind of thing?" Anisha asked.

"It's magnificent. The power of the horse reflects the power of the King who commissioned the painting."

"It's not very subtle, is it?" asked Anisha. "I mean it doesn't leave any room for insight, or interpretation, or compassion."

"And those are all very commendable qualities, but not what I'm looking for in a painting – speaking personally, of course."

"Of course."

"Tell me about FARIS", Anisha suggested.

They had left the Gallery and were headed to Gregory's South Kensington flat.

"Tell me about FARIS," Anisha repeated.

Grego turned and stared at her, his mouth open and eyebrows raised.

"Where did that question come from?" he asked her.

"FARIS popped up on a website and the logo looked familiar."

"Familiar from where?"

"From that reception you were at. Have you forgotten?"

"No, of course not but I don't remember any logos on display – it was a private function. What are you on about?"

Anisha thought for a moment; she wasn't about to tell Grego that she had sneaked inside; at least not until she knew a bit more.

"To be honest, I can't really remember. I may have seen it on some of the guests, as they left. Were they wearing badges?"

Grego shook his head. "No, not as far as I know; they weren't supposed to be."

"Is it top secret then?" She pressed him, smilingly.

"Not at all," he replied evenly, "Just….private."

"I can tell that much from the website. It looks like some extremely exclusive health club."

Grego smiled.

"Is that what it is?" She pressed him again. "There's a lot of emphasis on fitness…. But also on intelligence and other things as well. I can't remember the rest of it."

"Don't bother about it," Grego almost snapped at her.

Anisha looked hurt and Grego added, less brusquely, "It's nothing!"

"I'm not bothered!" Anisha replied evenly, "But it's obviously not nothing. There were a lot people with large bank accounts at that reception – probably off-shore ones too - as well as one or two faces I'm sure I've seen but I haven't put a name to yet. And a lot of champagne was flowing."

"How do you know there was champagne?"

Anisha pulled herself up short and improvised.

"You could tell by the way the guests came out: they were buzzing – they were on some sort of a high. And anyway, you told me."

He shook his head again.

"It really wasn't anything that interesting. Forget about FARIS it's nothing."

Anisha didn't like being patronised, and she didn't like being fobbed off either. Gregory could see she wasn't satisfied.

"It's nothing to do with me either," he went on, "if that makes you feel any better. It was work for me, being there. I had to go."

"Oh, bad luck!" she said sarcastically. "If you want to know what I think…"

"Look Anisha, I don't want to know what you think. Can we talk about something else?"

"Sure: like what? Life? The universe?"

He stopped walking and turned to face her, grabbing her arm and making her pull up short.

"Listen, I said let's change the subject – don't keep going on about FARIS!"

She was silenced- stunned by this response, then in a quiet voice,

"So FARIS is about life and the universe is it? You could have told me before. It's nothing to be ashamed of!"

"Forget it; I didn't say it was about life and the universe."

No she said to herself, you didn't say it, but I obviously hit a chord! Why should a crowd of expensive guests be treated to champagne and caviar just to listen to a dry talk about moral philosophy? She had food for thought.

For some time they walked on in silence. Eventually Anisha thought she should offer up a new topic of conversation.

"Are you keen on cars Grego?"

He turned to her

"Yes, in fact I am – why?"

"Do you have one in London?"

"Yes, of course. You'll see it. I'll drive you home in it, if you like."

"Yes please. What kind is it? And where do you keep it?

The car was a neat BMW sports model and Grego, having taken Anisha on a tour around London with, thanks to the mild summer night air, the roof down, dropped her outside the flat in Southwark at an hour which was thoroughly respectable for a girl who would cycle in to work for 8.15 the following morning.

"Thanks for the ride; the car is great!"

"It's fun; I enjoy it."

"I can see that!"

" Umm… another of my interests is polo. Have you ever been to a match?"

"Never! Is that an invitation?

"If you like. Do you want to come and watch at the weekend?"

"I told you – I'll be away for two weeks. Visiting my parents."

"Right; I'd forgotten. Have fun! I'll ring you when you get back. I'll be playing in the team at Cowdray Park soon after that. Will you come and spectate?"

"Not sure it's quite my scene" Anisha began doubtfully, then: "Give me a ring anyway: you might be able to persuade me!"

Chapter 8

The origins of Polo goes back to Persia. The game first played in Persia at dates given from the 5th century BC. or much earlier, to the 1st century AD and originated there, polo was at first a training game for cavalry units, usually the king's guard or other elite troops. To the warlike tribesmen, who played it with as many as 100 to a side, it was a miniature battle. From Wikipedia, the free encyclopedia

It was a Tuesday when Anisha cleared her desk for her trip. I may be well into my 70's but my eyesight is good and my driving licence is intact. I would go so far as to say that my casual acquaintances probably think I am a good five years younger than I am, probably because I like to dress well and have a most talented hairdresser who I should hate to lose. That Wednesday morning in March I had the privilege of driving my grand-daughter to Heathrow and an opportunity to catch up with her life and to hear about her plans. First she would be visiting Jessica and Alastair, her stepfather, in the newly purchased villa on the now world-famous Palm Island development; that would be exciting in itself. After that she was planning a week's adventurous trip with a company that ran desert safaris, over-landing from Dubai around the coast and ending up in Muscat. Having convinced Rob that a visit to the Water Resources Department of the university there would be relevant to his concerns about Akwa's plans for abstracting water, she was able to tack a few working days onto her leave allowance and also to offset part of the cost of her air-fare. From Muscat she would fly back to London. We exchanged warm hugs as I dropped her off outside Departures and I offered her some grandmotherly advice.

"First, do try to get on well with your stepfather. I know from your Mum that he desperately wants you to be friends."

Anisha looked doubtful.

"He'll give you a wonderful good time. And I'm sure he's looking forward to it," I told her "So mind you behave, young lady!"

She promised. "Don't worry! I'll be really well-behaved and nice to him."

"And the other thing is about the safari trip: – do take good care. Don't get dehydrated; don't let yourself get sick, and if anything goes wrong – make sure your phone is working and that you can contact Jessica. In fact you'd better have my number as well; you can always contact me if you can't get hold of your Mum."

"You know I've got it already Gran! Of course I'll take care. I'll text you if I have time, to let you know how everything is going."

"Don't worry about that," I urged her, "You'll have far too much to think about enjoying the trip. But I just want to know that you can get in touch if you need to. You're very precious to me, my darling, and I'm proud of everything you do. Don't let me down!"

"Of course not, Gran. Now, thank you for the lift and stop worrying. I'll have a fabulous time and I'll tell you all about it when I get back."

The Emirates flight touched down soon after 11 pm at the Gulf States International Airport. Anisha barely had time to register the heat, which was in the high forties, before she was inside the airport building and passing through customs. Jessica and Alastair were waiting for her. Mother and daughter hugged and Alastair enfolded her in an embrace which Anisha submitted to less willingly and failed to respond to with equal warmth, feeling still an instinctive distrust of this interloper – as she thought of him – in her life. Not just an interloper but obviously a wealthy one which, to Anisha, was something to be suspicious of. With little opportunity up to now to get to know her new step-father outside of a large gathering Anisha was struck again by the figure he presented. In his late-fifties, Alastair was tall and well-built with a cultivated sun-tan. He carried himself with the authority of a man with a purpose and the confidence and wherewithal to carry it through. Anisha found herself wondering what exactly his aims and ambitions were and how her mother fitted into his plans. But she had little time to dwell on these questions as Jessica and Alastair whisked her away by car and boat to the island. Soon she was unpacking in her own room in the magical island villa where air-conditioners hummed quietly, making the hot air bearable.

At one a.m. they sat looking out at the terrace where a fountain played in a blue pool whose submerged lights illuminated the surrounding vegetation and the red hibiscus flowers stood out against the blue of the water and the greenery.

"It's beautiful; just gorgeous!" Anisha exclaimed, the sleepiness of the 6-hour flight dispelled by the new surroundings and the pleasure and warmth of her mother's welcome and, she had to admit it, that of her stepfather as well.

"Wait till you see it in daylight. You'll love it even more," her mother told her.

"We've got it almost how we want it. I've spent hours on the furniture and getting the curtains and everything right. Your study has been a headache, hasn't it Alastair?" He nodded his agreement. Jessica rattled on, "The difficulties in getting his office equipment installed – horrendous! They told us that everything would go in smoothly but when it came to the point the various broadband, satellite and whatever else he has to have in the way of advanced communications and – you know! All the boys' toys!" She smiled indulgently.

Alastair nodded his agreement complacently and added:

"It's nearly there now. When everything is installed, Anisha, you could probably do your London job from right here!"

"Is that what you plan to do? Work from here." she asked him?

"Only part of the time, but I need to be in touch with everywhere and at any time of the day. Follow the markets from East to West, talk to people when I need to. In fact this is an ideal halfway house as far as global networking is concerned. It means I can be in touch in both hemispheres without too much disruption to the biological clock. Tomorrow you can see the video-conferencing facility; it has a room all to itself."

It was ten o'clock when Anisha woke next morning, her body still adjusting to local time. Pulling back the curtains she had a fine view of the villa's gardens. Her window was surrounded by bougainvillea flowers, brilliant shades of purple and scarlet with a fountain, the one she had glimpsed lit up last night, rising out of a blue basin of water, its droplets creating a rainbow. Beyond were flowerbeds and a lawn with sprinklers playing over the carpet of green. Graceful palm trees created the boundary beyond which Anisha could see a sweep of road, cornice-style, and beyond that, the blue of the sea. There were birds too, some which looked like small doves on the grass, others, perched on bushes were black and yellow with pointed bills and, near the palm trees two, the size of jays but vivid turquoise, performing acrobatic flights around the trees.

She made her way to the kitchen where she found her mother.

"It's like something from the Arabian Nights Mum; it's lovely; a long way from suburban Surrey!"

"I felt sure you would like it – and understand…?"

"Yes, of course!" Anisha paused. "I still can't see how it's going to work out though."

Jessica raised an enquiring eye at her daughter, who went on,

"I mean, I know you want to be with Alastair, that's natural. But is he going to spend all that much time here? And what will you do when he's away? You're used to running things; won't you miss your job at the Golf Club?"

Jessica looked serious.

"For the moment there's plenty to do, getting the house and garden how we want it. When that's done I will look around for something to keep me busy. I promise you – don't worry!"

"Will you get a job?"

Jessica shook her head.

"There's no chance of a work permit; wives of expats don't qualify and there's no way round that."

"So what will you do? You'll be bored out of your mind."

"Well, I don't need the money now but I'd like to find something - maybe with one of the local golf clubs on a volunteer basis."

Anisha nodded approvingly. "With all that experience of running the Clubhouse in Surrey they would be keen to have you. Anything else?"

Her mother looked pleased and went on to elaborate.

"There's the Polo Club which Alastair belongs to: it could be another possibility."

"That sounds interesting," Anisha remarked. "I've got a friend who plays polo. It sounds exciting – and expensive. I imagine the membership is pretty exclusive. What do you know about it?"

"Well, it's not a cheap sport – if you are a serious player. We've been a few times and the membership is very international. Are you interested?"

Anisha nodded. "I'd love to see a game…."

"We could go while you're here. Would you like to?"

Anisha nodded her agreement as Alastair came into the kitchen.

"We could go tomorrow, couldn't we Ali?"

"Go where?" Alastair enquired.

"To the Polo Club. Anisha would like it."

So the matter was decided. Next day, Friday, which was the weekend here, they would go for brunch at the Polo Club and watch the tournament that was scheduled to last the whole day.

Friday brunch at the Polo Club was a regular event and a relaxed affair. Members might start the day with a swim followed by breakfast from the buffet laid out on tables beneath the palms surrounding the pool. From the terrace spectators had a good view of the polo fields and, beyond those, the stables and the exercise fields. Distant sounds of hooves on stone stable yards merged with the patter of rain from morning sprinklers and the insistent chirping of sparrows in the bougainvilleas. While the dress-code was relaxed within the constraints of local custom, the host nation expected ladies to observe a covered up decency. Jessica had spent an hour agonising over what to wear and looked stylish in designer casuals whilst Anisha had picked her only spare white trousers and a flowered cotton tunic which covered her arms and came down to her thighs. Both carried sunhats and dark glasses in readiness for the glare of the sun when the tournament began. Alistair was relaxed in open-necked shirt.

"Are you girls going to have a swim before the matches begin?" he suggested. "I'll be over at the yard for a bit and then I'll join you for breakfast."

At nine in the morning the day had already heated up and Anisha relished the swim in the cooled waters of the pool. This, she reflected, was the luxurious part of her holiday and she might as well make the most of it because there would not be much luxury in the second stage. Diving into the pool she twisted and turned gracefully under water, coming up gasping, not for air but in surprise at the sight she had glimpsed. Taking a few more strokes she dived again to check her first impression; one side of the pool appeared to be a tropical reef, with fish of all colours apparently swimming in the same space as she was, until she realised that a thick wall of glass separated her from them. She came up spluttering. "That's really clever the way they've done that. You should take a look, Mum."

"Actually it's visible from the other side. When you go down to the changing room you can see the aquarium from the back."

"Come on in anyway – it's lovely!"

Jessica shook her head

"I want to keep my hair dry; not sure who we might be meeting later."

Anisha reflected how her Mum had changed. Getting her gorgeous red hair wet would never have been a worry in the past but now, the thought of Alastair's position, his interests and contacts seemed to have altered her outlook and changed her responses to all sorts of situations.

After Anisha's swim the two of them sat in the sun before it became too hot to bear. Anisha shook the water from her hair, knowing that it would dry in the tight curls that suited her well. Jessica patted hers cautiously back into place where the odd drop had moistened it.

"Tell me a bit more about Alastair and the polo club" Anisha prompted. "He's a member, but does he actually play for a team?"

"He used to, but not often now."

Anisha looked enquiringly, "Is that, er, age-related?"

"It's a young man's sport" her mother retaliated, defensively. "Aren't most sports?"

"Golf isn't!" her daughter retorted, "As you know!"

"Polo is quite different!

"Tell me about it!"

"You have to be ultra fit, not just fit. You need fast reactions and split-second timing – and that declines with age. Great horsemanship, of course, that goes without saying. And Alastair does play, when they are short of a man. Just not regularly"

"OK, I'm not winding you up about it."

"And I'm not at all wound up! There are plenty of other ways for him to keep up his interest in the sport."

"Such as?"

"Sponsoring his team for one thing; running a string of polo ponies doesn't come cheap. There's more to it than golf!"

"That's what I imagined." Anisha said thoughtfully. Her mind went back to Grego in London and she wondered how he could afford his sport.

"And do you have to be very well-off to play in a team?"

"Not, necessarily, but I think you would have to have connections; or else be utterly single-minded and determined."

Anisha wondered: which of these applied to Gregory: single-minded and determined? Probably yes. Well-connected? She didn't know but might find out if she were to accept his invitation to a match. Now, however was her chance to find out something about the sport and surprise him on her return.

Alastair joined them at the buffet for breakfast where once more Anisha felt she should take advantage of the selection. Every conceivable kind of fruit offered a colourful way to start and the variety of grills, omelettes and pastries would have been enough to last the day without thought of returning for lunch. Anisha helped herself generously and returned to the table to find her mother and step-father satisfying themselves more modestly with coffee and croissants.

"Tell me about the tournament," Anisha urged him, "Is it a big one? How many teams are taking part?"

"It's an international tournament – the most important of the Club's year today. Teams are from Europe, America – that's North and South, also India and naturally the Gulf States."

"So it's a really big event. But I need to start from scratch: what are the rules of the game?"

"Eat up!" Alastair urged her "We need to get over to the stands to get good seats. I'll tell you the rules if you're interested, and anything else you'd like to know, once we're settled."

Twenty minutes later they were seated in a stand, well shaded by awnings from the increasing heat. The walk from the pool terrace had been delayed by the acquaintances who stopped to greet Alastair, sheikhs in robes as well as westerners like themselves. Finally they took their seats and Anisha looked around.

"The pitch is enormous!" was her first comment.

"The field," Alastair corrected her. "It's as big as ten football pitches. That gives you an idea of the scale of the game."

"It certainly does. It's obviously not a sport which can be played in a city stadium!"

"Polo began as training for battle. It started in Persia and the game was a way of training the King's cavalry."

"A bit like fox hunting in the eighteenth century – the gentry being encouraged to ride hell for leather?" Anisha suggested

"Something like that – but chasing a ball rather than a fox" Alastair responded. "It soon became the national sport in Persia, with women, mark you, as well as men playing. You can see them in those old miniature paintings."

"And do women play today?"

"Yes indeed! There are some all-women teams and some mixed teams. But it will be mostly men today."

"Why is that? Anisha asked.

"Well now, it's hard to say. But wait until you've seen a few games," Alastair suggested.

Two teams were coming onto the field, distinguished by their colours,, one team sporting orange shirts and light blue helmets, the other in shirts of green and yellow with white helmets. The ponies were burnished and gleaming, their manes cropped and their tails plaited. The next seven minutes passed in a whirl that left Anisha breathless just from watching. The pace of the game, as the ponies thundered down the field only to wheel and turn in seconds of flying turf and thundering hooves made her gasp. She had to admire the skill and the nerve of the riders as they flung their horses – no, 'ponies!' she reminded herself – in the general direction of the goalposts at either end.

"That was breathtaking!" she admitted at the end of the first bout.

"It's called a chukka," Alastair reminded her.

"Chukka: that's a word I've heard before," Anisha replied.

"A chukka lasts seven minutes and there are six in a game, three in each half, with a four-minute break between. The aim of course is to score goals. At half time the riders change ponies and they have a longer break for that."

"It looks pretty dangerous: I mean, those poles could cause serious injury. How do they avoid crashing into each other or hitting the horses?"

"There's a whole set of rules which they have to follow. The umpires see to that. Basically, no rider is allowed to cross the line of the ball. That's an imaginary line that extends forward in the direction the ball is travelling. It changes frequently – obviously!"

" Umm, not sure if I follow that," Anisha said doubtfully. "How about the ponies? Do they enjoy it?"

"They wouldn't make good polo ponies if they did not," Alastair replied. "They are bred for it. It's in their blood."

"And do they always play on grass?"

Originally not. The '*maidan*' of Persia was just wide stony ground. And here in the Gulf at first they played on sand. Grass is obviously best for the ponies – and for the riders when they fall off too!"

One chukka followed another until Anisha began to get a clearer idea of the rules of the game. And match followed match in the tournament, with teams from around the world.

"Keeping up a polo team must cost a bit," Anisha remarked. Was it your idea to make your company a sponsor?"

"Mine and a few like-minded colleagues in the boardroom. There are several of us who used to play. What do you think? Is it a good game?"

"It's fantastic. Breathtaking is the word. I would love to have a go!"

"Really darling," Jessica interrupted, "You haven't ridden since Pony Club; and that must have been ten years ago"

"I don't think you forget" Anisha retorted, "What do you think Alastair?"

"I'm sure you don't forget, but you get out of practice – and you need to be fit."

"Fitness isn't a problem, but out of practice, yes I agree there."

"I'll take you round to the stables – when the tournament finishes and after the presentations" Alastair promised her. "Now, this is our team coming next. We need to give them plenty of support."

Applause broke out all round the stands for the six riders and their ponies that were one of the three local teams taking part. Wearing salmon pink and yellow, they raised their long sticks in acknowledgement of the applause before lining up to face their opponents for the start of the match.

When the match was over, Alastair, satisfied that his team were through to the next round, went to give congratulations and encouragement. Anisha and Jessica took a break and returned poolside to where the breakfast buffet had been replaced by an array of lunch dishes.

"Alastair's into polo in a big way," commented Anisha and Jessica agreed.

"It's his passion of the moment. He's on the committee and spends quite a lot of time here at the Club."

"And quite a lot of money too, I imagine. Flying a string of ponies around the world, putting your team up in hotels and all of that. It can't be cheap".

"It certainly isn't", Jessica agreed, "But if that's the way he wants to spend his money that's OK."

Anisha gave a shrug which her mother picked up on immediately.

"You really should get over this thing about money, darling. Now that you're working in the City I would have thought you would be more accustomed to the idea. Alastair has made his money: he can spend it how he likes."

Anisha responded sharply.

"I work in Ethicals, Mum, You know that."

It was Jessica's turn to sigh and remark ironically

"And you wear your halo very prettily too."

The conversation was threatening to take a wrong turn and as neither of them wanted a scene Anisha was happy to change the subject.

"Do you go with him to the international events?"

"Sometimes," Jessica replied. "I'll be going to Argentina with him in the autumn, which should be interesting. I mean, the hosts always entertain you lavishly and you meet a lot of interesting people."

"Like who for example?"

"Oh, leaders of industry, big names from international corporations, even academics and scientists. You'd be surprised just how many people take an interest in polo."

The final heats were being played when the two of them returned to the stand.

"Where have you been? You missed some exciting rounds," Alastair reproached them.

"Mother and daughter have a lot to catch up on!" Jessica protested. "Don't be hard on us. And the lunch was too good to miss! What about you; aren't you hungry?"

"I grabbed something over at the Players' Bar." Alastair reassured her. "Don't run away again; the final will be soon."

Jessica and Anisha settled into their seats again.

"So how is it going? Do we know who's going through to the final?" Jessica asked.

"I'm afraid our team got knocked out in the fourth round but their opponents will be in the final – so, no disgrace."

The final was if anything even more breathtaking as the two top teams battled for each chukka. Anisha lost track of which team was on top amid flying hooves and flying turf and the cheers and applause of spectators. When it was over and ponies were led away sweating and steaming, it was time for the line up and presentation of trophies and cups. An awning was swiftly erected at one end of the field and the Club's president, in white robes and with royal guard in attendance, presented the prizes to the winning team. Still red-faced from the final round, the riders had sleeked down their hair and smartened themselves up for the important moment. The trophy was large and beribboned and the individual cheques, Anisha guessed, were probably also quite large.

"I'm going to join the teams in the Sponsors' Bar. Would you like to come?" Alastair invited them. "There will be a good atmosphere."

Anisha and Jessica happily agreed.

The Sponsors' Bar was crowded but Alastair made light work of clearing a path, pausing on the way to greet or be greeted by acquaintances, locals in robes and ex-pats alike. Jessica too was known to many and greeted her friends enthusiastically. The women were well turned out in casual designer items to complement the understated cool of their men-folk, those not wearing national garb mostly in chinos and crisp open-neck shirts. Anisha followed along in their wake, observing. She had hoped to meet the riders, but it seemed that they had taken themselves off to party elsewhere. Instead Alastair introduced her and Jessica to his friends and fellow sponsors. They were a cosmopolitan gathering, brought together by a common interest. One detail, which she filed away in her memory to be taken out again later was something seen here and there among the jewellery, tie-pins and lapel badges. An elegant pin made up of five letters entwined around a fountain-like shape. Where had she seen that before? She racked her brain to remember. Ah yes, the reception: the hotel just off Jermyn Street, London. She wondered if she still had the lapel badge from that occasion.

"Mum, have you got one of those little badges?"
They were in Jessica and Alastair's bedroom, chatting over the day's events.
"Which little badges, sweetheart?" Jessica asked.
"The fountain with the initials" Anisha explained.
"Oh, you mean the FARIS pin?"
"Exactly! What's it supposed to stand for? Is it special?"
"Alastair did give me one and to be honest I'm not sure what it stands for. It's just rather pretty. I think perhaps it's the Polo Club. Let's see if I can find it for you."

Jessica took out a jewel box and looked through the different compartments.

"I remember that box," Anisha looked at it with pleasure. "You used to keep it on your dressing table at home. But you've got a lot more in it now than there used to be!"

"Well, Alastair is awfully good in that way and he knows what I like. Ah, here it is. What do you think?"

She handed Anisha the little brooch, the outline of a fountain with the initials worked into the droplets which cascaded from it. Jessica's version was embellished with diamonds that formed the droplets.

"It's beautiful! Why didn't you wear it today?"

"Alastair told me not to. I'm not sure why." Jessica responded.

"Told you not to what, Jessica?" Alastair had come into the room.

"You didn't want me to wear the pin today." Jessica replied. "Anisha was asking me about it."

"I was just asking what it was," Anisha told him. "I noticed several people wearing ones like it. What do the letters stand for?"

"It's just a Polo Club badge. Nothing significant, can't actually remember what the logo stands for."

"I can't think why you didn't want me to wear it today, though, Alastair."

"It wasn't that I didn't want you to wear it – just that I wanted you to wear something else," Alastair told her with evident irritation. "Now can we leave it at that?"

"Of course!" Jessica laughed. "I wouldn't have wanted to be seen wearing the same jewellery as half a dozen other people!"

"Quite right" Alastair agreed with her. "OK Anisha?"

"Fine!" Anisha replied, wondering what all the fuss was about and why this emblem seemed to be popping up in so many places

Chapter 9

Geographically, the Musandam peninsula juts into the Strait of Hormuz, the narrow entry into the Persian Gulf, from theArabian Peninsula. The Musandam peninsula is an exclave of Oman, separated from the rest of the country by the United Arab Emirates. Its location gives Oman partial control, shared with Iran, of the strategic strait. In the northern section of Musandam, around Kumzar, the language is Kumzari, which is one of the south-western Iranian languages and related toLuri and Persian. The Musandam Peninsula has an area of 1,800 square kilometers (695 sq mi) and a population of 31,425 people   From Wikipedia, the free encyclopedia

Anisha retired to bed, not to sleep but to think out the next part of her trip. Planning this second stage of her holiday hadn't been entirely straightforward. Her objectives were to visit the inland oases of one or more of the Gulf States and see for herself the ancient *falaj* system, while it was still working as it had done for a thousand years. She knew she couldn't organise the trip in such a short time on her own and she would need a knowledgeable guide to travel with her, someone who knew the area and the people who lived there. In the end, with her usual resourcefulness and refusal to let obstacles get in her way, she had gone back over some of her leads and succeeded in obtaining an invitation to visit the Department of Water Resources at the university outside Muscat, in the Capital Area of Oman

Having got this far, she booked herself onto a trekking holiday – a week travelling overland across all six of the Gulf States which make up the Emirates and down the coast to their final destination on the Gulf of Oman. In five days from setting out they would reach Muscat and, shortly before that point Anisha had arranged that she would be dropped off conveniently close to the campus and her meeting place.

She was unsure how much to tell her mother about her trip and in particular the final few days of it. In the end she decided she couldn't tell Jessica too much because Alastair would be bound to pour scorn on the idea. In any case, as he was still unaware of the precise nature of her employment she very much preferred to leave him with the comfortable impression that she was a high-flying fund manager and not a researcher in the ethical investment team. So to Jessica and Alastair she described the next part of her trip as a straightforward adventure holiday.

"It sounds exciting darling, but how well prepared are you?" her mother asked on Anisha's last evening at the villa. "It could be quite arduous …."

"We're travelling in four-wheel drives Mum, not on camels!"

"I know that, but you are supposed to be having a holiday. I presume these people know what they're doing…?"

"I think they do. They're an established company with five year's experience of organising treks in the region. They have all the right kit in case the vehicles break down or get stuck in sand and there really isn't much to worry about." Anisha assured her. "It's probably a lot less risky than the treks you did when you were my age!"

Alastair agreed. "It strikes me as very enterprising of Anisha," he told Jessica and, turning to Anisha, "I've driven that way myself – you'll have a fascinating trip. Make sure you stop at the villages en route; people are very hospitable."

"That's exactly what I want to do; and to see something of the old way of life before it disappears."

Early next morning Jessica accompanied Anisha on the crossing back to the mainland. A breeze had got up and the sea was bumpy. Once ashore, they found the pick-up point where the four-wheel drives and the team leaders were waiting. The wind was whipping up sand and dust, turning the air to a beige blur and blotting out the sun. Several members of the group were standing around, drinking Pepsi or Seven-up from bottles and making the first tentative steps of getting to know each other. They were to travel in a convoy of three Land-Cruisers carrying nine passengers, each with its driver who doubled as their guides. Jessica inspected the supplies they were carrying: food water, tents, first-aid and breakdown kit. Despite her own years of carefree travelling at Anisha's age, she was still not entirely at ease about the venture and needed to reassure herself on the smallest details.

"What about visas?" she asked Anisha. "You'll be crossing several frontier posts, won't you? Have they got that organised?"

"That's all part of what they do, Mum!" Anisha reassured her and, as they climbed aboard and made to leave:

"Think of me tonight as you relax with your G & T – I'll be sleeping under the stars!"

"Good luck – enjoy yourself, but take care!"

Jessica stood and waved as the convoy moved off and, after they had disappeared into the sandstorm she stood for a while reflecting; it must have seemed a long time since she had set out on her own travels, which had been considerably longer and less well-organised than Anisha's modest trip: she really needed to take a grip on herself and not fuss over her daughter, who had turned out to be so much more capable and sensible than herself at that age. It was, I think, at this point that the realisation began to sink in and Jessica may have felt regret that she had closed the door on the adventurous life. She must have sighed a little – but only a little - as she walked back to the landing stage on the creek where Alastair's power boat waited to take her back to the Palm Island and the comfort of the villa.

The first stage of that day's journey was unexciting. The convoy drove north along the coast road, leaving behind the exotic towers, the hotels and shopping malls of Dubai. Her fellow-passengers were eager to get off the coastal four-lane highway but also keen to catch a glimpse of places which until then had been merely names on a map. Approaching Sharjah, the convoy turned inland in an easterly direction. The highway was still good but less frequented and as the ground began to rise they took another turn, northward. Here, road-signs in Arabic and English pointed towards Ras al Khaima. It was mid-morning when reaching high ground the convoy pulled up for a break and, as they got out to stretch their legs, leaving the cool of the air-conditioned vehicle, the intense heat hit them like a fist. The road snaked away behind them and in front of them it twisted and turned to disappear behind rocky shelves of mountainside; the silence was overwhelming. To right and left the sea was visible in the distance through the haze, while ahead only rocky mountain could be seen.

"We're heading for Ras al Khaima, further along, on the coast," the guide told them, pointing ahead. "And from there north up the coast again to Ash Sha'm. It's a small settlement which makes the border with Musandam. There will be border checks, so passports ready please."

The travellers scrambled back into the vehicles and in a flurry of grit and dust they were on the road again.

The group was beginning to meld. For Anisha getting to know strangers was never a problem; people warmed to her open and friendly manner. Most of the travellers were like herself in age and likewise adventurous and enquiring in outlook. They were soon chatting, exchanging stories and travel experiences as well as details of how they had come to choose the holiday. Anisha mentioned her particular interest in water systems and irrigation and their driver/guide was able to tell her that they would be visiting a family farm, a chance to see how they managed for water in this drought-ridden part of the Gulf. Anisha was surprised that there could be anything called a farm in the barren rocky landscape they were passing through.

"There's a village not far from the border and you'll see what I mean," the guide told her. "We're expected, and there will be a chance to look around. For tonight we'll make camp nearby, on the coast."

From Ras al Khaima where they had rejoined the road they continued north up the coast. From that point they were driving on a simple two-lane hard-top, winding along the base of the mountains which, at this point, came right down to the coast. The road seemed new with signs in Arabic and English. Looking up to their right they could see clearly the engineering needed to prevent rock slides and its importance was even more evident when, rounding a bend, the three vehicles came to an abrupt halt where a pile of fallen rocks had blocked and cracked the road surface. A bulldozer and men were at work lifting and moving and one of the men, his head swathed in cloth up to the eyes to protect against the sun and the dust, guided their convoy through and past the obstruction. Soon they were on their way again.

The border crossing was straightforward; passports were produced, scrutinised and stamped and they were waved through. The road wound on without much change along the coast. The sun was now beginning to decline and the colours showed more clearly. They passed a few small villages – modern single-storey houses and a gleaming white mosque with a jumble of fallen stonework showing where the older houses had been abandoned for the new. To their left the road bordered the coast, which in some places was rocky and in other places consisted of stretches of deserted beaches. Near to any village the beaches were furnished with *barasti,* shelters woven from palm leaves and branches and in some places a pair of goalposts was a sign of beach football and modern life.

At the village of Bakha the road branched inland, passing a fine and evidently recently restored fort, after which the hard-top road gave out and they bumped and lurched up an un-made track for less than a kilometre. For the first time in many miles a few trees were growing and they were approaching a modern low building which the guide told them was the farm.

Alerted by the noise of the vehicle bumping over the rough track and pulling up, their host, dressed traditionally in dishdash, his neat white turban denoting a person of substance, appeared to greet them. He spoke some English and when he got stuck the driver/guides were able to translate. The party was expected and welcomed into the house. All of them were stiff and sore from the journey and glad to move their limbs and follow their host into the house.

Seated on cushions around the room in the modern single-storey family home where air-conditioning was at work, they were offered tea and dates by the host's wife, who smiled a lot but spoke no English. Afterwards the son, who was studying engineering in the capital, home on university vacation, led them outside to look around.

The family kept goats and a few wiry sheep, there were a dozen or more date palms and beneath these grew the alfalfa crop needed to feed the livestock and enough vegetables for their needs.

The palm garden was shady and, in comparison to the heat elsewhere, seemed cool. In the past, the young man explained, water had been near enough to the surface and animals powered the pump that brought it to the surface. Now it had to be pumped up from ever increasing depths and they ran a petrol-driven pump to do the work.

"My father has houses in the capital but our family like, when possible, to be here at the farm where our grandfather lived."

He pointed to the pile of fallen masonry at the far side of the palm garden. "That is the family house from my grandfather and grandmother. Today we have a better one," he smiled indicating the new modern house.   Anisha took some photos, for her record of the trip. There would be some which she would send to her mother and to her grandmother.

The visit to the farm was brief and their camp for the night would be down near the shore. The road ran along the coast and at a point where they could drive off and park the vehicles they stopped and walked down to the foreshore for a swim in the sea before pitching camp. While it was more a warm bath than a refreshing dip, they nonetheless splashed and dived and washed off the dust of the journey. As the sun went down cameras were brought out and the stillness and beauty of the scene was captured for sending home to families. They all joined in the work of setting up camp and preparing a meal before settling down for their first night under the stars. There was little comfortable sleep to be had however as the heat pulsated relentlessly off the mountainside with scarcely any abatement until near dawn.

The next two days were spent exploring the Musandam peninsula by boat, from the little port and main township of Khasab. Here there was no shortage of spectacular photography provided by a shoreline which Anisha could only compare to how the Norwegian fjords might appear if denuded of trees and baked dry in the merciless sun. The coastline was a fretwork of grey-brown limestone cliffs with inlets penetrating deep into the mountainside.

The safari company had arranged for their clients to join one of the regular boat trips carrying supplies to coastal villages. The main cargo, they learnt, consisted of tanks of water which were winched ashore to the tiny fishing villages dotted along the side of these fjords. Anisha was fascinated and wondered just how those communities had managed for water in the past before this service was provided.

As they chugged back to port in the evening crew and passengers took turns to make their evening prayers with mats laid out on the ship's deck. Anisha felt herself a million miles away from London and her desk in the City and struggled to maintain her focus for the purpose of her journey which would come in the next part of the week.

After exploring the peninsula the convoy began its drive down the Eastern coast. Blink once, thought Anisha, and you could miss any of the smaller states all together. From the tip of the peninsular which was Oman they crossed back into Sharjah and then Fujairah after which it was Oman again and the straight drive down the Batinah coast. Here the convoy followed the old route, driving straight along the firm sands, in the manner used before the hard-top road was built. They could see plantations of date palms stretching inwards and the coastal plane was dusty green with citrus fruits in walled compounds. They made camp in the evening away from the villages.

Chapter 10

Oman (Falaj)

In Oman from the Iron Age Period (found in Salut, Bat and other sites) a system of underground aqueducts called Falaj were constructed, a series of well-like vertical shafts, connected by gently sloping horizontal tunnels. There are three types of Falaj: Daudi with underground aqueducts, Ghaili requiring a dam to collect the water, and Aini whose source is a water spring. These enabled large scale agriculture to flourish in a dryland environment. According to UNESCO, some 3,000 aflaj (plural) or falaj (singular), are still in use in Oman today. From Wikipedia, the free encyclopedia

The convoy deposited Anisha at the gatehouse to the university. The rest of the group waved as they speeded onwards on their way towards the fortress town of Nizwa in the interior, which they planned to visit; they would meet again in three days, in time to catch their flight from Seeb to London.

Anisha was expected and received her visitor's ID at the gatehouse. Carrying just a light rucksack with minimal necessities, which included notebook and camera, she protected herself from the glare and the heat with her backpack held over her head to create some shade. The sun-baked grounds were laid out with gravel parterres and low palm trees, with an eye-arresting sundial at the focal point. The walkway led towards the main steps to the University buildings and here she was met by a small wiry man wearing the traditional white robe which Anisha had learned was called a dish-dash. His face was brown and crinkled by the sun under his neatly folded turban. He greeted Anisha curiously with hand outstretched and introduced himself as her host.

"Dr Ahmed! It is so very good of you to allow me to visit!" Anisha responded.   "Please don't mention it," was the response. "Come this way," he gestured as he held open the main door. "This way is my office and I will be happy to answer your questions – if I can!" he smiled.

"I hope to learn much from you about your ancient and fascinating irrigation systems," Anisha continued, chattily. She sensed that he was happy, intrigued even, to have someone from the outside world taking an interest in his special subject.

Anisha looked around the office of Associate Professor Dr Hayder Ahmed, noting the maps and the aerial photographs, shots of mountainous landscapes with pockets of dusty palm trees marking villages, which lined the walls. She was waiting for him to return with the coffee which she had willingly accepted. The office was small, and sparsely but practically furnished with shelves for books and files, desk, computer and a partial view from the window of the courtyard exterior where brilliant sunlight shone on a paved garden. Anisha was surprised by her sudden transition from holiday-trekker to researcher, but it felt good. She put on a business-like manner as she prepared to take notes.

They spent an hour in conversation as Anisha explained to him how she had come across the description of the traditional systems of bringing water to irrigate the palm gardens and supply village needs in the interior of the country.

"What I'd like to know is: are these systems still in use, and do they still work?"

"I can certainly tell you," the professor replied in almost perfect English, "that for the villages of the interior these are the most important system. In your country you have piped water for everywhere. It is the same here in our Capital Area and the other big places. Inland, the small villages now, some of them have the electricity. In some they use the generators. The water supply, it is the traditional methods - the old technology."

"So what I have been reading is still up-to-date?"

"Of course! What other way can there be?"

"Well, to give you one example, up north in the peninsula we saw water being carried by boat to the fishing villages. I was thinking that perhaps you would bring water in by lorry - by truck?"

"Why we should do that, when there is good system in these places?"

"Why, indeed!" Anisha echoed. "But is the system still that good? I mean, nowadays these old traditions are sometimes neglected; modern ways take over and old technologies are sometimes thought to be - well, out of date."

"These are very important systems to our people. While education is for all the children in all the villages the respect for tradition is encouraged."

"And how much of your work is connected to this area?"

"The department works in many areas; for example desalination is top priority. Here in the Capital Area we have a very large desalination research project for the Middle East. Also we have work with dams; in the mountains we have built dams which catch the rainwater, which falls very heavy and could run off into the sea."

"And do you pipe this water to the city?"

"That is not the idea at all. This water is to feed the aquifer - the groundwater supplies which today are getting low because of the cities and the agriculture and also the golf courses!"

Dr Ahmed stood and pointed to a map on one wall. "These aquifers feed the village systems. They also feed the big cities which are using too much. So here you can see the city where you came from just now is using the same groundwater as our small villages and the level is going down. So the dams are to replenish the aquifers."

Anisha nodded, standing up to look more closely at the map.

"But this groundwater comes from millions of years in the past. Can you really hope to replenish it with a few dams?"

"We must do what we can," was the reply.

"And do you work at all on the traditional systems? I mean the technologies for creating and maintaining them - you must be in a position to help to pass them on down the generations?"

"Because I come from one village like this, it is my personal interest. However, I do not have too much time allocated to this field."

"You said in your email that I might go with you on one of your visits - is that still possible?"

"Of course. Today we will go and my family is expecting this visit. I can take you to see the *falaj* system – that's the channels which provide water to our villages and palm gardens. Maybe also you can see how it is maintained and cared for by those specialised in this kind of work."

"That sounds marvellous - more than I could hope for. Thank you, Dr Ahmed!"

He smiled, pleased at her excitement.

"But first we can go to eat something at our faculty canteen. And please, my name is Hayder."

Lunch was taken in the staff cafeteria, a cool and spacious area where they were joined by two more members of the department. The food was good and they drank cold drinks and mineral water, which Anisha noticed was a local brand. She noticed also, with surprise, that one of the colleagues who had joined them wore the fountain symbol that she was becoming familiar with, as a lapel badge and she hoped that she might get a chance to enquire about its meaning; perhaps here too they played polo – if that was what it stood for. Hayder introduced the two colleagues.

"Saleh works on grey-water usage in the Capital Area, and Mushtaq has joined this semester, coming from three years in Europe and working in some special projects."

The men were intrigued and not a little puzzled by Anisha and her reason for visiting. The idea that a London girl should go to the trouble of seeking them out was unusual. Anisha explained about her job and also that she was quite simply interested in the way water was used around the world and in particular in the old, traditional systems.

"So I have been able to combine my holiday with my work," she told them. "And to research a subject that really fascinates me."

They smiled at her enthusiasm and Anisha continued in the same vein.

"I think with climate change and the way development is going, the traditional uses of water must be important for people living off the land. Perhaps these old systems have something to teach us in other parts of the world?"

"Such as?" enquired Saleh.

"Well in Africa, obviously"

"We believe that the new technologies will be more helpful in Africa," he countered. "Desalination powered by the sun or the wind - small plants for individual villages."

"But surely there is a place too for the traditional, especially when they are far from the coast?"

Hayder agreed. His other colleague however shrugged.

"Africa is a lost cause" Mushtaq commented.

Anisha was shocked.

"Surely you don't think it should be treated as a lost cause?" she asked.

"In some respects" he answered, "that is what I do think. And there are many others who hold the same view. And some of us who would abandon more than that…"

"I don't know what you mean by that but….." Something was clicking in Anisha's mind. "When you talk about 'us', do you mean an organisation? And does your badge have some connection….?"

She was looking at his lapel badge and fingering her own collar in the place where his was pinned.

"If you don't mind me asking…" she pointed to its pattern of letters. "What do those initials stand for?"

Mushtaq, who had been speaking with great energy, noticed what she was indicating and suddenly snapped shut.

"This is nothing. Just a fitness club that I belong to."

"Here on the campus?" Anisha asked?

"Yes of course; we go running together and train. We like to keep fit."

Hayder, while this was going on was beginning to look uncomfortable and tried to distract Anisha with offers of a dessert.

"No, but thank you!" She turned back to Mushtaq. "But really; I'd like to know more," she persisted while Mushtaq was looking as if he regretted having spoken.

"I know there's more to it than local fitness clubs because I have seen it in London; and not just in London, at the Polo Club my stepfather belongs to. And I'd really like to know what it's about. There must be more to it than keeping fit. Oh…." A thought had suddenly struck her. "Is it some kind of religious society? Is that why it's a bit hush-hush?"

By now Mushtaq had enough.

"It is only what I told you and nothing is more there to say. Please; no more question!"

Anisha felt snubbed but remembered that she was their guest.

"Well, I'm sorry if I was inquisitive," she responded apologetically, "I'll forget all about it."

She turned to take a second look at the dessert menu and when she looked up Mushtaq had stood and was abruptly leaving the table. Anisha tried to apologise to Hayder, her host.

"I think I must have upset him. I'm sorry. But, do you know what that badge stands for?"

Hayder replied uneasily.

"I have little knowledge of this thing. Mushtaq is new colleague; has friends and contacts from his old position…. He does not speak openly with me..." he looked enquiringly at Saleh, "or with the other staff."

And with this Anisha turned her attention to dessert.

As the giant sundial in the university grounds showed three o'clock, Hayder Ahmed with two passengers, Anisha and a houseboy, turned right out of the University's main gates in Hayder's Toyota pickup truck. They were driving up the dusty two-lane road headed towards the yellow-brown line of the mountain ridge ahead. The drive to the village would take an hour and a half, the last half hour of which would be on unmade road. It was at this time, to the accompaniment of Arab music from local radio, that Anisha began to reflect seriously on the FARIS symbol for it had popped up in so many places that she felt she had to discover what it meant. She tried to count the number of times and the places where it had come to her attention: at the hotel reception in Mayfair, at the polo club, her mother's pretty brooch and now worn by a member of the Department of Water Sciences at the University. She decided to have another try at finding out from her companion.

"Do you know what that badge means, the one your colleague wears?"

It took a moment for Hayder to understand what Anisha was asking about and even then there was little he could tell her.

"There are a few others around the campus who wear them. It is some sort of club I guess, but not my sort."

"What sort would that be?" Anisha asked.

"Me, I come from village life. My family is not rich. Those people have money, during the vacation they travel, maybe to Europe, America...." he tailed off.

"And they - the ones who belong to the club, or whatever it is, are they in all in the Water Sciences department?"

"Not at all. They are in all different faculties."

"And the letters; do you know what they stand for?"

"This is where we leave the hard-top road," was Hayder's answer as he swung the vehicle left off the highway. "Not so far to go now." And Anisha had to be content with that.

It was with a shock of recognition that Anisha met the *Arif*. Not recognition of a face but realisation that this was the person who fitted the description she had read in the research paper back in London, the paper that had first intrigued her and set her off on this adventure. For she was definitely beginning to see it now as an adventure and wondered where it would take her next.

Hayder greeted the Arif with "*Salaam aleikum*" and received a courteous "*Aleikum-wa-salaam*" in return. He explained to Anisha what the Arif's work was as they walked together, all three, along the side of the stream.

"This, we call it *falaj*" Hayder explained, indicating the cement-bottomed, shallow irrigation channel that they were walking along. As they walked its length from where the channel entered the village, he explained its various functions. At their first stop he explained:

"Here is the first taking place. From here all people take water; for drinking and for cooking."

They walked on, stopping again in due course.

"Here is for washing. Here men, and here ladies and children." He pointed to two enclosures built across the water and providing cover, showing where the water flowed beneath and on to its next appointment. Anisha nodded, taking it in, confirming what she had read. They continued walking, under the hot sun.

"Here is for washing clothes," Hayder indicated with a wide gesture where the bank sloped gently down to the water, allowing easy access for the women who would stand in the water to wash the clothes. A concrete block with ridged surface had been provided which Anisha recognised as a wash-board.

"Next is the palm gardens." Now Hayder was eager to move them on out of the sun and into the shade offered by the trees. Anisha, who had paused to wade into the water at the washing point followed. There was no coolness in the water: it was more like a hot bath than a cool stream.

The Arif all this time had spoken little; he had gone on ahead and, when they caught up he was standing at the side of the path which bordered the main *falaj* at a point where a channel led into a square of land shaded by palm trees under which a crop of green vegetation was growing. The trees - she counted six of them – were each encircled by a mounded-up ridge of the reddish, sandy soil which captured and retained their regular ration of water while the rest of the ground had also been well dampened by the flow.

"In this garden is growing herbs," Hayder told her. "Next garden is alfalfa and this is good for animals - they like very much eating this one."

Anisha looked across to the next garden, separated from where they stood by a low wall. She could see a white-robed figure bending and working with a hoe of some kind. As they looked he straightened himself and gave a salute of greeting. The *Arif* was engaged in altering the flow of water away from the first garden into this next one. He placed a large slab or slate to divert it from one path and lifted a similar block to allow it to flow into the next one. The farmer hastened to clear a way and ensure the flow reached the parts of the garden where he needed it. He stood then, scratching his head, in conversation with the *Arif* who nodded and shrugged and looked skywards.

As the Arif came back to where they were standing he addressed a few words to Hayder. Hayder translated for Anisha.

"He says the water is flowing slowly and is not good supply," he told her.

"Do you know why that is?" she asked.

"It may be that others are taking too much water: it may also be that watercourse is blocked higher up in the mountain. Tomorrow the men go to make their investigation; look inside water tunnel and find the answer. If it is blocked - this can be repaired. If is the other....." he shrugged.

"If it is the other, isn't it an issue for your department?"

Hayder shrugged again.

"If it is so – as we think – the matter is complicate; we in the University can tell the facts, but we cannot make the policy."

"No, I understand that," Anisha acknowledged.

"Countries have boundaries, but under the ground," Hayder stamped his foot on the rough ground beneath their feet to emphasise his point. "Under the ground where the aquifers run, there is not boundaries. One state takes water to make green and pleasant land with golf courses and this may mean that the next neighbour have no water for its villages."

"Of course; I begin to see how that can happen," Anisha thought of the green turf of the gardens and the polo field and the refreshing swish of the sprinklers turning her mother's new garden from sand to a riot of colour.

"And can I come with you to see how it all works?" She asked. Hayder nodded

"Of course; no problem.

Chapter 11

Qanat

The qanat technology is known to have been developed by the Persian people sometime in the early 1st millennium BC and to have spread from there slowly west- and eastward. The value of a qanat is directly related to the quality, volume and regularity of the water flow. Much of the population of Iran and other arid countries in Asia and North Africa historically depended upon the water from qanats; the areas of population corresponded closely to the areas where qanats are possible. Although a qanat was expensive to construct, its long-term value to the community, and thereby to the group that invested in building and maintaining it, was substantial.

From Wikipedia, the free encyclopedia

Hayder's family welcomed their guest to the village and their house with traditional hospitality; his nieces, who were both students at the secondary school, fired questions at Anisha about life in London, and two small nephews studied her with wide-eyed interest.

The next day Anisha set out from the village with Hayder and the work party who would be checking the shafts and the underground watercourse. They had again been joined by Hayder's colleague from the university, Mushtaq, who was keen to use the opportunity to explore the old waterway. He wore the white dishdash the same as the other men in the party with no badge on show today.

At six in the morning, while there was still a little coolness in the air, they left the village and followed goat tracks across rocky terrain where the only vegetation was dusty thorn bushes, nibbled by goats to a uniform height of the stretch of the animal's neck. As the path grew steeper they slipped and stumbled on the loose rough surface, dislodging rocks which went skidding down the mountainside. Anisha found the sweat running off her face, stinging her eyes and blurring her vision. Hayder was a little better and Mushtaq was taking it in his stride, keeping up with the village men without trouble. An hour of this exertion brought them to a high point marked by a cairn of piled-up rocks. When the stragglers caught up and rested gratefully they looked around over a vista of ochre and yellow peaks and slopes to where in the distance the village was marked by the grey-green blur of its palms.

At this height a shaft had been bored down, who knew how many hundreds of years ago or by what technology of water-divining, to tap into the aquifer which carried the precious supplies of underground water. Far below a tunnel had been excavated to lead the water at a steady gradient downwards in the direction of the village with, every few hundred metres, another vertical shaft giving access to the tunnel for maintenance and to keep it clear of rocks and debris.

"This is very specialised work," Hayder told Anisha. One family takes care of this work for many ...." He searched for the word: Anisha helped him out

"For many generations? Father son, father son, and so on...?"

"Exactly so" Hayder agreed. "For many generations the same family. Maybe for hundreds of years. And these people take care of other *falaj*..." He gestured expansively over the surrounding vista, "....other villages."

The two men from the village now set about opening the shaft, removing rocks and boulders to reveal a gaping black hole. Using ropes secured at the top they quickly disappeared down, leaving the others wondering whether to follow. The work would take them an indefinite time, depending on what state they found the tunnel and the watercourse in. One worker reappeared quite quickly and headed down the hillside carrying another coil of rope over his shoulder. Hayder explained to

Anisha that he was going to open up the next shaft and work from there back to meet his co-worker.

Mushtaq declared he was going down the top shaft and Anisha, to Hayder's, alarm said she would go too. He watched uneasily as she disappeared into the perpendicular hole.

The shaft was broad at first and, as she descended with the rope to steady her, following Mushtaq at what she judged to be a safe interval and careful not to dislodge boulders which might fall on him, Anisha was able to find footholds in the side of the shaft. The workmen who had descended first had carried candles and placed them at intervals and these gave off a very faint glimmer. As the light from above dwindled and she climbed deeper, so the shaft narrowed until it was barely wider than her shoulders. It was with relief that she found her feet on level ground and realised, from the fact that she was standing in water, that she had reached the bottom of the shaft. She could hear that the person ahead of her, which must be Mushtaq, was making his way along the tunnel and the noise of his footsteps in the water reached her. She called out.

"How far are you going?"

And his voice came back along the tunnel as a distorted echo.

"What did you say?"

She repeated her question and the reply that came back was even less audible.

Anisha had to decide whether to follow or stay where she was. She took a few steps, bent double, fumbled and tripped and decided that going back was the best idea. It was only a few yards and she could see the pin point of light high above showing the entrance to the shaft. Feeling around she failed to locate the rope but knew Hayder must be waiting there at the top and called to attract his attention. She called several times, realising as she did so that her voice was probably not carrying up that narrow shaft. It was a moment of heart-sinking disbelief and panic as, unable to find the rope, it dawned on her that she was stranded. The tunnel of the water course was low and the blackness totally intimidating and any sound from Mushtaq had long-since faded into silence. Nevertheless, after calling out several more times the sensible thing seemed to be to stay exactly where she was and wait until someone came back for her.

What time could it be? It had been about ten a.m. when they had reached the top of the shaft and perhaps half an hour had passed. Now she perched where she could look up to that pin prick of light, waiting for what seemed an age, although she had no idea how long it was. Her mind wandered and she came to with a start thinking she might have dozed off. Next she realised she was feeling hungry. How long was this going to last? She began to wonder whether she really had been abandoned and what could have happened that everyone had disappeared. Might there have been an accident elsewhere? The thought of a night here, when even that small point of light would disappear, filled her with fear and at this point she decided that even without a rope she should try to make the ascent. Cautiously she felt for handhold and foothold, hauling herself up the narrow tube, scratching and grazing her limbs and tearing her fingers until she could taste the blood. She made some progress, slipped, dislodged stones, almost gave up. She found a ledge where she could pause and give herself some rest and she forced herself to take slow breaths to calm the miasma of fear and panic, then on again to gain a few more hard-won feet upwards to where the point of daylight was at last becoming larger and clearer: she dared to think that she might yet make it.

Hayder's shout when it came nearly made her lose her foothold and she was barely able to call out in reply.

"I'm here! I'm climbing! I need the rope!"

Now the light from the top of the shaft went dim; looking up she realised it was Hayder's head and he was shouting down to her.

"Anisha! I'm going to drop the rope! I'll do it slowly so it doesn't fall on you but please be careful. Are you ready?"

"I'm ready"

"Tell me when you have the rope"

Anisha's arms and legs were trembling with the effort now of clinging and climbing, and when the rope came twisting and curling down she had difficulty in holding it and tying it around her waist. Finally she managed and shouted up to Hayder.

"I've got the rope and I've tied it around me. Can you help me up now?"

The rest of the climb was a struggle but Anisha was more confident knowing that the rope would hold her and support her as she moved from one foothold to the next. Near the top the shaft widened and the light began to flood in. Finally she was up and out and rolled in a heap on the blissful hard, gritty, rocky, baking hot and beloved surface with the blazing sun beating down on her.

She got to her feet to find Hayder staring at her with horrified eyes.

"I'm OK - I really am! Don't look like that!"

She glanced down to see her arms and legs grazed and bleeding and she imagined that her face must look as bad as she wiped her arm across it.

"What a mess. Thanks Hayder, but what happened? Where did you go?"

"To the next shaft. Mushtaq told me he was taking you with him and to bring the rope down to the next shaft. But he didn't arrive there. I wait, and then I come back here."

"And the workmen?"

"The workmen they are going on down, doing their work, moving the rocks that are blocking, the normal work."

As soon as Anisha was sufficiently recovered the two of them made their way down the mountainside hoping to find Mushtaq at the next shaft and it was as they hoped and he was waiting at the bottom of the shaft. This time Hayder fed the rope quickly down and hauled on it to take the strain as Mushtaq climbed and clambered up the ridges and ledges of the side of the shaft. He emerged, unscathed.

There followed a heated session of indignant question and answer, accusation and denial. Much of it Anisha was unable to follow, some of it was in English for her benefit.

First Mushtaq:

"I told him," gesturing at Hayder," I say to him to bring you up first then you come here for me!"

Next Hayder:

"You say me I pull up the rope and come to meet her and you at this point! I come here, wait and call and no-one is here."

Whatever the truth of it Anisha realised that it was she who had been insanely reckless in the way she had trusted that all would be well without clarifying the plan. She was too exhausted to pursue the question of blame. All she needed now was to clean herself up some more and get back down the mountain. She used the bottled water and her fingertips to gingerly wipe the mess from her grazed arms and legs.

"What about the two men down there? Will they be alright?"

Hayder assured Anisha that they would send others up from the village with the rope to check on their progress but that if all was going well, when the work in the tunnel was finished they would expect the men to make their way out where the water appeared in the *falaj*, on the hillside just above the village.

Progress back to the village was slow; descending the unstable rocky mountainside was trickier than climbing up it. By the time they reached the village the two workers had already returned; their work inside the tunnel had been relatively easy with no major blockages to clear. The fact of the matter was that the water was not being blocked, either by rocks or by fallen debris and was not leaking away though holes in the tunnel's floor. It was simply running slowly. And this was not good news, implying as it did that the water level itself was low and supplies were surely being depleted.

The three of them, Hayder, Mushtaq and Anisha left the village and reached the hard-top road before darkness fell. From there it was an hour's drive back to the campus. Because of Anisha's deadline for meeting up with the rest of the party they drove straight past its gates and another twenty minutes more of driving brought them to the airport where Anisha would meet them and board the plane.

On arrival in front of the airport building Hayder parked and went ahead carrying Anisha's rucksack. Mushtaq jumped out and made to help her down from the pick-up. He was wearing his jacket now, over the dishdasha and she could see the lapel badge which he was fingering in a deliberate manner; obviously he had something to say to her; she waited.

"Anisha" Mushtaq started. "You have had an experience which has frightened you. And I am saying to you: frightening things happen if you put too much curiosity into your investigations."

Anisha sensed that this moment was important and she listened intently.

Mushtaq looked down at the badge he was fingering and then back at her, seeking her eyes and emphasising his words.

"This is not something to be curious about, please. What I say is: No more investigating in this direction, OK?" His voice was friendly and cajoling but when she looked into his face she realised with something of a shock the implications; she was getting a warning.

"You had an unpleasant experience but thankfully no bad harm has come from it...." He paused before finishing his sentence,

"....not this time. Now be careful. No more questions and no more foolish investigations."

Anisha, as she told me afterwards, was lost for words. Mushtaq turned his back on her and walked away.

Speechless Anisha shouldered her backpack. She could see her companions of the trekking group already queuing at the check-in desk. She would be glad to be part of that group again.

PART TWO

Chapter 12

Space and survival

Space and survival refers to a position advocated by some that the long-term survival of the human species and civilization requires proper use of the resources of outer space. Its investigation is justified by the fact that space colonization and space science could prevent many human extinction scenarios. From Wikipedia, the free encyclopedia

Grandparents

In the history of modern humanity, around 30,000 years ago, the number of modern humans who lived to be grandparents began to skyrocket. It is not known for certain what spurred this increase in longevity. But it is believed that a key consequence of three generations being alive together was the facilitation of the passing along of information that prior to that point would have been lost; From Wikipedia, the free encyclopedia

In the summer that Anisha was pursuing her researches and seeking adventure, finding more than she had bargained for, at the end of the twenty-first century's first decade, events on the world stage were not making cheerful reading. Trade talks failed, oil prices rose, climate change, with flooding or water shortages, was hitting every part of the world and the wrangle went on to find out who to blame instead of doing much about it.

As I approached my eighties, blessed still with good health, I looked around at the world we lived in. So much more of it was visible than had been when I was Anisha's age: so many opportunities lay open to those who could take advantage of them. Ideals and vision were not lacking. In most countries there were many who lived well, scaled heights of ambition in their different fields of endeavour and worked to leave the world and the human race in a better state – or at least in as good a condition as they found it. On the other hand, a mood of deep cynicism was also evident in the trading of arms and narcotics and pursuit of power and there were some who, combining vision with cynicism, believed they had read the writing on the wall and had no intention of succumbing to the defeat of a planet past its prime. Some of these appeared to believe that the future of humankind lay beyond the boundaries of their own planet. They called themselves FARIS.

Of course for Anisha, when she stumbled across FARIS and started asking questions, nothing of that sort could have been further from her mind and I'm sure she would have dismissed such ideas as ludicrous and improbable, even though there were historical precedents; I recall, for instance there had been a similar movement in Russia in the early years of the twentieth century. But Anisha was unaware of anything of the sort and, as soon as she got back to London it was mostly down to her natural curiosity and unwillingness to be put off by obstacles - especially if someone seemed to be putting them in her path on purpose - that nagged her into asking more questions. There was only one person she knew in London who seemed to have a connection with FARIS and who could tell her more about it and that, of course, was Grego. She would ring him, but she needed to give some thought to what she would say.

Anisha's plane got into London in the small hours of Sunday morning giving her a full 24 hours to catch up on sleep and to pay some attention to her appearance before returning to work on Monday. There was not much she could do about the cuts and grazes except choose clothes which would cover them up. Even so her appearance caused alarm when she reached her desk the next day. In response to her boss' and colleague's enquiries she told a tale of rock-climbing - which was pretty near the truth anyway.

She spent the day putting the finishing touches to the report on bottled water and made sure to include a paragraph on aquifer depletion around the Gulf States and a note of caution about further investment in the industry in that area.

During her lunch hour she tried Grego's mobile.

"Hi Anisha - how was your trip?"

"Oh it was really great. Would you like to hear about it?"

"Of course. How about after work?"

They settled on a pub half way between their respective work-places and from there moved on to a Chinese restaurant for something to eat.

Anisha began to talk about her trip, starting with the villa on the Palm Island. Grego listened with keen interest and enthused about the project. Anisha mentioned her reservations on the score of water and environmental issues but Grego would hear nothing and brushed them aside.

"It's a brilliant project. If it can be done in those locations and under those conditions, think where else it could be done. The sky's the limit! And maybe not even the sky"

Anisha felt she should come clean and tell Grego about her role in the Green Team at Focus Asset Management but she still held back.

"Let me tell you about the rest of the trip; the trekking part."

There was plenty to talk about and she happily described some of the places they had visited. She stopped short of telling him about the detour she had made and the visit to the village, the water system and the mishap in the tunnel.

"You haven't explained how you came by the cuts and bruises" Grego reminded her.

Anisha gave a version of the story: "We were rock-climbing and I lost my footing, the rock gave way under me and I came crashing down! It was quite painful actually, but no long-term harm."

Grego nodded sympathetically.

"Anyway, to go back to the Gulf, I haven't told you about the polo match," Anisha continued. "That was while I was staying at the villa." And she added, "My stepfather belongs to the polo club there on the mainland."

Grego was keen to know more.

"Actually I remembered you saying you played and I thought it would be interesting, so we went at the weekend."

"And what did you think?"

Anisha enthused about the excitement of the match.

"And the club is magnificent. Not just for the polo; there are all sorts of facilities. It's obviously a very social place - for those who can afford it."

"And your stepfather can? If it's not a rude question."

"Oh no doubt about that! He's sponsor of a team and seems to know all the players and the other patrons. Apparently he used to play - and still does sometimes."

"Interesting. What's his line of business? If it's not another rude question."

"To be honest I'm not quite sure." Anisha had to reply. "At least, I know he is a lawyer as well as some sort of company director, but beyond that I couldn't really say. He hasn't been my stepfather for very long - that's my excuse for not knowing!"

"Obviously a successful lawyer!" Grego commented.

"How about polo in England?" Anisha asked. "Is it the same? A rich man's sport?"

"What do you think?" Grego asked, "Do I look like I'm made of money?"

"Well…" Anisha was unsure how to respond. "You do drive a BMW, so you can't be exactly hard up…"

Grego brushed the comment aside.

"I'll be playing at the weekend so if you want to come and see for yourself, you're welcome."

It was decided that on Saturday morning she would drive down to the club in Sussex with Grego and watch him and his team in the final of a summer tournament.

They parted company. On her way home Anisha reflected that she had not spoken once about the theme which had been preoccupying her; she realised that this had not been an oversight but a deliberate decision in the light of Grego's attitude towards what she had revealed about her job and her views. So why did she agree to go on seeing him? And why the trip to the polo match at the weekend? Her subconscious was at work warning her and at the same time prompting her. She knew that Grego had at least some knowledge of FARIS but what she knew of his views told her that she would do better to tread carefully. FARIS had been evident at her stepfather's club: would it be on view at all in Sussex?

Chapter 13

The surface of a polo field requires careful and constant grounds maintenance to keep the surface in good playing condition. During half-time of a match, spectators are invited to go onto the field to participate in a polo tradition called "divot stamping", which has developed to not only help replace the mounds of earth (divots) that are torn up by the horses' hooves, but to afford spectators the opportunity to walk about and socialise.
From Wikipedia, the free encyclopedia

What did you wear, Anisha wondered, for a polo match in the English countryside, as opposed to one in a sandy Gulf state. She decided against any attempt to look like the horsey crowd and settled for her white jeans and the soft leather jacket her mother had given her, last birthday. Grego picked her up in the BMW. The roof was down and she made him wait while she ran back in for a wispy scarf and sunglasses to act as a windbreak. The Saturday traffic had barely got going in South London and they made good time to the motorway where Grego could show off the BMW's paces. He was forced to slow down on leaving the motorway and they made their way through the Sussex countryside. Driving through narrow country lanes they were held up by a loaded farm tractor, shedding wisps of hay as it passed under low branching trees. Grego dropped back to avoid catching the debris on the gleaming bodywork of the BMW. He looked sideways at Anisha, who was attempting to smooth down the unruly mass of her black curls which had broken loose from the inadequate little headscarf.

"Did you enjoy the ride?" He asked.

"It was great!" she enthused, adding "But I need some time to repair the damage." She adjusted the sun- visor to make use of the small mirror concealed on its reverse.

"Don't worry" Grego told her, "You look good like that"

There was something serious in his voice that made Anisha take her eyes off the mirror. As she met his glance she registered that the bantering approach had changed and what was coming next could signify something more serious. Did she want that? For the moment there was no chance to find out. The tractor in front had come to a complete halt at the moment that Grego had taken his eyes off it speak to Anisha. He braked quickly, in time to avoid a nasty crunch and realised that the tractor was actually preparing to back up and the driver was signalling furiously at him to do the same. The lane, which curved at this point, was narrow and overhung with branches. Grego reversed cautiously, unable to see round the bend he was negotiating, but backing thankfully into a field gate just twenty-five yards along. The tractor did likewise and allowed the horse-box which was the cause of the manoeuvring to swing past, bringing down debris of branches which it strewed along the surface of the road in its wake. When it had passed, the driver of the tractor let them go ahead and, as they were now following signs to the polo park, driving was straightforward. The moment which Anisha had noted with some alarm had passed. Soon they were passing through the gates of the park and into the sweep of a driveway that led to a vast open space, green almost as far as the eye could see, set against a magnificent back-drop of Sussex Downs. Anisha was impressed.

"This is an amazing place –beautiful!"

They drove over firm turf to where cars were lined up and Grego parked the BMW alongside an array of 4-by-4s, open-top sports cars and old bangers. Beyond were rows of horse-boxes and Anisha stared with surprise at five or six jumbo-jet-sized vehicles from which strings of horses were being unloaded to be tethered in the roped-off lines, set up a short distance away from the polo playing pitches.

"These make me think of how the cavalry must have been organised when they were on military campaigns. It looks very well-organised with the roped off area for each horse, and places for their saddles and bridles and a net of hay for each one."

"That's right," Grego replied. "Each team has its lines for their ponies and the grooms are in charge."

The two of them moved out of the way as a horse came clattering down the ramp of the huge horse box they were passing, led by a girl in jeans and jodhpur boots .Grego obviously knew her.

"Hi Jenny, "

"Grego, hi! Are you riding today?"

"Certainly am. By the way, this is Anisha. Anisha – Jenny." The two girls exchanged smiles before the tug on the leading rope made Jenny look to her charge.

"Look out for Anisha if you have a spare moment, will you?" Grego called to her as she led the pony away.

"Will do. Good luck for today!" and Jenny moved away, busy with her work.

Grego had turned back to the car and was busy pulling on riding boots and looking for the helmet which he found in the boot of the car. It carried what must be the colours of his team and Grego swung it over his arm as he led the way to where his team were saddling up.

"You'll have a good view from here" he told Anisha. "The lads'll keep you company but just stay out of the way in the breaks when we're changing ponies. Otherwise you'll be trampled underfoot and not very popular."

"That's alright, I've already seen how it is – organised chaos was my first impression. I'll steer well clear." Anisha watched him as he swung into the saddle and took the mallet that was handed to him.

"Good luck!" she called.

"Hey, there's binoculars in the car," he called to her.

"Thanks – oh, keys?"

Already Grego's team were making for the pitch but he had time to fish the bunch of keys from his back pocket and toss them to her.

"Good luck!" Anisha repeated.

Thanks to the day with her mother and step-father Anisha had some knowledge of what was going on but even so, and with the ringside view less favourable than sitting in the stands, as she had done on the previous occasion, most of what she could see resembled a maelstrom of flailing mallets and thundering charges. After seven minutes came the break and the riders raced in for a change of mounts. Grooms were ready with fresh ponies and stood by to take the sweating, steaming animals off the pitch and lead them to the stands there to rub them down with handfuls of straw. Anisha had no opportunity to exchange a word with Grego or ask him how it was going although she gathered that his team were a goal down. By the time the four minute break was up the team had remounted and were cantering back down to the centre of the pitch where all action began.

This time Anisha decided she needed the binoculars for a closer view and made her way the short distance back to the car. She had no trouble in finding the binoculars and hung them round her neck. Clicking the car door shut she paused and caught her breath for Grego's keys hung on a fob with the fountain symbol and the initials which she was becoming familiar with. She walked reflectively back to watch the second chukka of the match.

Using binoculars Anisha was able to participate more fully in the action. Grego's team were on the defensive and time and again retrieved the ball from perilously near their own goal posts. She jumped up and down with shared excitement to see Grego hook it expertly and pass it to a team member; then the whole team were away, thundering down the pitch with the opposition in hot pursuit. Just short of the goal the charge was halted and she was unable to see what was going on until, once more, their team broke loose and headed for the goal. At this point the hooter blasted time and both teams trooped back to base for a short breather and another change of ponies.

As they came off the field Anisha stood by with water which she handed to Grego.

"You were brilliant!" she exclaimed. "I saw you get the ball away when...."

But Grego was scowling through the sweat streaming down his face.

"I was crap! We should have made it all the way. I messed up."

He brushed past her, ignoring the proffered bottle of water, to release his pony to the groom and reach for the next one. Then he was in a huddle with his fellow team-members and, the three short minutes break being over, they were out on the pitch again.

After the next chukka a ten-minute break was due for half time and Anisha, knowing better this time than to attempt any words with Grego, headed out onto the pitch with the other onlookers as they replaced divots and exchanged comments and conversation before play resumed. Chatting sociably they bent to lift and replace the clumps of turf, dislodged by the careering hooves of the ponies as they turned and twisted in the game.

The match ended in a win for Grego's team over their Argentinian opponents and satisfied smiles on the faces of Grego and his companions.

"That takes us into the semi-finals," he told Anisha with a grin. "We'll be against the winners of this match." They were standing by the board with the order of the day's play displayed, and he pointed to the two teams who were paired to go next – a home side playing against an Italian team.

"There's time for some refreshment. Let's go!" and he steered Anisha in the direction of a large marquee. There Anisha asked for a diet coke and Grego gulped down a double fruit juice laced with spring water; after that he ordered the same again.

Grego's team were knocked out by the Italians in the semi-finals and their opponents went on to win the trophy, so honour, thought Anisha, was satisfied. Grego took a fall in the final chukka, which was somewhat alarming, and Anisha found herself dabbing TCP onto some very raw and bruised shins as well as dabbing cautiously onto a gash dangerously close to one eye.

"This isn't going to look very pretty for a while" she told him. "It was quite a close thing – you're lucky it missed your eye."

Grego winced as the antiseptic stung but let her carry on. "Par for the course in this game, I'm afraid," he acknowledged. "My colleagues are used to seeing me arrive black and blue on a Monday morning. They've stopped asking who beat me up at the weekend."

In the tent where the trophies were presented Grego introduced Anisha to the team patron who seemed to sum her up appreciatively before addressing himself to Grego.

"Well-ridden Grego," he congratulated him. "And nice to see you have company today."

He turned to Anisha. "These chaps need someone on the sidelines to cheer them on as well as administer the necessary first aid."

Anisha found herself staring at his lapel badge, that fountain symbol, yet again. Quickly she tore her eyes away from it to respond.

"I can cheer with the best of them; and I'm not a bad hand with the TCP as well."

"TCP is useful, especially if followed by TLC in due course," he replied good-humouredly with an almost avuncular nod at the two of them as he moved away.

"You made an impression there" Grego told her. "He doesn't often pay compliments."

By seven in the evening while some of the company had settled in to make a long evening of it, others who had further to go were streaming from the car park snaking across the grounds towards the exit. Grego and Anisha made their way back to the car and Grego felt for the keys.

"You gave them to me, don't you remember? To get the binoculars. Here they are," Anisha dangled the keys, rather prominently highlighting the leaf-like fob.

"Ah!" Grego was startled. "I forgot. Actually, do you want to drive?"

It was Anisha's turn to look startled.

"Your precious BMW? Would you trust me?"

"Why not? And you're probably feeling less sore than me."

"True, but I don't actually drive; I gave it up as soon as I passed my test! Cycling is what I do best."

"Ah, well that settles it."

"Are you alright to drive?"

"Of course! No worries about that."

They joined the trail of cars to the exit and followed the slow procession through the winding country lanes eventually to disperse on trunk roads and motorways to their various destinations. As they hit the Saturday night London traffic they were forced to slow down again. Grego turned to Anisha.

"What did you think of the polo-playing scene then?"

Anisha measured her response. "I had a really good day. I enjoyed talking to the grooms and watching them work. The way they are dedicated to their horses and look after them; it's impressive."

"And the game? Do we strike you as just a bunch of rich play-boys?"

"You strike me as a fairly mixed bunch actually."

"Meaning?"

"What you have in common is that you are all skilled riders and all absolutely fearless. I think that is the strongest impression I had. And of course you must all be in good training; you must have to be fit to keep up that pace."

Grego nodded appreciatively. "Yes, I think that's what we have in common. Fit and fearless!" He grinned. "That sums us up."

Anisha sensed the significance. "Fit and fearless: and would there be anything else?" She was fishing for clues. Grego knew it and was uncertain of her motivation. He seemed fascinated – her looks and her quick intelligence were getting to him; on the other hand her persistent questioning about FARIS may also have acted as a warning. He seems to have been both attracted to her and wary of her.

After a pause and some more slow driving he turned again to Anisha.

"It's been really nice having you here today. Do you want to eat somewhere? I'd have to stop off and clean up a bit but we could…."

Anisha stalled. "How about we make it tomorrow. I mean, you could do with a bit of time to repair yourself and it's been a long day." She looked at him enquiringly. "Shall we make it tomorrow?"

Grego seemed good with that.

"I'll pick you up at seven and we'll go for a drink and a meal. OK?"

"OK. You've got my mobile if you need it."

Gregory dropped Anisha at her South London flat. As she let herself in Anisha knew she had twenty-four hours to do some serious thinking about this guy and work out in her mind

118

how she felt about him and about what he represented in his association with the mysterious FARIS.

Chapter 14

EXTREME CHARITY CHALLENGES
Push yourself to the limit in one of these ultimate challenge events!
Experience extreme mountaineering in Argentina, or marathon racing
across the Himalayas, climb some of the highest mountain peaks in
the world or traverse one of the widest deserts. You need to be tough,
determined, physically and mentally in top condition. Find out more
information about the challenges from the list below.
http://www.timeoutdoors.com/challenges/extreme-charity-challenges
Located in the heart of Central Asia, Kyrgyzstan is a land-locked
country the size of England and Scotland (or Washington State). It is
bordered by China to the east, Kazakhstan to the north, Uzbekistan to
the west and Tajikistan to the south. It is located at the juncture of two
great mountain systems (the Tien Shan and the Pamirs), and only
one-eighth of the country lies lower than 1,500 metres (4,920 feet).
www.discovery-kyrgyzstan.com

But Grego did not pick Anisha up the next day. Anisha took care to be back from work soon after six in order to be ready for seven o'clock. But had she done the 'serious thinking' she had promised herself in the twenty four hours which had elapsed?

"I did give it quite a bit of thought" she told me. "You know, in the shower and while I was cycling to work. The trouble was, I found it hard to come to any conclusion. On the one hand I was not mad about Grego – although I sensed that he was getting a bit serious about me, so it might have been best to have let him know, let him know that there wasn't going to be a big deal relationship. On the other hand I was definitely intrigued, as I'm sure you've gathered, by the mysterious FARIS stuff: the drip-feed of signs and coincidences which I kept encountering.

That was why I decided to let it continue. That and perhaps the BMW – his car was pretty cool!" She smiled mischievously at me.

When Grego failed to appear Anisha tried his mobile. No reply there, just the usual voice saying he was not available and inviting her to leave a message or send a text. She did both. By eight-thirty she decided he definitely wasn't coming and went out and bought a pizza. She went to bed that night feeling not just stood up but also somewhat concerned. The following day, Tuesday, she tried again, with the same lack of response. How could she find out if anything bad had happened – an accident perhaps, leaving Grego in a hospital bed? There was not a great deal to go on; all Anisha knew was that he worked as a parliamentary researcher; she was not even sure which MP he was employed by. Still, that did not have to deter her. After several phone-calls during her lunch hour to the House of Commons enquiry desk she succeeded in finding that out and in getting through to that particular MP's personal assistant. She made it sound as if her call was to do with Grego's work.

"I'm calling in response to an enquiry he made" she told the secretary. I'm afraid I don't have his extension number: could you put me through?"

"I'm sorry, no. He's not working for Mr xxx any more."

Anisha was surprised to hear this, to put it mildly. "Since when is this?"

"Yesterday was his last day."

"And is someone else dealing with his work?"

"He is not being replaced at present."

"I see. What about his enquiry then?"

"It is not important. Thank you for getting back to me, but there is no need to follow this up."

The tone of voice was telling her that her interest was not required but Anisha wasn't prepared to leave it at that.

"I see. As a matter of fact I did want to speak to him personally, but his mobile is not replying. If you could help to put me in touch I would be really so grateful."

But there was to be no cooperation forthcoming. The woman, quoting data protection refused to give out Gregory's

121

address and of course his House of Commons email address wouldn't be active if he had left his job. There was nothing for it. She had no means of contacting Grego even if she wanted to. The fact that he had let her down was irritating, the mystery of why was even more so but the only thing to do was to shrug her shoulders, write him off as not worth bothering about. And this was what she did, getting on with her work, enjoying the city life and forgetting about Grego. Until one day, some three months later, FARIS reappeared on the scene.

At first it appeared as an internet rumour, something mentioned on the blogosphere, which caught Anisha's attention when she was looking for information about a company that Focus Asset Management was considering adding to its green portfolio. She recognised at once the fountain symbol and the distinctive acronym but what surprised her was the company it appeared in, alongside a colourful spread advertising tours to romantic-sounding destinations in Central Asia along the course of the Silk Route.

FARIS appeared to be inviting readers to 'join us in Kyrghizstan, for the voyage of a life-time'.

It was an invitation, Anisha told me, that she had felt unable to refuse. In doing so she would again find her path crossing with that of Grego.

By responding to the advert she found herself looking at a choice of tours to Kyrghizstan which included many fascinating and unexplored parts of a country which had recently been opening up to tourism. The tours included walking and trekking as well as kayaking, travelling on horse-back and camping out. They were graded, from easy-going, suitable for any reasonably fit person, to the extremely challenging, requiring a high level of fitness, stamina and endurance and for these trips medical certification would be required and evidence of experience under harsh conditions. In other words the most

difficult of the tours on offer were, in reality, extreme fitness
and endurance challenges. Anisha had become aware of
'extreme challenges' since some of her friends had taken part in
one-day events. They tempted those young men – mostly men,
who wanted to test their endurance and fitness against what
seemed like a disturbing series of gruelling exercises. Taking
place in the coldest months of the year, usually in some
northern location, the participants waded through marsh and
mire, fought their way through near-impenetrable barriers of
wire and thickets, crossed lakes which might or might not be
frozen over but would in any case be very close to freezing and
competed against each other to complete the trial in the shortest
time possible, whilst at the same time raising money for
charities. No would-be participant was allowed to start the trial
until they had signed a document signalling their recognition of
the danger of the undertaking, the fact that they were putting
their lives in danger and waiving any right to take action
against the company that was organising and offering the day's
so-called entertainment. Anisha could name two of her old uni
friends who had been tempted to take up such a challenge; one
had completed the test, the other had failed and had spent
several weeks recuperating from the effects of his misplaced
belief in his own fitness and ability. 'Extreme challenge' was
thus a phrase which Anisha recognised and, because it appeared
to be linked to the FARIS emblem and the mystery of Grego's
association with the shadowy group and his sudden
disappearance from her scene, she felt bound to investigate.

    With no very serious intention of taking any of the tours,
she submitted an enquiry form. Within a day she received a
reply, welcoming her interest and explaining the choice of
tours. They came at different levels of difficulty, from easy
walking and horseback riding with porters carrying the luggage
and semi-permanent camps along the route for each night's
stop, through treks that presented a greater degree of challenge

and excitement: walking at high altitude, using canoes to cross lakes and rivers, pitching and striking camps evening and morning. The highest level of difficulty was flagged up as only for the outstandingly fit: young men and women who had already completed similar challenges and had proved their endurance and their ability to cope with heat and cold, altitude and absence of sleep and who could bring to the challenge skills like rock-climbing, swimming, handling canoes, running marathons while carrying their own packs and cycling for hours under the most gruelling of conditions. Anisha chose her level carefully, avoiding the extreme levels but nevertheless flagging up her experience of desert trekking in the Gulf, pot-holing (well, that time underground: what else was that?), as for kayaking and swimming, modesty compelled her to admit that swims and boating in the Thames would not count as real experience in the fields but at least, as a demonstration of an interest, worth a mention.

What came back, after a couple of days, was the suggestion that she might be interested in the 'Trek Kyrgyzstan; summer tour', moderate to difficult level. Anisha felt an almost visceral thrill rattle through her frame. Heck! Surely she wasn't going to let herself in for another trek, even more far-flung than last year's episode?

As her grandmother, I could only imagine her response: 'You bet she was!'

But before Anisha could even contemplate her next adventure there had to be a pause. She had been with Asset Management for just eight months. Her annual leave amounted to twenty five days, of which she had taken sixteen to make possible the Gulf trip and the Musandam Peninsular trek of recent memory. She thus needed to work another four months in order to earn the additional nine days of leave to make up a year's worth. And nine days, even when factoring in weekends and, if they fell neatly, public holidays, making it up to two weeks, was hardly enough for the initial journey to reach base camp Kyrgyzstan and then complete the ten or possibly the fifteen-day challenge of the trek she was offered. And then there was the cost. Flights, cost of tour/trek, but more seriously the expenses involved in the necessary kitting out for a trip of this type. Anisha was faced with serious problems .

Well, what could I say or do to help? I had to tell her that I felt she was simply asking too much. One exciting adventure holiday in a year was surely enough to keep her happy, wasn't it? Well, apparently in Anisha's view, if it were simply the case of taking a holiday she knew it was asking too much, but the FARIS factor, which she had already told me about, was what was getting her hooked.

Why, I asked, did she not ask her mother to stump up the funds?

She had thought of this but dismissed it; she wouldn't be able to explain the FARIS factor without Jessica taking the matter up with Alastair which, In Anisha's view was undesirable.

"Why so?" I asked her.

"To tell truth, Gran, I'm not sure but because I know that Alastair gave Mum that brooch, and because he and others were wearing it at the polo match, and because of the underground episode, and before that the odd occasion when I met Grego coming out of the champagne reception, and Grego's unwillingness to talk about – in fact he got quite worked up when I tried to get him to tell me about it – all these little things seem to add up to one big question mark."

"I can quite see why it has got you wondering. But there's no need to take it to the lengths you're proposing, especially if it means me lending you money, which you'd take ages to pay me back – if indeed you did."

"Of course I'll pay you back, Gran. I always pay my debts!"

"I know, but it's just that I might not have the heart to insist; and then we'd both end up cross."

"That wouldn't happen. You know I wouldn't let you pay. I'm earning a decent salary and you don't have to subsidise me." Anisha protested.

I adopted a soothing tone while trying still to persuade her not to rush at things.

"Why not wait six months and when you have the new annual leave allowance as well as the funds in your bank, go on one of the treks in the spring next year."

"That does sound like a good plan," she replied and I began to think I had won the argument. "But I think I've got to do it now!"

I reflected yet again that Jessica must have had second sight when naming her daughter; no obstacle was going to stand in the way of Anisha signing up for one of those challenge treks. The following week she had persuaded her boss to allow 4 days of unpaid leave to add to the days she was entitled to and a loan of £2000 was transferred from my bank account to hers, with a written agreement from Anisha that it would be paid back within the next twelve months. She even set up the standing order from her bank account to mine. With that sum she was able to go back to the travel company to book her trip and then go out and buy the recommended kit – the list came with the confirmation of the booking.

Chapter 15

*The Pamir-Alay (also Pamiro-Alai, Russian: Памиро-Алай) is a
mountain system in Tajikistan, Kyrgyzstan and Uzbekistan, part of the
Pamir Mountains. It stretches between the valleys of the rivers Syr
Darya (Fergana Valley) to its north and Vakhsh to its south. Its
highest summit is Pik Skalisty (Russian: пик Скалистый, "rocky
peak"), 5621 m, in the Turkestan Range.*
From Wikipedia, the free encyclopedia

The itinerary on her e-ticket was first to Turkey,
overnighting in Istanbul and then a mid-morning flight to
Bishkek, in Kyrghizstan, where she would take a connecting
flight to her destination, the city of Osh. At the checkout in
Istanbul airport Anisha tried spotting who if any among the
passengers checking in might be signed up for the same trip as
herself – a trekking holiday, with horseback and canoe stages,
in the still relatively unknown Republic of Kyrghyzstan. One
reason why this smallest of the central Asian 'stan' republics
was still relatively unknown was the political unrest which had
plagued the country on and off for the past two decades
following the break-up of the Soviet Union. Looking around at
her fellow-passengers as they sat waiting for instructions to
board, she failed to spot, among the suited and brief-cased men
and women, any candidate for a tough challenge of endurance
like herself. She did note with interest the variety of faces.
Some of the men had high foreheads, small pointed beards and
eyes which seemed screwed up against the light. These she
mentally noted as belonging to the peoples of the 'Stans' – so
near to China that they shared some features which she, while
acknowledging her ignorance, already thought of as 'Asiatic'.
Looking at them sent a shudder of excitement through her, as if
she was standing already on the edge of undiscovered worlds.

There was time enough to examine physiognomies on the
four-hour flight from Istanbul to Bishkek and then on to Osh, in
the course of which the tea and plastic-coated cake, served as

in-flight snacks, left her feeling glad that she had had the foresight to bring supplementary rations. She spent part of the time with her Lonely Planet guide, checking out the places which her trekking itinerary included. As she leafed through it she became aware of her neighbour's gaze moving across the pages and seeking her own gaze interrogatively. She glanced sideways and smiled encouragingly while pointing to the images.

"Do you know this place?"

He was startled and retreated momentarily into himself. She tried again, pointing and looking enquiringly, using one word at a time in the hope that his English might be more than her non-existent command of the Kyrghiz language… she still had not grasped quite what it was called.

"Beautiful…?" she suggested, indicating an illustration of a lush valley, river and mountains.

"Very beautiful!" the reply came.

Anisha proffered the book she was holding, inviting him, by gesture, to turn the pages. He quickly obliged, searching, it seemed. At one image he came to a halt and pointed. It was a family standing together, several generations, grandfather holding a grandchild, parents and siblings, and behind them a round, tent-like structure which Anisha knew was called a 'yurt' – at least that was the name she knew it by although she figured that her neighbour might have a different name for it. She took a closer look at her fellow-passenger's face and noticed the small narrow eyes with the wrinkled skin, browned, it seemed, by the sun and the wind. His cheekbones were high and beneath them the skin fell in a series of lined folds to a narrow chin where a wispy beard bobbed and nodded in time to the words that he was trying to say as he pointed happily at the image.

"My family…"

Anisha was surprised.

"This is your family?"

128

"No! No my family. "He paused, seeking words which he could assemble to make sense. After a pause he had another try.

"My family we…. Summer time my family here, this way, living."

Anisha got his meaning.

"Ah, I understand! In summer time your family live like this family. Right?"

The gentleman – for he clearly was, in Anisha's view, a gentleman – nodded enthusiastically. She attempted to move the communication forward.

"You – grandfather, like this?" She pointed to the picture. "You have a grandchild, like this?" She pointed to the small child in the photo, whilst reflecting that the best topic of conversation with strangers was always about the family. He nodded again and smiled.

"How many grandchildren?" Anisha asked. He looked puzzled and she repeated: "How many….?" Whilst pointing at the child. "One? Two? Three?" she used her fingers indicating the numbers and pointing to the child. It was easy. He showed on his own hands one – two-three- four fingers.

"Four grandchildren?" Anisha asked? "That's wonderful!" He looked puzzled and so, to elucidate she added: "That's very good!"

Her companion nodded, smiling.

The time was passing nicely.

After a while her companion leant across her and pointed out of the aircraft window.

"Pamir!" He mouthed at her, "Pamir Alay …"

Anisha looked and nodded back enthusiastically at her companion who had named the mountain range that they were flying over. The sun was going down and reflected pink tones on the tops where snow was lying. The plane droned on; she could feel that they had started to descend when the seat-belt sign came on and the steward's voice announced something in Turkish and in Russian and finally in what might have been English.

"Osh!" her companion told her, leaning across again to see and point to the lights of the city ahead and below them.

At the airport Anisha was pleased to spot her name on a placard as she came out of Customs. So good to be welcomed! Up ahead her travelling companion was being greeted by a crowd of family and as she headed for the exit he noticed her too and exchanged a warm hand shake. Seeing the family gazing curiously at her she paused and a general handshake ensued with greetings which were fully intelligible in spite of being in mutually incomprehensible languages. After that Anisha was whisked away in what she later described to me as a kind of camper-van to meet the team and the rest of the adventurers.

An hour's drive through unrelieved darkness brought them to the camp. After a meal and a good night's sleep they were ready to set out in the morning.

There were nine of them in the group, plus the two guides, an interpreter and a driver. Besides Anisha there were a couple from New Zealand, two Dutch lads, a Norwegian girl and her boyfriend, an American and a French girl. So far, so very international! Anisha confided. After the meal at the base camp outside Osh, the two guides briefed the group about their itinerary.

"You guys have all opted for the fairly serious challenge and we've got some exciting stuff in store for you. There were nods of appreciation from all except the French girl, who screwed up her nose and eyes signalling incomprehension.

Anisha translated. The girl, whose name was Elodie nodded gratefully.

"Really I speak alright but she is so fast. It is hard for me!" she confided to Anisha who nodded sympathetically.

"You'll get used to it" she told Elodie, encouragingly. "You will understand very well soon. Tonight – tired!"

Elodie nodded gratefully. The guide, whose name was Helen, continued and Anisha translated whenever Elodie gave her the sign that it was needed.

"Tomorrow's the long drive," Helen continued, "So, not much to do except relax and watch the landscape. Once we get up into the mountains it gets more exciting. You'll love the scenery. It's wild; it's fertile; this is the part of the world where humans first began to cultivate all sorts of fruits and in these parts you'll get an idea of what I mean. First night camp is a farm where they'll be harvesting apples and apricots and a whole bunch of other stuff. You'll like it but we'll not be staying long. Day two is on horseback and we'll be up before dawn. I know you can all saddle up – according to the information you gave us at least; so I hope you were telling it straight. The saddlery may not coincide with what you are used to but you'll sort it out. Three hours ride and we stop for breakfast at the top of this mountain pass." She pointed on the map. "You'll be ready for the break, I can assure you; but so will the horses. Remember, we look after our animals before we look after ourselves – right?"

"Right" came the expected reply and the group looked around at each other uneasily, gauging just how fit, truthful and up for it the members might be.

"OK – enough for today. Get some sleep. You'll be up at 5.30 in the morning."

Following this rather threatening introduction Anisha retired to the bunk bed she had been allocated. Her unpacking consisted of toothbrush only. After a quick visit to the washroom she opted to sleep in the clothes she had travelled in to be ready for the early start.   She fell asleep instantly and woke next day feeling ready for anything.

The days that followed were a whirlwind or a kaleidoscope of challenging physical activity, all set within the most inspiring scenery. Anisha kept busy recording moments on her camera – at least any moments when she was not fully occupied either keeping her balance on horseback, clambering along precarious mountain ridges or taking her turn at the oars of the boat as they negotiated a river-crossing or a lake. She has subsequently written up the diary and illustrated it with those photos and as a record for all to see. It was towards the end of the trek with just two days left that a conversation took place that was to change the course of Anisha's holiday, and much more besides. That night they were camped under cover in a woodman's barn which was used by the foresters only when they collected the walnut crop. At that time of year, their guide told them, the woods were transformed into part workplace and part picnic place as the villagers came up from their homes and farms further down the slopes to gather in the crop. That walnuts had been packed in boxes onto the old Soviet lorries which were seen everywhere and trundled off to the warehouses and markets in the lowlands of the Ferghana Valley, and the only evidence of all that activity was where the sparse undergrowth and grass had been trampled down and charred circles showed where cooking fires had been made. Now the woods were deserted and the barn was theirs to make use of for the overnight camp. The group made themselves at home, each one choosing a spot to roll out sleeping mat and sleeping bag. They made use of the nearby stream for a wash and a clean-up before setting about dividing up tasks for making the evening meal. It was Anisha's turn along with another to make the fire, collecting wood, seeking out the driest logs and branches from among the dead wood which lay strewn around. She was amassing a tidy pile to take back to build the fire when, Helen, the guide, joined her.

"Like a hand with these?"

Anisha accepted willingly. Helen was easy to get on with; her straight-talking and down-to-earth manner guaranteed that everyone knew where they were with her, what they had to do and how she viewed their performance. Dressed almost militarily in khaki cargo pants, sweaters with shoulder tabs and boots that looked as if they could go anywhere, she was respected equally, Anisha noted, by the boys in the company as much as the girls – although, to Anisha's mind she seemed to be more relaxed with the females in the group. Now Helen smiled as she offered to help Anisha with the firewood and Anisha responded.

"Thanks, that'd be great."

The two of them picked up a load each. Helen enquired how Anisha had found the day's adventures.

"Good fun. A big challenge, but that's what I like."

Helen nodded approvingly.

"I've got something rather special tomorrow, if you're interested…."

Anisha was curious because she thought she knew what the next day's programme was going to be.

"Isn't it the Lake day?" she asked, "At least that's what the programme has. I was just thinking perhaps I should have brought a wet-suit; or is that against the rules?" she laughed.

"No wet-suits allowed. The lake crossing is by kayak and getting wet is all part of the challenge: wet and cold!"

"I can cope with that," Anisha assured her.

"I'm sure you can. I've been quite impressed – the way you've handled things. You don't let much get in your way or put you off, do you?"

Anisha laughed and told her, "It's all in the name, you know. It means not deterred, something like that, and of course I do like to live up to it"

Helen smiled appreciatively. "I can see that you do. So, now, this 'something special' I mentioned. You might find it interesting."

"Tell me more," Anisha was intrigued.

"The thing is that I can only take two people on this little detour and I was thinking of yourself and Piet, the Dutch guy. I think he could handle it."

"Piet is up for anything", Anisha assured her, "And he is really tough, can keep going for hours in all weathers."

"Actually this would not call for much in the way of stamina. In fact if you want to test your powers of endurance more than you have already you might prefer to go on the lake day. This would be interesting though…"

"You haven't told me what it's all about yet," Anisha reminded her. "Tell me more and I might be able to decide!"

"You're right! It's a trip to an enclave, down on the other side of these mountains."

Anisha was puzzled. "Enclave? What exactly….? I mean I know the word, but I'm a bit hazy about the exact meaning…." she tailed off.

Helen laughed. "It's a word we all think we know: 'a group of people and their homes isolated within another group': the Chinese in Soho – we call them an enclave sometimes. It's the same sort of idea here in Kyrghizstan. There are little patches of land with communities and villages – towns too in some cases – which have stubbornly remained not part of Kyrghizstan. And for political and historical reasons, going back a long way, or some times not a long way, they have negotiated the right to remain part of the country to which their population – in ethnic terms – belong. Here in Kyrghizstan there are pockets of populations which are not at all Kyrghiz; some are ethnically Uzbek, some are ethnically Tajik. And actually throughout Kyrghizstan, as you will have noticed, the population is incredibly diversely made up of these three – and other – ethnic groups. But in the enclaves they are pretty well

134

ethnically all of one and, through the negotiations of history and of politics, they have achieved their aim of remaining part of what they see as 'the mother country."

"You've given me something to think about there. I mean, why should they feel so strongly....? On the other hand, I can see how they might feel. But it must create some problems, to be a small island of population in the middle of another country."

"I thought you and Piet might like to visit one of these tomorrow. Would you like to see how it works? Or at least how they try to make it work? What do you think?" Helen asked.

Without hesitation Anisha's answer came back.

"Yes of course, I certainly would. What time do we leave?"

"We should be away by 5.30. Pack your things up and they can go along with the luggage for everyone else. I'll tell Piet the same."

"What about the rest of the group?" Anisha asked.

"They'll be doing the lake trip as planned, *sans* wet suits naturally – using ice picks if they need to! We'll be back together at the evening camp."

"Will they manage without you? I mean, don't they need you along with them?"

"It's been taken care of," Helen assured her. "We have an extra guide, a local, fully qualified, knows the lake well. As far as the company's health and safety regs are concerned, we are covered. See you tomorrow at five thirty a.m., right?"

"Right," Anisha replied. "See you then!"

Chapter 16

In political geography, an enclave is a territory whose geographical boundaries are entirely surrounded by the boundaries of another territory. An exclave, on the other hand, is a territory legally or politically attached to another territory with which it is not physically contiguous. These are two distinct concepts, although many entities fit both definitions.

From Wikipedia, the free encyclopedia

Should you ever find yourself travelling in the famous Fergana Valley of Uzbekistan, you are well advised to take time for a side trip to Shakhimardan, the Uzbek enclave beyond the Kyrgyz border. Whomever you may ask about Shakhimardan, few have ever been there but for Uzeks, Shakhimardan is the equivalent of Shangrila and is also referred to as the Switzerland of Uzbekistan. At an altitude of over 1,500m and surrounded by most picturesque mountains, Shakhimardan offers the ultimate contrast to the oasis cities of the steppes and deserts. ..... For some years now, there have been disputes between the governments of Uzbekistan and Kyrgyzstan over this enclave. However, the enclave remains an Uzbek territory, with majority Uzbek population. http://www.discovery-central-asia.com

The sun came up when they had been on the road for an hour, turning the mountain tops to pink where early autumn snow had fallen. The road was surfaced with rough grey rubble and the 4-wheel-drive scrunched and threw up stones behind it as Helen drove at a speed which had no regard for the age of the vehicle. Tall poplars lined the road at intervals, their leaves beginning to turn to yellow and gold in the late summer sun. At times the road fell away steeply into the river valley that they were roughly following where Anisha could see small irregular-shaped fields whose crops seemed to have been harvested and figures could be seen working with hand tools to prepare for the next seasons sowings. After another hour Helen signalled that they would be stopping for a break and the stopping place was worth being awake for.

She pulled the vehicle off the road in a level space where the view down the narrow valley was spectacular. Anisha drew in her breath and reached for her camera.

"How about that? The two rivers meet at that point. It's a fine view."

"What's the name of the river we've been following?" Piet wanted to know.

"It's the Ak-Su. And this one which joins it is the Kara-Su."

After consuming coffee from a hot flask with hard-boiled eggs and cold potatoes from the previous night's meal they were on their way again. Another hour and a half brought them to a check-point, beyond which a jumble of urban buildings lined the steep sides of the seemingly interminable river valley. Their documents having been scrutinised and a few words exchanged, they were waved through.

"What language is that you were speaking there; was that Russian?"

"The Kyrghiz version of Russian," Helen replied. "It's still the lingua franca in these parts, though the official language was changed to Kyrghiz when the union broke up. With so many different nationalities mixing here, there has to be some middle meeting ground and Russian is what they were used to for so many years."

"And how did you come to learn Russian, Helen?' Piet asked. "I don't think so they teach it in English schools....?"

"I did it at uni, along with French and German."

"So you can read the script too I assume?"

"Yes, of course. That's the first thing you learn. It's not so difficult."

They had entered the outskirts of a town and she slowed down as a checkpoint came in view.

"Now, we're nearly there!"

Signs at the check-point greeted them in several languages and scripts. 'Welcome to Uzbekistan city of Shakhimardan' Anisha read. After showing their papers they were waved straight through.

Helen drew the car up in front of a monumental building with inscription in Cyrillic lettering over a high, arched portal.

"What's this?" Anisha asked.

"This is the tourist information bureau." Helen replied, jumping out and beckoning to Piet and Anisha to do likewise. "Come on, they are going to give us their speech."

"In English, I hope" Anisha muttered under her breath as she stepped stiffly down from the vehicle.

"Where next? I take it that's not everything?" Anisha challenged Helen as they came down the imposing steps of the Tourist Bureau and regained their vehicle. "Frankly that was something of an anti-climax and not as exciting as the lake challenge which our colleagues are doing right now. I'm not sure if I would not rather be with them!"

"That is by no means all," Helen replied. "Our next stop is a kilometre or two from here: it's called 'Shakhimardan Exploration'."

Piet too appeared bored and enervated by the tedious and difficult-to-follow presentation of the Tourist Board.

"What's Shakhimardan Exploration and why is it of interest?" Anisha asked

"It's a company that is taking advantage of two things, firstly the remoteness of this area and secondly the purity of the atmosphere up here."

Anisha looked at Helen in surprise.

"You mean, by that, a western company…?" she demanded "And taking advantage for what purpose?"

"Wait a bit. Soon you'll see."

138

At 11.30 as they set off again, the streets of Shakhimardan were crowded with stalls, barrows, loaded donkeys and mostly very old cars and trucks blaring their horns to make a way through. Helen followed suit with the horn and steered a cautious way along the main street where the action was taking place. The majority of merchandise was agricultural, with a fair quantity of wool and woven goods on display as well.

"It's what they do here." Helen shouted above the noise. "Most of the people are small-holders growing veg and stuff and a lot of it goes straight off to Russia. There are the herders and livestock farmers who keep cattle, sheep, and goats up on the mountains. Hence the clothes and textiles that you see. It's traditional to wear them, mostly over the top of the sweaters and jeans and mass-produced stuff that we all wear wherever we come from."

Anisha and Piet were looking around expectantly, searching, like the tourists that, basically, they were, for the unusual and noteworthy. So far Anisha had failed to find it.

"Actually I don't see what's so very special about this place. It seems much the same as the other various towns we have passed through in the country...." She ventured.

"Except that you are not now in Kyrgyzstan; you are in Uzbekistan." Helen pointed out.

"We are roughly aware of that because of the check-point – or I suppose you call it frontier post – that we passed through. It wasn't very noticeable and there was hardly any hint of a change – in the atmosphere, or anything I mean"

"Not today – you're right", Helen conceded.

Anisha went on. "I mean if you are in UK and you go from Northern Ireland to the Republic today – well, you really don't notice it. You can't even tell where the line lies these day, since the troubles ended...."

"Well it's not like that here", Helen retorted. "And it's only a few years since there were horrendous problems, with all the mayhem and massacre which goes on when neighbours turn against each other."

"And what sparked it off on that occasion? Was it a cultural or a religious thing?" Anisha asked.

"I think those were part of the mix" Helen replied thoughtfully, "But the spark – not the right word really – at the heart of it was the question of water."

Anisha, despite her tiredness now paid attention. The same old problem, everyone's basic need, the one which could set a community against its neighbours or give it power to dominate and control them. Anisha's mind jumped back to the palm garden of Oman and the contradictory watery scenes of Andalusia. Here, however, she could see no evidence of shortage.

"There seems to be plenty of water here; what is the problem?"

"You can see how dependant people here are on the crops they raise. Every family has its market garden to supply the household and to sell to the market – to Russia in particular."

"I still don't see the problem. They have the river running almost through the front garden!"

"Exactly! And the country that surrounds them claims the water rights and controls what the people here in Shakhimardan can use."

"How can they do that?"

"Very easily. Hydro electric dams are a most effective way of controlling what actually flows in the river bed. Turn a few screws and levels can be reduced – at any time of the year they choose to do so but most easily in summer, when river levels are naturally lower and when the need to water crops is at its highest."

"Yes, I can see. It's obvious, as you say." Anisha was thoughtful now. "The powerful neighbours can put the screws on this little enclave at any time they choose."

"Not just by controlling the water level; here the electricity supplies come from outside – from those very hydro-electric plants that are using the water. And the neighbouring government can decide to ration the electricity that drives the pumps that should be pumping what small quantities of water remain, to irrigate the fields."

"So being an enclave has very definite disadvantages. You wonder why they stick it out...."

"Well, they do get help from their 'mother' country – as they call it. Uzbekistan supports them and encourages them. It also plays them off against Kyrghizstan, the country that surrounds them. So, in some ways these enclaves – there are several of them – are pawns in the bigger game; the game of power politics. And don't imagine that old Mother Russia is far removed from any of this."

Helen had been driving as she spoke and had left the main streets to cross by bridge to the other side of the river and uphill, via smaller lanes, to emerge into a square with poplars and a startlingly modern building alongside apartment blocks and a couple of warehouses in the old Soviet style.

"We're here," Helen announced. "Shakhimardan Exploration!" She gestured to the bold sign in English and Cyrillic script over the entrance.

The sleek clean curving lines of this building stood out in cool contrast to those that surrounded it. In front were gates where Helen drew up and an official stepped forward to greet them. Not a government official, at least Anisha thought not, perhaps just a janitor or member of staff on gate duty. He did ask to see Helen's identification and, although it was all in the foreign language, Anisha deduced he was asking about their appointment. He looked cursorily at the passengers, pointed to where Helen should park the vehicle and indicated the steps of the smart cool building where they would be received. Stiff and tired from the journey Piet and Anisha stepped down from the 4-wheel drive. Anisha looked around, rubbing her eyes.

It was only as they entered the building and stood at the reception desk that Anisha started to wake up and take notice. Above the desk, flanking the company logo in its Cyrillic script, indeed, as she couldn't fail to see, decorating the visitors' passes which were handed out to be worn around their necks, the sign she had come to know so well. Before she had time to think further the three of them were directed to a lift and, as they emerged as instructed at the second floor, a figure was there to greet them.
"Hello Helen, Piet," he turned to her "Anisha…."
Anisha paused and replied, slowly, quietly.
"Grego! Well, hello."

They were sitting drinking coffee. Grego had taken them to a room furnished as an executive office and they sat on sofas with a view of the town and the river valley that ran down the middle. Anisha, still stunned and with no idea what to make of the situation gazed blankly, registering the figures which crossed the bridge which they themselves had recently crossed, figures carrying bundles and baskets of market produce, driving even more heavily-laden donkeys or weaving in and out of the crowd on motor bikes with the occasional truck and car nosing its way among them. The contrast of the view with these sleek twenty-first century surroundings could not have been greater.
"Is someone going to tell me what this is about – at all?" Anisha enquired faintly, looking around at Helen and Piet. Did Piet know more about this than she had thought? He and Helen were exchanging complicit glances and looking in turn to Grego who shrugged apologetically.

"The boss will be with us any minute, he must have got held up. He'll explain; really it's not up to me Anisha; I'm just a junior assistant here."

"And since when is that?" She asked with unconcealed sarcasm. "Since you stood me up last June on a particular date in London?"

"I couldn't help it, Anisha. Believe me. You were getting too close, and it was too soon."

"Close?" Anisha's jaw dropped with astonishment. "Me, getting close? It was you who was making all the running!"

The others were looking on with embarrassment at this exchange as Grego was obviously squirming with some degree of discomfort. He sought to explain himself.

"You're right. I'm sorry. I didn't mean close in that sense…not in the sense I think you're taking it."

"What other sense am I supposed to take it in? Too close for comfort? Can I remind you that the date was your suggestion – I could take it or leave it but you seemed to want…"

Helen cleared her throat preliminary to entering the fray.

"Anisha, I think I know what he's talking about and…."

But Anisha wasn't to be distracted and rounded on her.

"You don't know the first thing about this, so kindly keep out of it Helen. This, this…" She searched for a suitable word. "This idiot tried his hardest to impress me in London with his smart car, his polo-playing friends, his Westminster connections and champagne receptions; stood me up on a date and has the cool nerve now to say that I was the one who was getting too close! Unbelievable!"

"I think he means 'close' in another way altogether. Not close too him, but close to…" She hesitated.

"Close to who then – if not to him?"

"No, not 'close to who?' 'Close to what?' You were getting to close to…."

"Go on", Anisha goaded. "If not close to who, then what was I getting too close to?"

There was silence; a silence in which Anisha looked from Helen, to Piet, to Grego and back to Helen again. Eventually Helen offered a response of sorts.

"It will all become clear quite soon but, as Gregory said, we need to wait for….. Ah here he is! Here they are!"

Anisha turned to see where Helen was looking towards the double doors behind her which swung wide to allow what she could only afterwards describe to me as 'a posse of white-coated boffins', spear-headed by a figure which it took her only a split second to identify as her stepfather, Alistair Singleton. The now-familiar FARIS badge was displayed on his chest and embroidered into the white coats of the figures behind him. She looked from Alistair to Grego in disbelief, then back to Alistair again.

"It's you! Oh my! My wicked stepfather and who would have thought it? On the other hand – why am I surprised?" Her eyes fastened onto the curiously shaped badge. "OK, so I was getting close, was I? Close to what?

To….?" She pointed to the symbol.

"That's right, my dear, to FARIS. Didn't you realise it?" Alistair moved over and put his arm round her shoulder. "You're a smart girl, Anisha, and we could see you were interested. And yes, you were getting rather close. I believe one of our members, acting rather rashly, tried to warn you off. I'm sorry if he frightened you in that tunnel. I hope the scars did not take too long to heal."

Anisha was gazing at him in disbelief. Alastair continued. "In the end we thought it best to get you out here among us, to invite you to join us." And he added, reassuringly, "Don't worry too much, you will learn all about us in the next few days."

He looked around; the faces were serious, the company needed cheering up.

144

Meanwhile Anisha's mind was working overtime trying to make sense of the situation and of what she was hearing. She concluded that the best she could do was to show little, or at best, no obvious reaction, feeling instinctively that it would be disastrous at this stage to betray her feelings, even if she was able to identify what these were, which she was emphatically not able to do right then.

"Come now," Alastair was speaking again. "A glass of the local wine would do us good. It's a bit of a shock for Anisha – look at her, still quite baffled! So we had better all make her feel at home and put her in the picture. Eh Anisha?"

While Anisha struggled to keep her composure many questions were racing through her mind. First and foremost, what was the nature of this FARIS thing that she had been tripping over for the last six months? And secondly, where did Grego come into it? And then, her stepfather? His appearance filled her with a mixture of feelings, from indignation to something near to fear since he obviously had some leading role in whatever FARIS was. And Helen and Piet: were they in it? Or were they just here by chance? No that could not be right: there must be some connection through Helen and Piet that had drawn her in and culminated with her finding herself in this futuristic space, in the middle of this odd little enclave and surrounded by a country that she knew next to nothing about.

Alastair, who seemed to be in charge, took them through to a space which he called the FARIS seminar room, equipped with pc, projector and screen. His first click on the pc brought up the fountain-shaped FARIS symbol. Alistair cleared his throat.

"Some of you," he looked at Helen and Piet, "have heard this before, but it won't hurt you to listen again. For Anisha, most of it will come as news, but to what extent it will surprise her....well, I wait to see."

Anisha was aware of her heart beating fast; her mouth was dry and her stomach felt as if it had been tied in a knot.

"Anisha," Alistair continued, looking long and hard at her. "What we have here – this place, of which you have seen only the outward-facing ante-rooms – is an installation for the future. Does that mean something to you? Does that ring bells in your vivid imagination? Evoke perhaps a sense of challenge? I know you are always up for a challenge and that, once you have taken one on, no obstacles are allowed to get in your way. As a quality, that could be very valuable to FARIS." He was looking at her now with amused affection, a look which Anisha, who had never felt comfortable with her stepfather, instinctively tried to evade.

"No false modesty please! I have heard about your abilities and have seen you at close quarters. What we have here is exciting, challenging, and..." here he paused and sought the eyes and affirmation of all who sat around the table, ".... and possibly of unparalleled significance for our shared future. Not just this year, this decade, or this century, but far, far ahead, into a future which we here and now are quite unable to envisage. A vision which, if we play our parts, may indeed mean that the human race does have a future and is not to be extinguished, in the space of the next two centuries, overcome by its own inability to act, to organise and to foresee."

As she listened to this, she told me later, Anisha's thoughts were a jumbled blur and she tried her best to focus and to pull apart the different strands which were tangled up in her head. On the one hand she began to wonder if her step-father was in some way seriously unhinged – a mad professor, some kind of Dr Strangelove. On the other hand, knowing what she did about him – his connections, his wealth, his business success, it seemed unlikely that he should turn out to be an irrational eccentric. And where did Helen and Piet fit into this? She tried to remember how Helen had persuaded her to come on this particular side-trip to her main holiday. Was there more to the holiday itself than she had realised? How had she made the decision to come on this particular adventure trip…..? Thinking back she began to wonder if she had been manipulated right from the start. In any case she still had very little idea of what FARIS was all about. She needed to know, but she also needed to keep her opinions to herself. And, to keep her composure, she put on a smile, a smile, she hoped, of the puzzled bewilderment of one who is anxious to learn.

"I'm lost" she told him. "I'm not sure what this is all about; I know the world is in a dire state but….? Do you really foresee the end of the human race? Surely you don't believe that?"

"Anisha," her step-father gave her a long and serious look. "You're a sweet girl, and an optimist. That's part of the trouble. The young are optimistic; they think that all will be well in the long run. The old on the other hand have no illusions; they know that in the long run the outcome is unlikely to be good, but at that stage they are too tired and dispirited to do anything about it, or else they retreat into some fantasy of another life when they move on – an afterlife where all will be well."

"I'm not sure that's true," Anisha replied. There are plenty of young people who are only too aware that it's up to them to clear up the mess left by the older generation."

"You're right there but then we find they go about it in the wrong way; as if planting trees and putting up solar panels was going to save the human race and its civilisation. But let's not get into arguments about environmentalists. You at least have your feet on the ground and that's why FARIS has brought you here. First though, what do you know about FARIS? And what would you like to know?"

"Well, first I would like to know…."

147

At this point Helen interrupted.

"First, Alastair, remember we're hungry! We left camp at 5.30 this morning. We could all do with some refreshment!"

"Of course! Thoughtless of me. I get carried away."

So Anisha was left in suspense again, dying to know at last what FARIS was all about but equally glad of the chance to refuel. And as she ate she took the opportunity to look around at the well-stocked and western-style canteen. The FARIS symbol was everywhere visible, etched into the glass panels of the doors and decorating the china and cutlery, embossed on the backs of chairs and embroidered onto linen napkins, everywhere she looked the sign which she had first noticed.... Where had she first noticed it? She tried to remember. Wherever it had first occurred, it seemed to have cropped up with increasing frequency until about six months ago. Then it had gone quiet but now, here it was again and she could wait a few minutes to satisfy her hunger and assemble her thoughts, get prepared for whatever revelation was imminent. The important thing, she reminded herself, was to keep her opinions strictly private until she could get some insight into what FARIS was all about. Until then she must keep her own counsel.

Chapter 17

Space tourism is space travel for recreational, leisure or business purposes. A number of startup companies have sprung up in recent years, hoping to create a space tourism industry. Orbital space tourism opportunities have been limited and expensive, with only the Russian Space Agency providing transport to date. From Wikipedia, the free encyclopedia

In the seminar room Anisha allowed her mind to wander. There were some fifteen of them, many of whom, she gathered, had also recently arrived and they had been sitting round the seminar table for at least twenty minutes, listening to someone in charge of administration telling them about the building, the safety arrangements, their accommodation and meal-times.

Her mind was in a strange state in which a feeling of unreality blended with very real sensations – aching muscles from the rough car ride as well as from the exertions of previous days, the warmth of the sunshine slanting in through the windows, the light it cast broken by the movement of the swaying branches of the tall poplar trees outside, the smell of coffee from the next room, the voice of the speaker as it rose and fell to emphasise a point. She had a note-pad and pen in front of her and with the ball-point with the fountain-shaped symbol engraved on it, she was doodling patterns. At the top of the page she had written out those enigmatic and irritating initials, with spaces between: F - A - R - I - S.

When the admin session finished Alastair returned to the room and prepared to address them.

He started the session off with a welcome.

"It's good to see you all. Some of you have been here before and will have heard what I have to say. Others are newcomers and I know there are many questions, which I hope I can answer. So, who wants to go first?"

Anisha raised a hand.

"Right Anisha, fire away. What do you want to know?"

"What the letters stand for, of course," she smiled as she spoke.

"Certainly. I can see how that has been teasing you. I'll start with the final letter. 'S' stands for 'survivors'. That's what we are, what we intend to be, survivors who will pass on our civilisation and our culture as well as our genes down the ages to come." He paused, looking around the room at his team, before adding "But not necessarily in this place," and Anisha saw the responding smiles of – what was it? Complicity, anticipation? from several of those present – yes, she thought, both Piet and Helen were certainly in the know – whatever knowledge that implied.

"Survivors," echoed Anisha. "Can you tell me survivors of what?"

"In due course, yes, I'll explain but I need to finish the puzzle. What kind of survivors do we want? The best, naturally. And for that they must be…" Another pause as he looked around the table, nodding first at Helen who responded:

"Fit and active"

Then at Grego, who added with panache and a smile:

"Intelligent and resourceful!"

"And there you have it," Alastair concluded the presentation, "Fit and Active, Intelligent and Resourceful Survivors: that's FARIS for you, in a nutshell!"

"I see," said Anisha, feeling that she really did not see or understand anything at all. To fill in the time she doodled the rest of the conundrum onto her note-pad.

"What does that mean to you, Anisha?" her stepfather asked. "Don't you find that exciting?"

She responded cautiously, "Well, maybe, but …." She paused. "I mean, when I signed up for this holiday I suppose that's just what I hoped I would be. I knew I had to be fit and active. Intelligent and resourceful seemed to be requirements as well. And at the end I hope I would turn out to have survived: to be a survivor. Is that what you mean?"

She noticed Helen and Piet, and this time Grego also, exchange glances before directing their gaze towards Alastair for his follow-up.

"Yes, you would be a survivor, Anisha, simply because you possess those qualities. But we aren't talking about adventure holidays; our mission is more significant than that. Are you ready to know?"

"Of course; you've kept me waiting long enough. Put me in the picture, please. What is the mission?"

Now Anisha was normally wary of words like mission: they started alarm bells in her head. : Already the day had taken on surreal dimensions – futuristic building in the midst of a city of medieval squalor, geeks in white coats, staff with an adoring regard, which amounted it seemed to reverence, for Alastair, the apparent leader. All these, even though her default mode was not one of caution, amounted in Anisha's mind to a warning. Keep quiet, go along with the revelations, appear interested, this was the strategy which suggested itself and, in her judgement, was the way to deal with the unusual situation until she knew more about it. She had no idea what to expect.

Even if she had had a clue as to what was coming it would not have prevented the incredulity Anisha felt. There followed a presentation that Alastair and his team had clearly given a good few times before as they rolled it out for her in the most matter of fact tones and terms. Apparently, and as Anisha recounted to me afterwards, for a decade or more a group of well-placed individuals had come together under a shared conviction that, because the world, the planet and, in particular the human race were headed in the direction of disaster and annihilation the best hope for saving civilisation was to

151

transport it, or as representative a sample of it as possible, to a new location and start again. Anisha's stepfather gave the initial overview, clarifying that he expected significant progress to be made to the project within his own lifetime. He described his role as chief fund-raiser and recruiter to the project and it was to this end that he had established his base in Dubai from where he travelled extensively meeting and extending the network of those who supported FARIS.

Anisha was impatient to ask him who or what kind of people these might be but she decided to save her questions until all the speakers had had their say. The next speaker described how life would be sustained on the inhospitable surface of the new planet. As she had already heard of biomes and geodesic structures Anisha was able to take some of this in but when it came to tunnelling and excavating and constructing a city underground – well, that left her with so many questions she would not know where to start. After this she listened to a discourse on the cultural and scientific resources that were to form part of the transportation; here, it appeared there was still considerable disagreement and the matter was very much open to discussion. What had been agreed however was that the major arts should be included and music and drama should present little in the way of problems, being readily available in digital format. For the visual arts a start had already been made and Anisha learnt now the true destination of various iconic paintings which had been sold at auction to unknown bidders whilst the possibility that the objects of art theft, items which had disappeared and never been heard of again, might also end up in the same destination was not entirely ruled out.

When this speaker finished his talk, Alastair signalled a short pause indicating that tea and coffee were available.

"All well so far, Anisha?" Alastair queried as she thoughtfully sipped her tea.

"Utterly fascinating!" she replied then added cautiously "It does sound rather like science fiction though. I mean, how are

152

you going to get there, with all the stuff that will be needed for survival?"

"Ah, an outline of the technical stuff is coming next. Suffice to say that we are much further ahead than is generally known and the exciting thing is that sufficient people have become convinced of the rightness of the cause as to pour in a really astounding quantity of resources. And that's what it's all about: the cash to get on with the job and the brains to make it happen."

"I still don't see…. I mean," Anisha struggled for words. "I mean, however many powerful, rich and brainy individuals you have on board your project, however can that be enough to make it happen?" She paused. "There must surely be more to it than that?"

Alastair looked at her appraisingly.

"What are you thinking of?" he asked

Anisha hesitated: how should she put it? Drawing a breath she plunged in with her question.

"Why here? I mean why have you set up your headquarters in this remote and difficult backwater? As I understand it this place is an island, belonging to one country inside the boundaries of another? I feel sure you have a reason for that?"

Alastair nodded appraisingly. "You are on to something there and you'll find out shortly why we are where we are. Of course, this is not the only place where FARIS operates, as you'll see."

Anisha hoped he was going to say more but it was not forthcoming and Alastair continued -

'Buttering me up!' was how Anisha described it to herself.

"I always thought you had the intelligence to understand the plan – as well as, hopefully, the common sense to get involved, to commit yourself to it. It was, of course, a stroke of pure serendipity that your path crossed with Gregory's. He's a bright boy, by the way and I think he really likes you."

"Hmm…. Well, I'm not sure that I like him," Anisha replied. "I couldn't say that I found him reliable – not after the way he disappeared without trace."

"Our instructions, I'm afraid. I hope he didn't break your heart?"

"Couldn't be further from it!" Anisha replied emphatically. "It just confirmed my impression of him all along: a cold fish, vain, too much money, power-hungry as well."

"Whoa! That's harsh! Alastair laughed at her response. "He's a good lad; eyes and heart in the right place. Maybe a bit hot-headed at times, but he will learn."

"Hmm; trouble is one doesn't know what is going on inside that head. Not that it matters as I'm not the least bit interested in him. What I am interested in, on the other hand…" she continued, but her stepfather had moved away and was signalling that the break was over.

The next presentation was what Alastair called the 'rocket to the moon and beyond bit'. Alastair introduced two of the FARIS team who, he told his audience, had come over especially from the base at Chong-Kara to explain just how far they had come and how far they had to go.

"Gentlemen and ladies," Alastair summed up. "It is thanks to the interest, collaboration and support of certain powers that so much progress has been made in so little time. It will, however, be another ten years before the mission can realistically begin. And in that time our focus must be relentless in all areas of our endeavour while at the same time maintaining that discretion and secrecy which has so far kept the project successfully out of the prying eyes of the media.

"The focus of our efforts over the coming two years will be on recruiting supporters to the mission. These, as you know, include financial backers, academics distinguished in many fields, not just scientific, with particular need for the young generation of future high-flyers in their fields, those who will be prepared to take the risks and endure the harsh conditions which setting up the first colony on an inhospitable planet will undoubtedly require."

Anisha listened from her seat in the audience with increasing disbelief; either she was taking part in an advanced piece of make-believe or else..... looking around her she found it equally difficult to believe that she was in the presence of a lunatic fringe; the people around gave no hint of derangement – on the contrary, they appeared to be thoroughly practical and down-to-earth, although down-to-earth was exactly what they were not discussing. Is this what insanity looks like in its early stages, she wondered, one man with an obsession and others who are willing to follow? But was Alastair, her step-father, that one man, or was he following someone higher up? She was not convinced that Alastair had the sort of charisma it took to lead a project like the one he was describing, even though he seemed to command complete attention from this audience.

Her attention wandered and she realised now that he was calling for questions. A man in his mid-twenties had got to his feet.

"Can you tell us about the base you mentioned: Chong Kara? Where and what is Chong Kara?"

"About eighty miles, or one hundred kilometres from here. Known also as Qalacha. It's another enclave. Very small. Uninhabited for years; that is until FARIS came along and requested to lease it from Uzbekistan. FARIS has the use of it – a ninety-nine year lease. As a base it is ideal: far from any significant population, clear skies not bothered by light pollution and freedom to set up whatever equipment and installations we choose. We have good communications and easy access to our neighbours, China to the north east, Russia to the North West. Both are happy with the concept of space-tourism, which is what we have leased this piece of land for. We keep a small number of staff at Chong Kara, and our best scientists and engineers rotate on tours of duty between there and this enclave of Shakhimardan, where we are today."

He stopped and looked around enquiringly for the next question. A woman got to her feet.

"I'd like to know more about FARIS's backers."

"Of course! I think everyone would. I cannot tell you a great deal."

"Does that mean you can't, or you won't?"

"Some of both but more of the second. I have a fund-raising role and that means I know many of our individual sponsors, but as they insist on anonymity I observe that confidentiality. I'm not alone in this work and there will be other supporters, financial supporters, who I don't know about."

"You mentioned the 'collaboration and support of certain powerful and well-placed entities'" another questioner began, checking against his notes. "Can we know who or what this refers to? And what kind of collaboration and support?"

"I certainly wouldn't have made mention of that if I had wanted to conceal the fact that there are power-bases that support the idea of FARIS. Their identity cannot be disclosed at this point – I'm sure that is understandable."

"Certainly!" the questioner responded. "But can we know the type of support they're prepared to give to the project? Even if not the identities of the entities – by which I assume we mean nations – are concerned?"

Alastair came back quickly in response.

"That's not to be assumed at all. The case is altogether more complex and delicate. All I can say is that there exist power groups within national administrations who see the world's future in terms similar to FARIS but possibly not in the same way as the governing consensus. In these cases, and where FARIS has contact and leverage, it uses them to the advantage of FARIS and the FARIS philosophy. Does that make sense?"

The questioner nodded and sat down, apparently satisfied. Anisha struggled to keep up. Finally, as the question and answer session was drawing to a close she got cautiously to her feet with her question.

"I'm sorry; this may be naïve, but I'm a newcomer here..."

Alastair smiled. "Anisha, of course! Let's have your question."

She told me later how nervous she felt but, not wanting to let it show, she took a deep breath and smiled confidently as she spoke.

"Just that you mentioned the 'philosophy of FARIS' and – as I have never exactly had it spelled out to me, having, as it were, picked it up along the way, could you give it to me in plain English?"

"Of course I can do that – or better still invite the team to do it for me. It's very straightforward."

He indicated two of the team with a smile.

"Andrea? And who else....? Mike, could you give Andrea a hand?"

Andrea – one of the team with her name badge on her shirt – got to her feet and Mike followed.

"The FARIS philosophy consists of three strands. Firstly, human civilisation as we know it is in danger."

She looked toward Mike who picked up the cue.

"Secondly, the planet where human civilisation was conceived, nurtured and bloomed will not continue to support it."

His gaze returned to Andrea who concluded:

"To survive, human civilisation must emigrate. Like the emigration to the New World, only in the 21st century we will leave behind a dying planet and carry our treasures to survive and flourish in a new environment –however inhospitable and daunting it may seem."

As Anisha took in these statements Alastair added a final comment.

"The project needs infinite resources. Since civilisation will survive here on earth for a limited time only – we are talking in terms of one or two centuries as opposed to a limitless future elsewhere – FARIS also opposes the wasteful use of resources in such fire-fighting manoeuvres as green environmentalism, combating climate change, fighting disease, poverty and corruption. They are measures which use up scarce funds and intellectual energy. That's why FARIS values the power-groups mentioned already who are ideally-placed to discourage the well-meaning but ultimately counter-productive initiatives of many national governments."

He concluded, looking around the room and resting his gaze finally on Anisha.

"I think we have answered your question, yes?"

Anisha shook herself.

"Yes, indeed. And thank you!"

Anisha knew she had to have a conversation with Grego. Much as she disliked the idea of a second encounter following that first bad-tempered exchange, she needed to know how far he had been involved in drawing here to this place and what his links with her stepfather were. The chance came after an evening meal when people had drifted into groups for coffee or had taken themselves off for a night's sleep before the next day's early start. She found Grego keeping an eye on her as she filled her coffee cup; he was definitely not avoiding her.

"So, do I have you to thank for finding myself here?" She began, with barely suppressed sarcasm.

"Possibly," he replied, with a smile, "A concatenation of circumstances might be more accurate though. Do you remember when we met?"

"Was it at that river party? Of Ben's?"

"Of course. You made a big impression on me, you know."

"If I remember rightly, you were trying to make a big impression yourself. And not just on me; you were showing off unashamedly."

Grego smiled, seemingly unaware of her sarcasm.

"It's good to know I succeeded," he replied with a smile.

Anisha chose to ignore the smile; if Grego was impervious to sarcasm it was time to exercise the kind of put-down which could hardly escape him.

"So you think I'm the kind of girl who is impressed by fast cars and polo ponies; time to think again Grego!"

But her comments failed to find their mark.

"Of course, working for FARIS, as I was, it soon came to their notice that I was going out with the step-daughter of a leading member."

"'Going out' would be putting it a bit strongly. We did have one or two dates and I can say that I found it hard to make up my mind about you."

"Ah, but not me! I didn't find it hard at all. Hopefully now you'll find it easier? I mean, now that you are involved with FARIS too, we'll be seeing each other a lot. And that's great!"

"Hang on a bit Grego; you're running ahead of me. I need to know a few things first."

"Of course you do. Fire away!"

"First, is it down to you that I'm here at all?"

"Well yes," Grego smiled modestly. "I think I can claim much of the credit for that."

"How, precisely?" Anisha demanded.

"Once the movement knew you were interested in me they simply trailed this 'extreme challenge' holiday in front of your nose. You fell for it!"

"I found the website myself with no trails being led, I think you'll find" she retorted indignantly. "And as for being 'interested in you', you really have an exaggerated idea of your own importance!"

"That's the way it looked – and that's the way FARIS works."

Anisha felt furious. The idea that she had been led by the nose made her seethe inwardly. But she kept her cool with Grego.

"So Piet and Helen are members too, is that right?"

"Yes indeed. The extreme challenge concept has a big part to play in identifying the sort of young people we are interested in attracting. We rely on them quite a lot. Anyway, I'm so glad you are here."

Grego attempted to take her arm and draw her away from the crowd but Anisha pulled back.

"I really need to know why you joined FARIS, Grego. I mean, I would like to understand what makes you tick, how your mind works."

"Of course! You'll get to know me better as we spend more time together."

"You can forget about that Grego. I'm not so easily won over. Just explain to me what the attraction of this organisation is."

Anisha was beginning now to see that what FARIS represented might be precisely the opposite of the things she herself believed in. But she still needed to get more from Grego. She certainly saw that she had been right not to let on where she stood as a member of the Green Team.

"So what is the big attraction of FARIS for you Grego?"

"Basically, for me it's the idea of a new beginning," Grego began. "The world is in a mess – from all perspectives, it's obvious. Patching up is not going to solve the problem. A new start is the only way – the obvious way. It's going to happen and we want to say we were part of it. And the sooner the better, which is why the FARIS agenda resists wasting time, money, energy or any other resources on propping up the old state of affairs."

"And do you really believe I can go along with it?" she asked him seriously.

Equally seriously Grego replied.

"I know it. I know you can – I've been observing you and I can see how determined you are. That's something I admire in you."

"Are you sure you've got me right? "

"Of course, that's not all I admire in you. You turn me on in every other way. Come with me now." His voice was urgent as he drew Anisha towards the door. She rounded on him.

"I really don't mean to be hurtful Grego but it's just not like that for me." She disentangled her arm from his and hugged her jacket protectively around her. She could sense how he recoiled, shocked.

"Grego, I mean it. I'm sorry if you misunderstood me; I mean if it's my fault that you misunderstood me."

He answered her stiffly.

"So there's someone else?'

"No! I mean, there isn't anyone; I'm independent, on my own and happy with it."

Grego's next comment made her pause before she replied.

"So you are in with FARIS absolutely independently and for yourself? Nothing to do with…. nothing to do with me?"

Her reply was cautious, careful still not to tell of her reservations about the whole project; best to leave everyone, Grego included, with the illusion that she believed in FARIS.

"I'm sorry but it has nothing to do with you at all that I am here, Grego. I just thought I was going on an adventure holiday. That, as you know, is what I like to do."

But Grego was not allowing himself to be wholly put off.

"We'll be seeing plenty of each other. I'm not letting go. Meanwhile we'll be working together, on and off, and in touch. "

161

"Don't get your hopes up Grego: it's better not to," Anisha told him – firmly, but less unkindly. "I have to go and get some sleep now"

And thus Anisha made her escape, thankfully and not a little disturbed by the force of the encounter coming, as it did, at the end of a very strange day.

Chapter 18

Anisha listened with increasing interest to the presentations
which took up the rest of their afternoon and evening there at
Shakhimardan Exploration. After hearing her step-father's
summing up of the FARIS philosophy she had begun to realise
that she was involved in a serious scientific movement which
appeared to have gathered significant support. It required a
considerable effort of the imagination to realise the serious aim
of the project was, indeed, to take the human race and its
civilisation – how this was to be defined and which components
included she had no means of knowing - and re-launch it
somewhere out in space. Was this possible? These people
obviously believed so and were committed whether or not they
would see the outcome in their own life times. That FARIS
could exist as a shadowy organisation but at the same time
attract so much support was surprising, to say the least. Anisha

163

reminded herself that power, money and intellect could combine behind closed doors, to be revealed only when they had gathered unstoppable momentum to create all kinds of havoc. If the aims of FARIS were as single-minded as their philosophy implied, then with money and influence they might go to all lengths.

"What happens to the rest of the people here – the billions who are left behind?" she asked Helen who sat beside her.

"Oh, rather like it happened to the Neanderthals, evolution will not be kind. They will die out eventually."

"Sad, don't you think?" Anisha commented.

"Yes, of course, but it won't happen overnight; it will be more a gradual decline, a winding down. Sad, but, given the numbers on the planet now, it's inevitable."

The base at Chong-Kara, although hidden from general public view, is not unknown to the small but growing number of wealthy adventurers who make up the clientele of space tourism, for it is a departure point for that most expensive of package holidays. The FARIS group arrived next morning, helicoptered in from Shakhimardan to learn just how much more there was to it.

The newcomers were taken to see the launch site and the capsules which would carry the first of the torch-bearers to their destination. Candidates for this assignment were already in training and Anisha spoke to one, a Chinese woman not many years older than herself, named Zhenzhen Sui.

"How do you contemplate the time it will take for the voyage, Sui?" Anisha asked

"We have practiced; we practice regularly," she smiled.

"Does that mean living in these pods for months on end?"

"Certainly. Three hundred days is the maximum I have experienced – that's the time it will take for us to reach first destination. I have good psychological ability for supporting this test. For me this is successful; but not everyone can succeed."

"And when do you expect to begin this mission?"

"When resources are sufficient then we need five years of more training and planning. After that we go."

Anisha shuddered as she viewed the cramped quarters of the capsules and wondered how Zhenzhen Sui or anyone else could contemplate almost a year in that environment. And that was only the outward trip, the one that would carry the first supplies of equipment for building an environment in which they could survive.

"How about the return journey; how long does that take?"

"No return journey," her informant replied, still smiling. "One-way trip – same as New World explorers. They also made one-way trip."

"Yes, but they knew they would find…" Anisha paused "…well, trees and grass and – and certainly air to breathe. And they could reasonably hope that there would be water to keep them alive!"

"Those travellers were very brave, courageous people. Maybe more than we are," Sui replied seriously. "They did not have the technology that we can use, no communication with home. We are so lucky! We can speak to our control right here; we can send emails to our friends and family; we can keep right in touch – even do Facebook and all – if we want!"

"Even so, I think that your future and even the possibilities of your survival, are much less than those of the Pilgrim Fathers."

Her companion smiled understandingly, apparently quite relaxed.

"I mean," Anisha went on, "They thought that God would protect them and that they were somehow doing what he wanted. Do you have anything like that to keep you…. To keep you in good spirits?"

Zhenzhen Sui considered Anisha's question seriously before replying thoughtfully.

"People like me…. I mean Chinese people, have very strong beliefs but not same as Pilgrim Fathers' beliefs. Our culture teaches us to be strong."

"How many of you are there?" Anisha asked,

"We are eight who are training and working together. We do not know if all of us will go when the time comes. We shall see."

Sui paused to attract the attention of another of the trainees who had been talking to the visitors.

"Sujit, come!"

A young man, probably in his late twenties or early thirties, strolled across and shook hands with Anisha. Sui told him:

"My guest has too many questions. Please help!"

"Sure, no problem – try me!" he smiled at Anisha.

"Well, first: why are you doing it? I mean, surely you must be leaving so much behind you. What's the payoff? …." She paused. "I mean….."

The response was an enquiring smile: "Go on…?"

"Well, even if things are not looking good here, it's not going to be all that bad, not during our lifetime, is it? And not if you are educated, intelligent and capable of earning a good living. Why abandon all that?"

She could see he was taking her seriously.

"It's a good question," he paused. "I'm sorry, I didn't get your name….?"

"Anisha. I'm called Anisha."

"An Indian name. Are you….?"

"My father was Indian."

"Ah, that explains!"

"Maybe is Indian; I never knew him."

"And your mother is…?"

"She's English. And Alastair, Alastair Singleton is my step-father. I rather think that is why I'm here."

He looked at her with considerable curiosity until Anisha reminded him.

"You haven't even started to answer my question: 'Why are you doing it?' why are you part of the FARIS team?"

"How much do you know of Indian culture?"

"Not very much. I've never been there."

"In my culture, my religion, each one must follow his *dharma*. That is why I am part of FARIS. This is my duty, my role, what I have to do."

"I've heard of dharma, but could not say what it is all about. Some kind of fate?"

"Not really - no, I would not say so. It's more complicated than that. Perhaps you will let me tell you about it some time?"

"I'd like that! But I don't think we're staying around here for very long. As far As I know we're being taken back to FARIS HQ, Shakhimardan, tonight."

"I'll see if I can get back there before you leave."

He moved away and Anisha turned to join Helen and the group. When she looked back she glimpsed Sujit in conversation with Alastair, who looked over his shoulder to where Anisha was standing. He nodded briefly in apparent agreement to the younger man. Anisha could tell that she had a date lined up and that she was looking forward to it. The rest of the afternoon was spent visiting the workshops and control rooms deep underground and listening to explanations of the different phases of the project over the next ten years. Anisha's head was spinning and she was longing for some time on her own when she might begin to process some of what she had experienced, seen and heard over the last forty-eight hours. There was no time for that however as there were underground levels to be visited. They were split into small groups and Anisha lost count of how many levels they visited as one technical presentation followed upon another. Eventually they were brought to the surface to regroup in the staff's canteen. Here they were offered refreshment before the flight back to Shakhimardan and FARIS HQ.

As the helicopter rose into the air the outline of the base on the little enclave of Chong Kara was sharply defined in the gathering darkness. Lights around the perimeter fence showed just what a small area of land the base occupied. That small area was more than doubled, Anisha reflected, by the extensive underground spaces. They must have taken a considerable time to excavate and construct and she began to wonder just how many years FARIS had been in existence as a project. Judging from the equipment she had seen, both above and below ground, which was ample evidence of the financial resources at its command, its membership must have been growing steadily since the beginning of the century at least.

She was grateful that the flight back to Shakhimardan would give her the space of an hour to put some order into her thoughts for the noise from the rotor blades and the engine made conversation impossible and her companions mostly seemed to be settling down to catch some sleep. At last she could give some thought to the question: what had she got involved in and how had she got herself involved? Was it something she had done or had others been manipulating her, pulling the strings and steering her in the direction they wanted? And what part, if any, did Jessica, her mother play in this? After all, without her involvement Anisha would not have stumbled upon Alastair – and he appeared to be placed right at the heart of all this.

And perhaps most crucially, what more did she know now about FARIS, the organisation, project, the plan?

She asked herself where and when she had first seen that beguiling small symbol. It was hard to remember now because, once stumbled across it seemed to crop up everywhere. Had it really been an accident that she had turned it up on the internet when looking for something entirely different? It wasn't FARIS, was it? that had led her to that oasis village in the Gulf? Where she had so nearly come to a sticky end? And encountered it again, first in a university setting and then in the polo pavilions among the fashionable crowd who were on such good terms with her step father and her mother. Anisha's head ached with so many questions until she drooped as the drone of the engine lulled her, like her companions, into sleep.

She woke again with a start. A fellow-passenger was clambering across her and almost fell into her lap as their aircraft lurched in a patch of turbulence. Anisha struggled to regain consciousness, unable for the moment to grasp where she was or who she was with. As she came to her senses and recollected the images of the day just past, she tried to imagine herself in one of those capsules, cramped together with the same people, not just for the space of an hour but for some three hundred days. And no return journey! Never to feel the sun or the wind on your face or hear the running of a fast river like she had experienced in recent days, feel the strong muscular effort of the pony that was taking her up the mountainside or exchange greetings with the people who lived in the villages that they passed through. All these were the sights and sounds that she had experienced in the challenge trip of the past week; how could anyone imagine spending the rest of life in a pod or breathing with a tube from a tank of oxygen – or whatever the arrangement was going to be? And it was not just the open spaces, the mountains and the countryside she would miss; imagine never again waking in the morning in her London flat, dressing for the day – choice of gear dependant on who she might meet – getting on her bike, dodging the traffic, the blare of car horns, the traffic fumes, the narrow city streets, the tall glass towering buildings.

The helicopter was descending, the sound of the blades growing louder is it approached the ground and with a small bump they were down, clambering out and heading towards the brightly lit building of Shakhimardan Exploration or, as Anisha was now beginning to think of it, FARIS HQ.

Chapter 19

Dharma
Dharma listen (help•info) (Sanskrit: dhárma, Pali: dhamma; lit. that which upholds, supports or maintains the regulatory order of the universe) means Law or Natural Law and is a concept of central importance in Indian philosophy and religion. As well as referring to Law in the universal or abstract sense dharma designates those behaviours considered necessary for the maintenance of the natural order of things. Therefore dharma may encompass ideas such as duty, vocation, religion and everything that is considered correct, proper or decent behaviour.
From Wikipedia, the free encyclopedia

Anisha found the short nap on the journey home had done wonders and after a shower and a meal she was wide awake. A second helicopter had landed and the occupants made their way also to the canteen to eat. As she chose a window seat for a quiet moment before bed Sujit, the Indian boy she had met in Chong Kara, who had arrived with the second group, joined her.

"I managed to get away! Are you ready for a seminar on 'dharma'" he asked, smiling.

"Of course – why not? I think it's time I started to learn about my Indian heritage." she replied. Together they occupied the window seat and for the next half hour he held forth.

Anisha found herself enthralled, not just by the subject of dharma but, as she admitted afterwards, by the dark eyes, earnest brow and that far-off expression of somehow seeing into the future that Sujit transmitted. She sensed something extra special about him, vibrations that resonated with her in ways which she had not known were possible. I think it was at this stage that Anisha was emotionally hooked and that Grego, had he known it, could there and then have thrown in the towel and avoided any further heartbreak from Anisha's direction.

After thirty minutes of listening to Sujit, and adjusting to the wavelengths she sensed from him, Anisha asked for a pause.

"I don't think I have taken in half of what you've been talking about but at least I know that I need to start reading up.
"

"A good start!" Sujit smiled.

"But, even if 'Dharma' means duty, I don't see why it has to be your duty to put yourself into a pod and…. Well, never be seen again – isn't that what it amounts to? I find that….sad…." she looked thoughtful and added, "considering that we have only just met."   There was a question mark in the way that she said it, which Sujit was quick to respond to.

"Yes, Dharma is duty, but if you like you can call it my vocation. It's not quite the same, but you can call it that if you like, or if it helps." He paused, but getting no response continued. "Anyway, let me tell you about myself."

"Yes, please do!"

Sujit had stood up and Anisha could see him assembling his thoughts as he paced deliberately to and fro. Although by no means a light-weight in his physique, for he was well-built and a good eight inches taller than Anisha, there was something about the elegance of his movements that appealed to her. The figure of a panther occurred to her before she quickly chided herself for such a flight of fancy. All the same…. She settled herself more comfortably and prepared to listen as Sujit launched into his story.

"My family are well-off, privileged and Hindu." Sujit began. "That brings obligations with it, in life choices and also at every turn of life. My education was the finest that India and then the USA could offer. I studied physics and worked hard – that was my duty, what I had to do. My parents taught me that

172

and my father had good reason to do so, since he felt that, along the way, one mistake, one departure from the right path of duty, leads only to havoc and unhappiness. So I studied hard, but played hard as well. Please don't imagine I was only ever a swot!"

"No, you don't give that impression." She told him, smiling. "And was it physics that brought you to FARIS?"

"FARIS was looking for sharp minds and the field of quantum physics attracts some of the sharpest scientific minds today. There are many of us Indians working in the field, in the USA and elsewhere as well as in India. And the fit between that discipline and Hindu philosophy is a perfect one."

"And your parents – today – do they know what you are involved in? Do you ever see them?"

"Of course! Not frequently and they have not followed my intellectual development. They just know that, in my own estimation, I am doing what I'm cut out for. I'm well-paid and I send much of what I earn to benefit the people and my family back home. So in that way a duty is also being fulfilled. I think my parents are proud of me."

Anisha nodded slowly feeling somewhat bemused by this high-minded, self-denying, sacrificial approach.

"I'd like to know more about you Anisha. Why did you decide to join FARIS?"

Now Anisha hesitated. How far should she go in talking frankly to this man? She felt, instinctively, that she could trust him but was not sure why. What reason might there be for feeling there could be some underlying bond with someone she had known for the space of just a day? Because he was Indian he had made her aware of how superficial she had been in enquiring after her own origins and she realised this must seem very strange to him. Perhaps the fact that he seemed to be taking such a genuine interest inclined her to be open in her reply – and those deep brown eyes which looked at hers so seriously were having an effect which, whilst she was acutely aware of the process did not render her immune. Maybe that was what made her reply cautiously, but nonetheless with a degree of openness which she hoped she would not regret.

"That's just it," Anisha continued. "I haven't joined FARIS! I kept stumbling across it and its funny little insignia in all sorts of different places. But until I came here I had no idea what it was all about. I think my stepfather wants me to be part of it though; I suppose that's why I am here. As far as I can see it is not just by accident."

Sujit nodded confirmation.

"Of course he does!"

"Why of course?" Anisha was surprised.

"He has told us all about you. How you work for a City of London firm of investors and how smart you are."

'He's got the wrong end of the stick!' Anisha felt like saying; instead she turned the conversation back to Sujit.

"Do you really believe in the project? Believe that everything here is a lost cause?"

He sighed. "Not exactly in those words but on the whole I do think, yes, that we have to be prepared to move on and it's no good waiting until the last minute."

"So you can confirm that it is no accident that I am here. Does that mean that Helen and Piet who organise the Challenge trips are part of FARIS?"

"Yes, again, of course! Their work is crucial to the network."

"I don't follow you; how can a holiday tour company be so important to FARIS?"

"My dear girl – think only of what those letters stand for – it's obvious!"

Anisha's hackles rose.

"I'd rather you didn't 'dear girl' me; that's patronising and unnecessary."

He looked contrite.

"You're right and I apologise. It's easy to forget when you're living the organisation, that to outsiders things are not at all clear."

"Alright," Anisha replied, "I'll let it pass this time. But go on....You were saying...."

Sujit started again.

"It's like this: the organisation needs its backers, financially; it needs the academics and not just scientists but literary men and women, philosophers, men and women of vision who can articulate that vision. It also needs young people who are bright and energetic: fit, active, resolute and intelligent, remember that? Young people with an eye to survival, not just for the human race in the long-term but who will train themselves to survive in all sorts of situations and conditions. Isn't that what your Challenge Trip proposed?"

Yes," she replied thoughtfully "It's certainly what they were advertising."

"Well, there you are"

"What do you mean 'there you are,'? Such challenge trips are quite popular with a lot of people. 'Extreme Survival' they're known as. You can join one back in UK for just a day; lots of people my age do it. The twenty- to thirty-somethings. If you're stuck in an office job, however well-paid, it's a chance to prove to yourself and your friends that you are still hard. Or you can go off and do it in some far-flung location and have a great holiday experience. Which is what I thought I was doing. And in any case I did not go for the toughest option, the Extreme Survival. And there was certainly nothing – how shall I say? - nothing remotely ideological in my mind when I signed up!"

"I believe you there. But don't you see? It's an idea which lends itself to our purposes just perfectly. Helen runs a smart adventure travel company very successfully, but she has also been signed up to FARIS and its aims for several years. Through her we identify potential supporters and if they seem

175

the right type we introduce them to the organisation. Just like has happened with you. And don't tell me you aren't impressed!"

Anisha could only nod silently, lost for words. Was this how she had come to be here? Thinking back, yes, perhaps it was Grego who had told her about Extreme Challenge Trips and certainly it was Helen who had skilfully guided her choice so that she ended up on this particular trek. Did they all believe that she would be in sympathy with the FARIS aims? How had they got that impression? And now that she had learnt what FARIS was all about, did she begin to feel that there might be something in it? Anisha had a sickening moment of vertigo when she felt that perhaps that was the way she was heading. Without brushing the thought aside she breathed deeply and let the moment pass. Perhaps they would convince her; perhaps Sujit, who she admitted she found both persuasive and attractive, would succeed in bringing her on board where both Grego and her step-father would undoubtedly fail. Perhaps, as she learnt more, he might persuade her that its aims were worthy and benign. In any case, she was due to return to London – and she could not risk not turning up for work on the appointed day - she would keep her counsel and see what transpired.

"I'm due back at work on Monday. I hope Helen has got that in mind. I hope that I haven't been hi-jacked!"

"I'm sure you haven't been hi-jacked. In fact Alastair will be as keen to get you back to your desk on time as you are." He smiled reassuringly. "Now, tell me more about yourself."

Well, Anisha was hooked. She couldn't resist the invitation and told him about her life in England, her friends and her mother. She described her mother as "slightly scatty, but I'm really fond of her!"

"As soon as I was big enough she got herself this job with the golf club and that's what she's been doing ever since. That is until about a year ago when she married Alastair and went off to live in a gilded cage in the Persian Gulf."

"Do you know how they met?" Sujit asked.

"No, but I imagine it would have been at the Golf Club. It's a smart place and Surrey is near enough to London. I imagine Alastair used to go down there for a round of golf with his contacts from time to time. I do ask myself what the attraction was though. I mean…. Money isn't everything, although he obviously has pots of it."

"Don't you think that she was just lonely?"

"Maybe…."

"And if she had loved travelling when she was younger, perhaps she liked the idea of more of that. After all, if she had seen you through university and established in a regular job, there was nothing to prevent her from indulging herself for once." Sujit commented adding, "I know we have only just met but, if you don't mind me saying, don't be too hard on her!"

"I'm not being hard on her!" Anisha exclaimed. "Of course she has a right to her own life…."

"But….? You're still not reconciled to the idea, are you? Don't you think that she has been carrying a burden of guilt for rather a long time?"

"How do you mean?"

"Bringing a fatherless child into the world. Do you think it was just a fling, or did she take it really hard when this guy left her. Left her to find her own way back to England and to find out that she was pregnant as well. In my view that was a completely shit thing to do. Perhaps, after the burden of carrying that hurt all through your childhood and growing years, she was finally able to let it go when she saw you so capable and launched on your career."

"Mmm, maybe. But I find it hard to think in those terms. I don't know who my father was – other that he was from India and his family lived in Delhi, from what I understand. For my own self-respect and pride it is hard for me to think of him as 'a shit'. That's not something that I can own up to. So that's why I have always made excuses for him, perhaps romanticised him a bit. Perhaps you can help me sort out his image."

"That's a challenge. I'll give it some thought. Will I see you in London?"

"Will you be going to London?"

"Who knows?"

She gave Sujit her email and cell-phone number.

Anisha attended the final briefing at FARIS HQ before leaving the compound in the company of Helen and Piet in the 4-wheel drive.. They departed the way they had arrived, which seemed so much more than two days ago. The farewell briefing turned out to be more of a pep talk from Alastair. He reminded the assembled group of the core beliefs of the FARIS movement: that the future of humankind lay beyond its present confines and that they were the vanguard, leading the move out into the cosmos. He exhorted those about to depart to keep in touch, keep tuned in and keep faith with the ideals of the organisation. Each one had his or her role to play and theirs was, in particular, to focus on the recruitment of people who would be invaluable to the organisation. After his speech he took each one aside to speak individually. When it came to Anisha he was warm and affectionate.

"Anisha, it's great to know we have you on board and I know your mother will be as pleased as I am."

"I've been wanting to ask you about that; is Mum with you on the FARIS idea?"

"Of course!" Alastair replied reassuringly. "And I am so very grateful for her support."

"And does she know what it's all about?"

Alastair hesitated.

"Your Mum is not one for a great deal of detail, but, yes, she's with me here. And I'm very happy and grateful for that."

Anisha may have wondered to herself about the extent of her mother's commitment and indeed her awareness and understanding of the FARIS project, but she kept those reservations to herself.

"Mum was always one for a big idea; at least when she was younger. It's her old character coming through again I think," Anisha responded.

"And she's pleased to know you'll be with us."

Anisha nodded thoughtfully.

"So there are things you want me to do?"

"There certainly are!" Alastair assured her emphatically. "You have an excellent vantage point inside Focus Asset Management and what you can do is spot those companies and those investors who might be potential FARIS supporters."

Anisha must have looked anxious because he hastened to reassure her.

"Don't worry, I'm not asking you to make any kind of approach, only to pass the details on. You can send them straight to me, seeing as we have direct contact, and I shall pass them on, if they seem alright, to the guys that deal with financial backers. How does that seem? Nothing too complicated? You will simply be a link – a very vital link – in a growing chain of supporters from around the world. Does that seem do-able?"

Anisha kept her thoughts to herself and nodded in a relaxed way.

"That doesn't sound too complicated. How do you want me to send these details?"

"Not from your office pc, that's for sure. But let's keep it as simple as possible. Use your web-based email address and send it to me at this address." He handed her a card. "I'm assuming no-one shares that email with you; is that correct?"

Anisha assured him that it was.

"Good luck then! And we'll see you again on the Palm Island, yes? Any time you need a break in the sun!"

"Lovely. Thanks."

The farewell to Grego was a prickly affair. They said goodbye stiffly, Grego aware, not only that he had blown it completely with Anisha but that she had never really been interested in him, for himself, in the first place. Now, seeing her so close with Sujit, gave an extra sting to the wounds."

"I hope it goes well for you here, Grego," she told him. "And I hope you know where you are going."

He looked at her and replied in an expressionless way.

"Yes, I'm sure of that."

Anisha could not resist a slight tease:

"Next stop the stars?"

Grego remained serious.

"It won't happen as quickly as that. But it will happen."

And soon after this conversation the three of them, Piet, Helen and Anisha, were rattling across the bridge, through the now darkened town, pausing briefly for formalities at the check-point before leaving the enclave of Shakhimardan behind them.

On the plane from Ankara to London Anisha was able to marshal her thoughts and impressions. It was clear that her stepfather, Alastair, saw her as a hard-edged city girl working in the investment sector and someone who would be well-placed to attract capital for the FARIS venture. And he was unaware that her interests lay in the opposite direction, that her commitment was to the green movement and to working, in however small a way, towards goals of sustainable development. How or why her mother could have failed to put him in the picture regarding her views remained a mystery, but

180

one she was prepared to overlook. She felt pleased with herself that she had resisted revealing her true colours in that seminar when the aims and objectives of the FARIS project were outlined to her and the other participants. The most startling part of the last two days for her had been the revelation of the measures the organisation was prepared to adopt to hasten the realisation of the project. If, as seemed likely, FARIS had penetrated to the heart of those international institutions which held the levers of change and improvement to the lives of many and if they were prepared to use their influence to impede all kinds of works which would make a difference, then they were a sinister force.

But why should they see it necessary to engage in that way? Her mind flipped back to the chilling presentation: the speaker had told them with conviction that to try to improve the present situation was simply throwing good money after bad when all their efforts should be directed towards the new era which would begin when FARIS took to the skies.

Anisha had kept quiet and even when Alastair outlined the role he expected her to play, she had kept silent and appeared to acquiesce. Now she must face the question of how to proceed when she got back to work. She doubted that Rob Underwood would take her seriously – not even for a moment!

Chapter 20

Russian cosmism was a philosophical and cultural movement that emerged in Russia in the early 20th century. It entailed a broad theory of natural philosophy combining elements of religion and ethics with a history and philosophy of the origin, evolution and future existence of the cosmos and humankind. It combined elements from both Eastern and Western philosophic traditions as well as from the Russian Orthodox Church.
From Wikipedia, the free encyclopedia

Back at her desk on Monday morning Anisha responded to the usual enquiries about her holiday with enthusiasm.

"I had a great time! It was a real challenge! Tough going!"

Rob, her manager had news for her.

"There's been a new sidelight on the water company that you were researching. Somebody has been circulating images on YouTube. I've sent you the latest."

Anisha powered up her pc and took a look straight away. It was a shot, or rather several successive shots of a ship, the size, as far as she could tell, of a tug-boat, towing what looked like a small mountain of glass. It was clearly being used as a publicity stunt for the Akwa logo was painted large on the side of the ship and on a banner which flew proudly from the peak of the mountain of glass – if that was what it was. More startlingly for Anisha, however was the appearance alongside the Akwa logo of the instantly recognisable FARIS sign and symbol.

FARIS, it seemed to her, was everywhere. Anisha had not yet made up her mind whether or how to bring the subject to the attention of her boss fearing that he would dismiss what she had to tell as beyond ludicrous. As she studied the U-Tube images she realised that there was a subtle difference between them. It was not just in the background in which the seas which started off in the first shot as grey and tempestuous became successively bluer and calmer. The shots must have been taken over the course of a voyage, from high latitudes to somewhere sunnier and warmer. But in addition the size of the glass mountain changed and became progressively smaller. This was not a glass mountain but a very real iceberg which was being towed from the ice fields which had shed it to somewhere warm and sunny. She remembered reading about the possibility of towing broken bits of icebergs as a way of transporting water supplies to arid lands. It had seemed an absurd and unworkable idea. This, on the other hand, seemed to be pure publicity; Akwa had taken their trade-mark sign and captured it in solid, if melting, form and FARIS was in there too.

Anisha spent some time staring at the images and trying to work out the meaning. The only obvious answer was that Akwa were collaborators in the FARIS project.

"You had better go back to Akwa and check out what they are doing here." Rob told her. "This publicity stunt is sending out very ambiguous messages on the environmental front. I don't think our investors will approve of the melting ice-cap being used as a advertising material."

"I'll get on to them and perhaps go down to Swindon again."

"The sooner the better. Now, do you recognise this other logo?" He indicated the fountain symbol."

"I've seen it before." Anisha responded with caution. "In fact I've seen it repeatedly over several weeks. It could be a worry and I'd like a chance to tell you about it."

"Fine, but not right now. I'm supposed to be elsewhere," he looked at his watch, "In fact ten minutes ago. It will have to wait until tomorrow. Ten-thirty tomorrow; and you can tell me all about it then."

Anisha was relieved that at last she was going to be able to share her thoughts with someone she trusted.

183

The following morning as she cycled to work Anisha thought through again what she was going to say to Rob and how much of her story to tell. She had puzzled far into the night over the question, fearing that Rob would find what she wanted to say too far-fetched to believe.

She spent the first two hours that morning working on a set of notes; putting some order into what she knew about FARIS and setting out in sequence her encounters with it from the beginning under the heading 'Notes on FARIS'

1. Found FARIS by mistake on the internet when looking for Arif (Gulf water systems)

2. Noticed it next at Westminster reception where I met up with Grego. First sight of the fountain logo

3. Same sign found when staying with Mum and her new husband, Alastair; viz Mum's brooch and the badges worn by some members at the polo club.

4. Adventure trek holiday: same badge seen worn by one member of university water resources team.

5. I was subsequently 'warned off' sticking my nose into it. Frightening episode in the irrigation tunnel: was it an accident??

6. Polo match with Grego; FARIS symbol in evidence there.

7. After Grego disappeared from London no further sightings until the 'Extreme Challenge' holiday. I am taken on a side trip and find myself in FARIS HQ. located in an enclave in Kyrghizstan. There, along with some other visitors, I learn about FARIS and I am invited to 'come on board' by my step-father.

Anisha drew a line and started a new section to her notes: 'WHAT IS FARIS?'

'Fit, Active, Resourceful, Intelligent Survivors'.

184

1. Apparently distantly related to an early 20th century movement called Cosmism, which advocated space travel and the colonising of other planets as the next step in the history of the human race. This 21st century version involves actively planning for such a venture and is preparing to make it a reality in the next 20 years. Selected personnel have volunteered to go as the first pioneers and are being trained.

2. FARIS itself is a movement with a network of recruiters and supporters. Target recruits are either wealthy, influential, or leaders in a number of academic fields.

3. FARIS is a secretive movement. The reason why it likes to keep a low profile is ideological. Its philosophy is that life on this planet as it is currently heading contains the seeds of its own demise. To hasten the forward thrust of the movement, and to strike out into space, it considers that resources have to be concentrated in that direction and that resources poured into 'patching up' the current situation on our planet, e.g. fighting poverty and sickness, are wasted.

Anisha paused at this point. Had she included enough detail? Or too much? It would have to do. Would she have to explain to Rob – always assuming that he hadn't dismissed the whole affair as beyond ludicrous - her own situation at the present moment? That would involve telling him so much about her personal life that she felt pale at the thought of it. Perhaps she could duck that part? And did Sujit have to be mentioned? She thought she could leave Sujit out completely.

A little before 10.30 Anisha tidied up the final bullet point in her notes and decided they would have to do. She hardly had time to worry any more about what Rob's reaction would be. It was time to engage personally with her boss – and with her own convictions.

Rob took it all quietly. Simply asking her:
"Is that all?"

Anisha had run out of steam and could only respond, "I'm afraid so. What do you think?"

He sat beside her, drumming his fingers on the desktop.

"It's hard to say. On the one hand, I could say that groups like these spring up, here and there and from time to time. Then they become part of history. Like the Cosmists that you mention. They did not succeed in changing the world. The difference is that, now, such ideas seem to have a very distinct possibility of becoming reality."

"That was the frightening thing about my visit – especially seeing the base in Chong Kala with all the technology they have there."

"And you kept quiet throughout, is that right?"

"I did. What else was I to do? If I had protested, or told them my views, they would have steam-rollered all over me. And it was scary to think what they might do to shut me up, to stop me from telling the world. But isn't that rather ridiculous? I mean, if they have gone so far down their road, how come they haven't come up against people with views like mine before?"

"It's the obvious question, I agree." Rob replied.

Anisha was immensely relieved to find that her boss was taking her seriously and not dismissing what she had to say as some kind of illusion. But she needed to be sure.

"So you do believe me, do you?" she asked anxiously. "Sometimes I think that I must have dreamed the whole thing. Except that I do have a few mementos, to prove my point."

She felt in her handbag and produced a selection of items with the FARIS logo: a ball-point pen, a paper napkin, a notepad."

"Hmm…. Nothing very conclusive or incriminating there. It's probably enough to convince me, simply because I know you and have confidence in you, and also – and this may surprise you – I have indeed heard rumours of some such grouping and this is not the total surprise you may have anticipated."

Anisha was so relieved to know she was believed that she was lost for further words.

"The problem is knowing what to do about these people – if indeed anything needs to be done."

"Do you think they can just be left alone? That they will come to nothing?" Anisha asked anxiously.

"That is certainly what happens to many of these slightly loopy groupings," Rob replied. "On the other hand, there are groups which have a pernicious effect. I could quote PNAC, that so-called 'Project for the New American Century' which was hugely influential in bringing the US and UK into conflict with Iraq after the attack on New York. Some people see the Opus Dei as another shadowy organisation. And the Freemasons were seen in the past, as the hidden hand behind some unexplained political events."

"So, do you believe me? And do you see this FARIS organisation as significant?" Anisha hardly dared ask him.

"Significant? In what way is this going to be significant – in your view?" Rob appeared to Anisha to be genuinely asking for her opinion.

So she gave it.

"In my view, these people, this organisation, FARIS, as they call themselves, have as their aim, their goal, to emigrate a very small proportion of the earth's population to the nearest and most accessible planet. Their idea is to restart civilisation there and to leave behind the one which is worn out and moribund."

There was a pause and Anisha waited.

"To start anew on another planet is not such a bad ambition, is it?" Rob asked her? "After all, isn't that what the Pilgrim Fathers did?"

Anisha thought her reply through carefully.

"The Pilgrim Fathers set out to start anew but in no way did they deliberately junk, undermine or sabotage what they had left behind."

"Do you believe this is what FARIS is doing?" Rob asked.

"I am sure of it," Anisha replied without hesitation. "It's clear from their presentations, their online material, their targeting, and their networking with the rich and powerful. Everything they do and say is aimed at attracting funds which might otherwise have gone to climate change, poverty alleviation, healthcare causes like AIDS, malaria and TB. All of these, in the mind of FARIS are not just a waste of time but a waste of resources as well: resources which should be funnelled into the FARIS project."

"Hmmm," Rob was thoughtful. "It seems far-fetched. And even if it were remotely true, to expose it – if that is what you are suggesting – would perhaps do them more good than harm. You must realise that there are more than a few people who support just such an idea".

Anisha shook her head doubtfully.

"For heaven's sake, Anisha! Your own mother has been convinced by the plan! Who else might not be tempted? The idea has the pioneering spirit! And it also deals with the dire problems which we, so-called enlightened ones, wrestle with daily: how to alleviate the unsolvable ills of this world? How could people not be won over?"

Anisha's shock was profound.

"You're saying they have a point?"

"Of course they have a point!"

Anisha felt faint.

"And what's more, they have money. Once they go public, people will be bound to listen to them."

At this point Anisha was genuinely at a loss. She had not known what reaction to expect from her boss, but that he might find in favour of the FARIS project had not crossed her mind.

"I thought you might not believe me but I never thought that you might find them credible and take their side. How can you say that? You're my boss, my line manager – fund manager of the ethical investment fund. What you're saying goes against everything that it stands for!"

Rob smiled and sighed.

"Anisha, that's not what I'm saying. Hey, calm down! What I'm saying is that this is an idea that could really catch the attention of some sections of the public. Not to mention the backing of some sections of the press – at least in this country."

Anisha breathed again.

"I'm sorry. Perhaps I misunderstood."

"Well, listen carefully now. To expose this movement to the public gaze could easily backfire seriously. On the one hand it could drive the movement underground and on the other hand it could work in FARIS' favour and draw sections of the public to them and attract more wealthy and influential backers."

"Of course, I can see that. So you think that nothing should be done? What about me? What am I supposed to do?" Anisha paused, to make her point. "Alastair has actually asked me to recommend new backers. I remember his words clearly: 'You have an excellent vantage point inside Focus Asset Management; you can spot companies and investors who might be potential FARIS supporters."

"Is that what he asked you to do?" Rob was concerned.

"Oh, he didn't ask me to approach anyone directly: 'Just pass the details on. Send them straight to me,' he said. He said I would simply be the link – 'a very vital link in a growing chain of supporters from around then world'. Of course he doesn't know I work in the Green Team – I told you that before!"

"Hmm…" Rob thought for a moment. "That puts you in a corner, doesn't it? We can't have you recommending investors; and in any case I don't see how you could realistically do so. Not from your current position."

"Thank goodness…" Anisha agreed. "But if I do nothing he's going to have a go at me. I don't see how I can respond."

"I need to give this some thought Anisha. We'll talk about it again in a couple of days" He put an arm on her shoulder reassuringly. "Thank you for telling me the whole story – fantastic though it seems. Meanwhile it would be best not to discuss it with anyone. Especially not your Mum."

"Don't worry; I'm being very careful of what I discuss with her."

Anisha spent the rest of the day trying to focus on the work on her desk. By five o'clock she was ready to leave. She retrieved her bike from the caretaker's lobby, bid him a reasonably cheerful goodbye and cycled off into the evening traffic.

Chapter 21

What is Culture?

Culture is a powerful human tool for survival, but it is a fragile phenomenon. It is constantly changing and easily lost because it exists only in our minds. Our written languages, governments, buildings, and other man-made things are merely the products of culture. They are not culture in themselves. For this reason, <u>archaeologists</u> can not dig up culture directly in their excavations. The broken pots and other artifacts of ancient people that they uncover are only material remains that reflect cultural patterns--they are things that were made and used through cultural knowledge and skills. http://anthro.palomar.edu/culture/culture_1.htm

Friday evening, the end of the week and returning home by her usual cycle route and wondering what the weekend held, Anisha took a call on her cell-phone. Sujit was in London! That solved the problem of what to do at the weekend.

It was with some trepidation that Anisha looked forward to meeting him. She knew that he had visited London before so he would not need to do the usual sights. They arranged to meet at the British Museum.

"There's an exhibition of Indian art on; would you like to see it and tell me more about my cultural heritage?"

Sujit agreed readily.

He was an interesting and informative guide and took great delight in explaining to Anisha the periods of art which were on display.

"How much of this would you take with you when you go on the great migration?" she asked.

He shrugged "How much would be possible? But in digitised form – then the possibilities are limitless! Did you know that the whole of Shakespeare's works has been stored in a minute sample of DNA?"

Now Anisha looked more doubtful than ever but Sujit was determined to convince her.

"DNA storage has hardly begun and its significance certainly not appreciated: the possibility of all the art and culture of the world being stored and taken wherever in the universe you want!"

"That is quite beyond me," Anisha replied slowly. "But, just supposing it happened – this dream of yours...."

"It will!" Sujit assured her smiling.

"Just supposing it happens then, what kind of experience would it be, looking at art on a small screen as opposed to walking around...." she gestured at the expanse of the domed building, which at that time of day was abuzz with crowds of visitors of all ages and nationalities , "...walking around this amazing space with all these people with their different outlooks and interests?"

"Yes, it would be different."

"And if this is living art, where would it go from here? Can you see a future for art out there on your new planet?"

Sujit was silent, thoughtful.

"Will there be artists? What will they do, who will they do it for?"

"Fascinating questions. We can only speculate."

"And languages? Which language will be used?"

"Oh, it will have to be English – don't you think?"

"Unless Chinese has overtaken English by that time!" Anisha suggested. "And what will happen to the others that are left behind?"

From the British Museum they headed for the park and somewhere to eat. Regents Park was in high summer splendour, rich borders of colour in the flower beds, office workers taking the sun, visitors trooping towards the open air theatre where a performance of Romeo and Juliet was pulling in school parties, in high spirits for a day out.

"I'd find it hard, leaving all this sort of thing behind," reflected Anisha. "Life in a biosphere would be dull, to say the least of it."

"What you're doing, Anisha, is trying to wind me up. No, I can tell," he insisted as Anisha protested. "It's simply a question of the pioneering spirit versus the stay-at-home. Of course there'll be sacrifices. Wasn't that what the Pilgrim Fathers recognised? But when it's a question of taking the human race to a new level or settling for slow extinction, for me the choice is obvious!"

They walked on, hand in hand and Anisha realised how comfortable and at ease she felt with this relative stranger. Something to do, perhaps, with a common heritage, one she had never known or investigated on anything but a superficial level. With Sujit there was a comfortable feeling of not having to explain herself, of coming back home, they were at ease together. Except, of course, for the very small matter of the FARIS project. That Sujit could seriously be planning to take part, if chosen, in an emigration to another planet was not something that she could get her head around. Not just a voyage of discovery but a voyage of no return – ever.

"Would you really leave all this behind?" she gestured around them.

"I agree it would be a wrench, but to be out there at the front of that venture: well, what a privilege! Can you see that?"

"No, frankly I can't." Anisha replied emphatically. "You would be leaving your family behind you; how can you contemplate that? How would they take it?"

Sujit looked serious.

"You asked about my family and my culture and I told you about our philosophy, of dharma. Dharma is our role in life and if this is my dharma, my family accept it joyfully and with pride."

"And your friends and your home? You might never see them again."

"Not 'might';" Sujit corrected her. "Never is unqualified. I would never see them again."

"Is there anyone else?" Anisha asked seriously. "Someone you would take with you? I mean, one imagines if you are going to start a colony that you will have to – well, 'be fruitful and multiply' to borrow a phrase."

Sujit smiled.

"At the beginning there would be very few of us. Later I feel sure that more would follow. Who knows, perhaps you might be tempted?"

It was Anisha's turn to smile.

"You must be joking!"

"No, in fact I'm not. I should like it if you were with me."

They walked on hand in hand and Anisha reflected sadly that she did, indeed, feel very comfortable with this strange man.

In the afternoon he came back to the flat with her and it was an unspoken assumption how they would spend the rest of the day. It was the first time that Anisha had had a man stay with her at the flat but before leaving home that morning she had made sure that the place was presentable, the kitchen tidy with a vase of flowers. Even the bedroom and bathroom had received her attention for she was not at all sure what the evening would bring forth. She was glad she had taken the trouble.

As Anisha recounted it to me – and I am grateful that she feels close enough to her Gran to take me into her confidence over these matters - they talked long into the evening as the light faded, then ate at the kitchen table before retiring for more of what she described to me, her eyes lit up and dancing, as 'the most wonderful, blissful, sunny, soul-music you could imagine or wish for,' and her eyes took on a faraway look until she spotted me laughing with her.

"Gran," she said, "I'm afraid that he captured my heart that night and I'd have gone anywhere with him. Even if it did mean another planet – absurd though that may sound."

I nodded sympathetically.

"I believe you. And I do remember what it's like. And I'm glad it was so good for you."

"Thanks Gran," she said, "Because what came next was not what I'd expected."

Anisha was due at her mother's house in Surrey for the Sunday afternoon. Jessica had hung onto the house and she spent several weeks there, to cool off when it was exceptionally hot in the Gulf. Sujit was more than happy to go along with Anisha for he was curious to meet this woman who had lived and loved dangerously and produced such a remarkable daughter.

Jessica was waiting at the station and appeared somewhat taken aback to see her accompanied. Over cups of tea in the garden she drew Sujit out, getting him to talk about his home and family. Anisha was delighted and grateful to her mother for taking such an interest, as she too got to fill out the picture of this man who by now so fascinated her. On the way back on the train Sujit told her how much he liked her mother and how insightful she had been in her questions and comments.

Sujit was due back at FARIS HQ soon after that so they only had one more evening together, which was Monday after Anisha had finished work. The next day he should be on a plane to Ankara and then onward to his destination. When would they meet again? Anisha was left wondering.

195

"I think it's really up to you Anisha. You see I'm committed. If there's one thing certain in my life it is FARIS. FARIS is the non-negotiable. I'll never give up the project; it's my bottom line."

"So what does that mean for me? For us?" Anisha asked.

Sujit's reply hit Anisha like a stone. "I'm not sure that there is an 'us'" he told her bluntly. But Anisha quickly dodged the issue.

"I could come out there again, to FARIS HQ ….perhaps?"

"Perhaps, but it's a long way to go – not the sort of thing you would do twice and in any case, given your reservations, it would hardly be possible. Probably it's best to regard this, these last few days, as something good that happened, and then just move on?"

Although Anisha found that hard to take there was no way she was going to lose face by pleading with him.

It was later that evening, after Sujit had left for the airport and Anisha was back at the flat that Jessica rang.

"Anisha, has he gone?"

"If you mean Sujit, yes, he's gone. And I'm feeling really, really flat."

"Darling, don't feel that way. Please don't think any more about him. Forget him. I know he's attractive and I can see you've fallen for him. That's what happened to me. I don't want to see it happening to you. Please follow my advice and think of it as a pleasant interlude. Don't see him again"

"Really Mum, that's extreme! I like this guy, but it doesn't mean it's going to be a tragedy, like it was for you."

But Jessica, at the other end of the phone was getting more and more worked up.

"It's important that you don't see him again. You've been brought up in England and his background is, well, so far removed from your own. Don't let it go any further."

196

"Mum, you're beginning to sound like a racist; I mean you can't be; that wouldn't make sense. You've got me and you can't start having racist prejudices now!"

"It's nothing to do with racism. Nothing at all! Just that I want you to forget him. Don't see him again."

"Why ever not?" Anisha demanded.

"I can't tell you why not. Please, just believe me."

"Mum, you're being quite ridiculous! It's my life and I'll see who I want to see. And sleep with who I want to sleep with for that matter," she added. "And I don't think you should be preaching to me on that score!"

"Oh my God! You didn't sleep with him did you? Did you have sex with him?"

"Mum! For heavens sake, it's my business and none of yours!"

"Were you protected? Did you take precautions?"

At this point Anisha felt she had taken enough from her mother. Jessica had given her very little in the way of guidance on sexual matters, preferring to leave it to the pastoral care of Anisha's quite expensive school. "Well, that's part of what we pay for, isn't it?" She told me when, with grand-motherly concern for Anisha I had once questioned her on the subject. Knowing what a lively and attractive girl my grand-daughter was, and the competitiveness of the girly culture in the face-book and twittering generation I felt that the least Jessica could do was talk thoughtfully and lovingly with her daughter – not least on the subject of how she had put in her appearance as a daughter of the flower-power generation. Jessica hadn't felt equal to it. Surprising? I have reserved my judgement not least from a remnant of guilt about my own contribution to her in her own generation. It was all so different back then – I reflected – and Jessica had taken things into her own hands and refused to listen to me then – as she still did now.

But now Anisha had had enough of being preached at and being told what to do with her love-life by her mother and she put down the phone. It rang again almost immediately but this time it was Sujit; he was calling from the airport where he had just had news from FARIS HQ. The news concerned Grego and it was startlingly bad. Grego, whom Anisha had last seen a week ago and had parted with in terms of uncompromising finality, had been found dead. A search party from Shakhimardan Exploration had been sent out to look when he was reported missing. They found him, lying in a pool of blood a kilometre outside the checkpoint at the entrance to the enclave of Shakhimardan. The team were in shock and Alastair appeared to be struggling to know what to do. Grego's family needed to be informed, the body flown back to London but the local police of both nations were involved and no-one knew how long the investigation was going to take.

"Anisha," Sujit's voice was unsteady. "I need to see you again. I think you'll be able to help. I've decided to miss the flight. I'll see you in an hour - OK?"

Anisha's mind was racing to keep up.

"I'll be here. I'll see you soon.

Chapter 22

The concept of using icebergs as a water source has been around for a long time and commonly is seen to lie in the realm almost of science fiction but not quite; it has always been seen as something that is vaguely possible one day in the not too far distant future. Even though icebergs are floating in salt water, the ice has no salt. It's compressed snow. If you melted an iceberg you would get drinkable fresh water after you killed any germs.
http://www.freedrinkingwater.com/water_quality/quality1/13-08-icebergs-for-drinking-water.htm

As she waited for Sujit to arrive Anisha tried to calm her thoughts and pin down the different elements of the turmoil going on in her mind. Of course, she had given Grego the brush-off, and in a way she wished she had never met him, much less somewhat frivolously allowed him to engage her curiosity and go along with his fast car and his polo-playing, and his Westminster village connections. Without Grego, she reckoned, she would never have become involved in this whole FARIS thing. Or would she? Was it Alastair who had drawn her in and Grego been only incidental – a mere coincidence? Certainly he did seem to have been a core part of the events which had alerted her to FARIS and led her ultimately to their headquarters in the remote enclave of Shakimardan. And what, she asked herself, had led Grego to get involved in the first place? And now he had fallen victim to some possibly motiveless crime in a lawless country: or was it motiveless? Or had she unwittingly played a part? Surely the way she had put him down could not have had anything to do with the way he met his end? But why had he left the FARIS compound? Supposing he had simply walked out and walked and walked in an attempt to exhaust himself and to suppress the anger and frustration of her recent harsh words?

Oh for heavens sake, she told herself, you flatter yourself too much if you really believe you affected him to that extent!

It was over an hour until the buzzer on the door announced Sujit's arrival. Anisha went down to the street door to find him paying off the taxi.
"I'll have to borrow a couple of pounds off you, Anisha. I'd used up most of my sterling before boarding the plane. I'm cleaned out!"
She had to go back up to the flat and when she came down with the money it was to find the driver revving away down the street.
"He said it wasn't worth his time to wait" Sujit told her. "Too bad for him!"
"Never mind. Come inside and tell me what has happened. And why do you think I can help?"

They sat drinking coffee and Sujit told Anisha what he could.
"There's really not much more than I told you on the phone."
"How was he found? Where? Was he dead already? What had happened? You must be able to tell me something!"
"He was found on a road, fifteen kilometres outside the Shakhimardan boundary. He seems to have been knocked down by a vehicle and left there....where he fell"
"That's ghastly! Is there no other information? Do they know how long he had been dead?"
"Nothing has been reported. Investigations are still going on," Sujit told her.
"So it could have been deliberate....? Or it could simply have been an accident... a hit and run, with the perpetrators simply not willing to own up!"
Anisha wanted to know what action had been taken by FARIS HQ. When had they been alerted? What did they know?

Very little, apparently, except that Grego had gone missing the day before and the team and Alastair in particular were worried about him.

"I can believe that," Anisha agreed. "The compound is so hermetically sealed against the rest of the town. It's a separate world. I can't see anyone actually going out for a brisk walk – at least not on their own."

"That's right. There's no reason for people to go into the town; not to buy anything, that's for sure. Everything you could possibly need is there, brought in – I think by special concession. The only reason would be for a change of scenery maybe."

"And are they allowed to do that?"

"There's a strict rule about signing out, going with at least one other person and giving a definite time of return. The people on the gate record all such movements."

"So it would look as if Grego somehow evaded the regulations...."

"Yes. And there will certainly be an enquiry into that as well as into his movements afterwards. The question is why he should decide to go off like that, and in such a furtive manner." Anisha could not hide her anguish.

"And you're suggesting that I can tell you something? How could anyone think that?"

"You knew Grego," Sujit spoke quietly. "Your reaction when you arrived and he appeared was quite startling. How did you know him? And what sort of relationship was it?"

So Anisha recounted everything she could remember about her encounters with Grego, from that first weekend barbecue on the island in the river Thames, the evening when she met him at the FARIS reception, the day out at the polo match and the planned date which never took place. She told him what she knew about Grego's job as a parliamentary researcher.

"He loved the buzz of Westminster, I could tell that easily."

"And what about the two of you; how close were you? "

201

"Anisha replied quickly; "No sex! I mean we weren't sleeping together, if that's what you mean. Far from it – at least a far as I was concerned." She paused, worried. "When I think now that I might have been stringing him along I feel bad about it. I was just curious about him – and about the whole scene that he represented."

"In what way?" Sujit asked her.

"Well, it was quite glamorous, flashy in a way, sophisticated. A sort of 'Hello Magazine' lifestyle – with all the people he seemed to know. And yet at the same time he did seem lonely – insecure perhaps – out to impress. To be honest I'm not sure why he thought I was worth impressing."

At this Sujit managed a smile.

"You do yourself an injustice. Perhaps you haven't been looking in the mirror much lately!"

"If it's looks there must be plenty better-looking around the corridors that he frequents! Or frequented," she added sombrely.

"You worked in the city and for a big City firm. That would have been another attraction."

"Of course; I should have thought of that. And he thought I could be useful to FARIS."

"In which, of course, he was right," Sujit assured her.

Anisha let this pass. The time for the discussion about the rights and wrongs of FARIS with Sujit had not yet come and Anisha decided that it could not be raised at this point. However she had to tell him about her last encounter with Grego.

"You know, he spoke to me before we left…before Helen and Piet and I left. That's when I realised that he was serious about me and I had to tell him that it was not the same for me. I may have been a bit brutal. If I had thought he would take it so badly I would never have….." She trailed off helplessly.

"But we don't know that was how he took it, do we? Unless back there something else has been discovered, short of that there seems no way of knowing why, or even how, he left the compound, or where he went in the time before his body was found."

"What a mess! What a tragic muddle and mess!" Anisha groaned. "And the thought of his family and telling them doesn't bear thinking about."

"Do you know anything about them? Where they live? That is something I was asked to find out."

"I know next to nothing," Anisha replied. "He mentioned a sister; that's pretty well all I can tell you. There must be a next of kin on his passport – isn't there?"

"I guess so... Yes, they must have some information – Alastair at least must know. In any case, I will try following up a few leads tomorrow. Then I have to book myself back on a plane as soon as possible. Meanwhile, I'm afraid I'm throwing myself on your hospitality – again. And you've got to be up in the morning. I can sleep on the sofa...."

"No question of that. I'm lucky to have you back again but I wish it wasn't in this situation."

Anisha thought that the turmoil in her head would leave no room for anything else. She was wrong and she was startled to find that the shock of events simply heightened her delight in their love-making and brought release and forgetfulness of the confusion and contradictions of the last 24 hours. She was still discovering the smoothness of his dark skin and the places where it lightened, the hollow place where his shoulder met his chest; the way that he responded to her own excitement enchanted her and led her on. And when they lay together afterwards, limbs entwined, in her own words, she couldn't tell which him was and which was her, so comfortably and perfectly did they fit together.

"I would have liked to stay like that for ever, Gran," she told me, "but I knew, too, that while we were so perfectly physically matched, in other ways we were poles apart!"

"You mean about FARIS, is that it?" The grandmother in me knew that she was living in a divided world and that it was tearing her apart.

"Exactly that! But I couldn't bring myself to broach it or to break the spell. He really did have me..... How can I say? Spell-bound, enthralled. It was not just a physical thing – oh I know you might say it was, but it was much more than that; right then I was convinced that it was a body and soul thing; that you could not have put a sliver of paper between the two elements. He was so obviously clever, intelligent, a scientist and, with his Indian traditions something of a philosopher as well. It was a strong mixture. And yet...."

"And yet?" I knew that there was more she wanted to tell and I suggested to her; "There was this real difference of opinion, of approach, wasn't there? Which you, surprisingly, had not even hinted to him about. That's quite unusual for you, isn't it?"

"Yes Gran, you're right, as usual," Anisha replied. "But you saw how I had done the same all along with the FARIS thing. I suppose I felt that if I was to find out more about FARIS I needed to conceal my own opinions and so I was becoming this different person, different from what I had always been, someone who could play a double role. But when it came to Sujit, there was this added reason: I had found him and I could not abide the thought of losing him."

And so it was that Anisha found herself leading her life on twin tracks, as she described it to me subsequently. On the one side, work at the office and the environmental agenda to which she was entirely committed; her manager, Rob, had set her to look into what Akwa the water company was doing advertising on a hoarding made of solid ice and dragged half way down from the North pole, something which the fund's ethical investors would disapprove of completely and which might mean the company would have to be dropped from the fund's portfolio. On the other side, the other track, she was living just to hear from Sujit and every free moment was spent checking her cell-phone for texts and waiting for his calls. She ran endless conversations with him in her head: cycling to and from work she described the scenery to him and any little incident that occurred along the way, in detail, longing to share the moments and to have him see it as if through her eyes, to understand the things that gave her pleasure or caused her concern. If some music moved her, she wanted to share it: if someone or something made her laugh, likewise. But in their texts and conversations the distance that separated them and the difference in their surroundings left little opportunity for the sharing of such mundane detail or everyday occurrences, and that was a source of anguish for Anisha. At the same time as revelling in them she puzzled over the strength of the feelings he aroused in her: why had this character, so different from her in many ways of background, upbringing and education made so strong an impression on her?

Back at her desk at Asset Management and with Sujit departed, Anisha followed up the Akwa question. It involved another trip to the Swindon office, to meet the elegantly-dressed Ursula Lemoine, and on her return she reported to Rob.
"It appears that this was an advertising stunt that was somewhat foisted onto the company," she told him.
"And who was responsible for the 'foisting'? She must have told you that?"
"Actually I drew a blank there. Oh I tried, believe me! 'Information confidential to the company'. That was all she would say, even though I reminded her that Akwa might get dropped from the fund's ethical portfolio."

205

"And that didn't make any impression?"

"I asked her if they would continue with that particular advertising campaign, making use of icebergs and she said that yes, they would."

"And what about the other logo, the FARIS one. Did she have anything to say about that?"

"She actually denied that there was any other company logo involved. I told her that we had seen it, that we had video evidence. At that point she showed me photos with yesterday's date on them. The iceberg has docked now – in the Gulf, as we expected. And, lo and behold, no logo other than the Akwa one."

"I see," Rob mused. "It was a ridiculous stunt, unworthy of that company. Whoever was behind it, given Akwa's intransigence, we can't afford to keep them on the ethical fund in view of it."

Anisha nodded.

"It's sad; they seemed a good company, but I can see why you have to take them off the ethical list."

"And seeing the FARIS symbol there," Rob added, "However briefly, makes me doubly uneasy in view of what you have told me."

That evening at the flat there was a queue of emails waiting in her in-box. Scanning the list she noticed there was one from Alastair and, with a somewhat sinking heart she opened it first.

My dear Anisha,
It is with great sadness that I have to write with the news, which our colleague Sujit informs me that he has already told you about. Gregory was found dead approximately one kilometre outside the boundary fence of Shakhimardan, two days after you left for London. He had gone missing – or at least his absence had been noticed first, the previous day and a

206

search had taken place. As you are probably aware, colleagues do not under normal circumstances leave the compound without registering their absence, and never alone. The situation at present is that the next of kin – his parents – have been contacted. They are keen to come here to Shakhimardan. That does present some difficulties at present; there is a police enquiry going on, with police from both jurisdictions involved and it is not clear how far they are collaborating.

I know that you and Grego were good friends and so, my dear, although this will be hard for you, I have to ask you to undertake the difficult task of making personal contact with his parents. I would ask you to do your utmost to persuade them to delay their journey. In any case they will find that the process of applying for visas will hold them up considerably and, all being well (if I can use that expression) we may be able to repatriate their son's body without the need for them to undertake the journey. It is not clear to me what understanding they had of their son's line of work. Whilst FARIS does not have an 'official secrets act' all employees sign a confidentiality agreement when they join the organisation. You too will feel yourself bound by the conditions you signed on entering FARIS HQ and will not be tempted to pass on any of your experience here.

I know that I am fortunate in having such a (step-)daughter and I can have full confidence in you.
Always affectionately,
Alastair

Anisha was dismayed; not just by the contents – the request to visit Grego's parents was bad enough and the strictures of secrecy made it even more difficult – but the whole tone made her flesh creep: this semblance of grief for Grego and of affection for herself: how dare he use brackets around the step

207

of daughter, as if laying claim to the right of fatherly affection for her? - How dare he! And the assumption that he appeared to be making about her and Grego: 'good friends' what sort of conclusion was he drawing here? And was there a veiled threat that he would use the assumption of such a friendship? She would have to put him right on that subject: she and Grego knew each other: 'friends' – alright, but 'good friends'? That was going too far.

She realised with shock that her feelings towards Alastair had been piling up, to the point where now, with this request, she couldn't ignore them any longer. But how to respond to the email was a puzzle. She decided to delay.

She turned next to Sujit's email.

Anisha's heart skipped a beat as she waited for it to come up on the screen: how would he write? Would it be Dearest Girl, I'm missing you already – more than I can say....

She held her breath. The screen seemed to take an age to open. When it did, the message she found was an anti-climax:

'Hi there! Safely back to base. London was great but it's good to be back; I'm needed here. Hope you are fine.'

Swallowing her disappointment, she read on, keen to see what he had to say about Grego and the turmoil his death must be creating at FARIS HQ.

'Things here are at sixes and sevens. People are upset about what happened to Grego. No-one knows why he went off like that and got himself killed. The police are interviewing and taking statements but there are two sets of police involved and, as you can imagine, there's a language problem as well as a shortage of interpreters. And the police seem equally bewildered about the setup here. It's a mess! Saw Alastair when I got back. He said he was thinking of asking you to contact Grego's parents. I said I felt sure you would do that....'

"Hey, hang on a bit!" Anisha exclaimed to herself. "What made you feel you could say that?' She read on: 'I can

208

appreciate it may not be easy, but you'll be doing us all, and FARIS, a favour. Alastair says he's emailed you but here are the contact details.'

There followed details of where Grego's parents lived, their address and a phone number. 'Let us know how you get on,' Sujit concluded. 'Cheers and take care, Sujit' followed by a smiley face.

Anisha felt deflated but knew that the full force of her disappointment was yet to hit her. When Grego had stood her up and disappeared from her London scene she had been annoyed and indignant but this was different and this time her feelings were deeply involved. The memory of her time with Sujit stirred her deeply, and this cheery, chummy message, with its business-like request was like a bucket of cold water and did not begin to address her expectations. Question number one: had she got Sujit completely wrong? Had she totally misunderstood the way he had been with her? She had memories enough for several hours of heart-searching to try to find an answer. Question number two: where did she stand now in relation to him, to FARIS, to her own beliefs and credentials and to the job on the team of ethical investors at Asset Management? Question number three: did she really have to go through with it and contact Grego's parents? It was more than a mess, it was a nightmare.

I'm glad to say that at this point Anisha did the sensible thing; tired out and knowing she had to be at work the next day, she went to bed and slept on the whole problem.

PART THREE

Chapter 23

Consanguinity

Consanguinity ("blood relation", from the Latin consanguinitas) refers to the property of being from the same kinship as another person. In that respect, consanguinity is the quality of being descended from the same ancestor as another person. Consanguinity is an important legal concept in that the laws of many jurisdictions consider consanguinity as a factor in deciding whether two individuals may be married or whether a given person inherits property when a deceased person has not left a will.
From Wikipedia, the free encyclopedia

And this is where I feel I, as her grandmother, have to step forward and take up the next part of the story, for Anisha did not put in an appearance at the office for quite some time. Rob, her manager, was, naturally, first annoyed – that she had not called in sick or in any way let him know the reason for her absence – and then concerned. And so I received a phone call from Rob.

"I'm sorry to bother you and I don't want to worry you but, as Anisha's next-of-kin, you might be able to tell me where she is, what she is doing – if she is unwell or anything has happened to keep her away from work?"

Of course I was concerned and also surprised: surprised that Anisha had given my name as next-of-kin and concerned that she had gone off the radar.

"That's not like her at all; Anisha is most conscientious, especially when it comes to work, and I know she hates to let anyone down," I told him. "Can you tell me anything?"

Rob did not give me the full story at that time – or even hint at the half of it, which is not surprising because I am sure he did not know the half of it himself. Instead he told me:

"She's been very quiet since she came back from her holiday. Do you know about that big challenge holiday?

"Yes, yes," I replied – probably a bit testily – "I know she was determined to give it a go. And there's not much point in trying to stop Anisha once she has set her mind on something."

He asked me if I had heard from her since her return.

"Just a brief phone call to say she was safely back." I told him. "She said she had gathered a few more scars! But she also added that the scars were not all of a physical nature, and I got the impression that there was a new romance involved somewhere along the line."

I added that it would hardly be surprising if she had fallen for someone on holiday and was feeling wounded.

"Holiday romances often end in bitter-sweet parting, don't they?"

And Rob agreed that, yes, they often do, adding however that they don't usually lead to un-notified absences from work.

But while I was most concerned that something might have happened to Anisha, or that she might be ill and alone, I was also puzzled that she had given my name as next-of-kin. Why not her mother? I wondered aloud to Rob.

"To be honest, I had no idea that I was phoning her grandmother and not her mother," Rob replied. "But I think, from what she said recently, that she doesn't get along too well with her mother. And if she doesn't trust her that would be the reason for giving your name instead."

I assured him that I was going to do everything I could think of to contact Anisha and would get back to him with my news.

My first action, after trying Anisha's mobile and her land-line without success, was to ring my daughter. Now Jessica was dividing her time between the Gulf and her old house in Surrey. And particular moment she happened to be at home in Surrey.

"Jessica? What's up with Anisha?" I asked.

The reply was, I thought, an attempt at playing for time.

"How do you mean, 'what's up with her?' Nothing as far as I'm aware."

"She hasn't been to work for the last three days. Is she unwell? Is she with you?"

"Of course she's not with me! She's never here during the week. In fact she hasn't been down here for weeks. What's all this about her not going to work? She loves her work. Has something happened to her?"

"That's what I'm asking you, Jessica! You're her mother; you should know! When did you last talk to her?"

"On Monday. Oh my God!" Jessica's voice rose rapidly to a squeal, "What's happened to her? What's she gone and done?"

"So you talked on Monday? What about? Was something upsetting her?"

"I don't know! Yes – No! I'm not sure!"

Really, my daughter, well into her fifties by now, was giving a very fair impression of a 20-year-old having hysterics. Not for the first time I could have shaken her until her teeth rattled, but it would not have helped. Jessica, although intelligent had been born with barely one ounce of common sense and since birth had never acquired any more. How she had managed to run a golf club was, to me her mother, an unexplained mystery. How she had given birth to a daughter with so much courage and, I had always believed, plenty of common sense was another mystery. Now I had the feeling that something had passed between the two of them which was the clue to Anisha's disappearance.

I could hear sobbing at the other end of the phone.

"Jessica, please calm down and tell me what you and Anisha talked about. When was it you talked? On Monday?"

Jessica appeared to make an effort, although it was still hard to make sense of what she was saying.

"It was about her boyfriend; the Indian boy. I wanted to warn her! Sleeping with someone like that...."

"So she has a new boyfriend. Is that what it's about?" I felt, for a moment, quite relieved. After all if it was a case of a broken heart, while not excusing her absence from work, at least it was understandable. But Anisha was quite able to manage her own affairs and if Jessica had put her oar in and voiced some disapproval.... No wonder that Anisha had taken offence. All the same – to go *awol* for several days... there must be more to it than that!

"Tell me what you know about the young man, Jessica. Why do you disapprove of him?"

The sobs were returning.

"For goodness sake, get a grip on yourself," I scolded her. "Why should you disapprove if she has an Indian boyfriend? You had one yourself!" I couldn't help reminding her. "It's just a pity that Anisha never knew her father. But we can't go back over that again. The upshot was Anisha, for whom we are all profoundly thankful."

"That's just the point, Mummy"

When Jessica called me Mummy I knew there was a problem. It was what she called me when she was in the grip of a panic and, child-like, came running to me for help. I tried again to calm her down.

"Take your time, my dear, and tell me what the problem is. I know it's not the boy's nationality or the colour of his skin you are worried about, so there must be something else."

I could feel that she was making an effort and I just needed to wait, patiently. Soon enough the sobs and sniffs subsided and, in a choked voice, she told me about her fears: fears

213

which, if they had any foundation in fact would provide an explanation of why Anisha would have been upset enough to take herself off, although no clue to where she might have gone or what course of action she might have decided on. I learned that Anisha had met this man, whose name was Sujit on her holiday. The thing must have been serious enough as he came to England soon after Anisha had returned here. Anisha had taken him down to see her Mum. Jessica had seen exactly why Anisha found him so attractive, memories of her own romance were immediately revived, but along with them, and in the course of conversation she had with him about his home and his family, Jessica had conceived the unlikely notion – or was it entirely unfounded? – that here she might almost be looking at Anisha's sibling, had there been one.

After the two of them had left, Jessica could not get the idea out of her head and became more and more obsessed with the idea that Sujit's father was none other than the man she had loved and who had left her before any idea of a child crossed their minds. When Jessica returned to England, pregnant, it was too late. They had parted and they would not meet again. Now, she was convinced that Sujit was Anisha's half-sibling. She had phoned Anisha two nights later, when Sujit had left the country and tried to persuade Anisha, without, of course, telling her why, to forget him and certainly not to take the relationship any further. Anisha's response had been to tell her mother not to interfere and that she would choose whoever she wanted to have a relationship with, and to sleep with. In other words she had told Jessica to mind her own business and had rung off, resolved not to speak to her mother so long as she took that ridiculous attitude. Jessica however could not let the matter drop. She told me how, some evenings later she had rung Anisha again and told her all her fears; that Sujit could well be – indeed in Jessica's mind it was already certain, that he was Anisha's half-brother, and thus the relationship was utterly out of the question. Anisha, her mother said, must give him up.

There were plenty more fish in the sea and she should put him out of her mind and forget him.

So now I knew why Anisha had taken herself off. But where to? And what was she doing? Had she simply gone somewhere to be alone and lick her wounds? That was not like the Anisha I knew, the girl who, in the face of opposition would turn and confront the problem or the people causing it. But what, in this case, could she do? I had to think myself into her situation and work out what I would do, or would have done, in her place.

Chapter 24

Investor. An investor is someone who puts money into something with the expectation of a financial return.
From Wikipedia, the free encyclopedia

It was not easy. The parameters of the possible situation were so far off my mental map that I had no idea where to make a start to the task of finding out where Anisha had disappeared to. Where to look or concentrate one's thoughts and efforts? I had to think myself into Anisha's mind. And that was not easy.

I had known Anisha since she was born. I had baby-sat her, taken her to the park, introduced her to games and stories, read books with her. She was my one and only grand-child.

When she moved on to school I followed her progress and kept up the conversations.

We were close: as close as grandmother and grand-daughter can be. When finance was needed I chipped in. Not to an excessive extent: just with what was needed to keep her education and aspirations afloat. And, most importantly in my opinion, we kept in touch – lovingly and trustingly. That trust was what I relied on now as I groped around in my attempt to fathom where she had gone – where she had taken herself off to, at this hour, a moment when the decisions she made might affect her life in the years ahead.

There were two quite distinct areas which were of concern to Anisha in my view. The first of these was, of course, Sujit. Anisha had fallen for him in a big way – not to put too fine a touch on it she had fallen, body and soul, for this man and she had found the two aspects, body and soul, inseparable. Whilst he attracted her physically, there was also (she told me and I can believe her), something else, another bond, which she sensed as inseparable from the here and now of the physical need that she felt, to be together with this other person. As she related it later there was a sense of correctness, rightness, of everything falling into place as their relationship evolved.

I do not know what I would have done in her position but I felt sure that Anisha would simply want to be with Sujit and would do everything possible to get back to where they had met. Her visa would most likely still be valid, making it in theory possible.

I got on the phone to her workplace and spoke to her manager, Rob. With his help I might be able to contact the airlines and find out if she had booked herself back to ..... I was still not entirely clear where she would have to fly to.

Meanwhile, Rob was treating the information which Anisha had given him regarding FARIS seriously. Anisha had been unsure, at the time, how he would take her story; indeed once she was back in the surroundings of Focus Asset Management the whole thing seemed so far-fetched she was not sure herself how seriously it should be taken. Rob, however, was convinced enough. He got to work.

How would you go about uncovering the backers of an organisation that wanted to keep itself out of sight? The weakness of FARIS lay in the fact that they were so keen to recruit well-placed, influential and, if possible, financially helpful supporters, and that was the opening that Rob thought he could exploit in order to get closer to them and discover whether they were a threat, or if in reality they were just a group of crack-pots. If FARIS were by some improbable means to become successful in its stated aims then might it not be a real threat to the foundations of civil society? It seemed far-fetched and he was unable to force his mind to see further; the whole concept was so improbable. And yet something told him that the possibility was real enough and had to be exposed.

Anisha had told him of her step-father's insinuation that she might use her position in Focus to supply him with more backers, and that was the route Rob decided to follow. Using Anisha's log-in and email address, as the proverbial sprat to catch the mackerel, he hoped was the way that access to FARIS might be gained. Her log-in and password were retrievable via the company's network systems and Rob was able, quite quickly and with their agreement, to trail the bait of two significant investors beneath the nose of FARIS, as represented by Anisha's stepfather.

Using her name and company email address he baited his line.

'Dear Alastair, (he wrote),

Here are a couple of names that you might try. I think they could be interested!

Love

Anisha'

And he did not have to wait long for Alastair to take the bait.

'My dear Anisha,' came the reply. 'Delighted that you have been able to put these names our way and I'm sure they will be intrigued by what they learn. I will naturally be cautious in my approach and not involve you or FAM in any way. This confirms my view that you are really 'on board' with FARIS and I was right to trust my instincts about you. There will be a warm welcome awaiting you next time you are here. I look forward to more names in due course.

Very much love

A.

What Rob did next was sit back and wait for Alastair Singleton to contact the two names. There was not long to wait. The two names received their contact from FARIS via entirely different and circuitous ways but the message was the same in both cases. It was, Rob told me later, a 'soft sell' of FARIS like the one Anisha had heard at the end of that reception with Grego, painting a picture of a pioneering organisation dedicated to taking the best of human civilisation 'out to the stars' and claiming the usual parallels with the Pilgrim Fathers' opening up of the continent of America – the 'New World'.

The pitch came across as maybe ahead of its time, maybe unrealistic but who, on the whole, could object to the idea?

Under Rob's guidance communication took place offering ever deeper insights into FARIS. As the picture became clearer Rob and his two collaborators began to see what Anisha had felt about the undermining of the progressive work of so many institutions, international, humanitarian, charitable, and so forth. It became evident that at the core of FARIS was a far less attractive philosophy, one which held that since the human race's future on planet Earth was beyond hope of recovery, any attempt to improve matters was worse than wasted effort, that the time to make the move had come and that FARIS was where scarce resources and funding should be concentrated. Anisha had seen and understood this but what Rob was not clear about was how seriously FARIS should be taken. Was it simply a bizarre adventure or did the organisation indeed have the capacity to undermine and do serious damage? To learn more he would have to delve deeper. Meanwhile, where was Anisha? She had been off work now for two days with no phone-call to account for herself. Rob gave her another two days, until the end of the week, and then took action. He sent her an email to the effect that, following his 'discovery' of her 'treacherous leaks' of private investors of FAM and her continued absence from the office with no word of explanation, he had no option but to announce her dismissal for gross misconduct and contravention of the rules of client confidentiality. The terms were instant suspension and a month's notice of termination of contract. Any appeal had to be filed within fourteen days.

He felt bad as he typed this but consoled himself with the knowledge that it was Anisha who had brought the FARIS affair to his notice, clearly with the hope and expectation that he would do something about it. Since she had disappeared – and he had no idea why this should be – it was the only way he could see of locating her and clearing up the mystery. At this stage he did not include me, Anisha's grand-mother and, as I now knew, her named next of kin, in the manoeuvres and I would only learn about it later It was in that state of ignorance I sat down to think myself into Anisha's mind and ask myself where she had gone and what she could be doing.

With Rob's help I discovered that she had indeed booked herself back via Turkey to Osh in Kyrghizstan, thence, presumably, to travel onward to the enclave of Shakhimardan and FARIS HQ. I would learn the full story of how she had done this from Anisha, later. Meanwhile I had to find some way to calm Jessica and assure her that Anisha had reappeared, but without mentioning the boy-friend who had caused Jessica's hysterical outburst.

Chapter 25

UN Millennium Development Goals

*"We will spare no effort to free our fellow men, women and children
from the abject and dehumanising conditions of extreme poverty, to
which more than a billion of them are currently subjected. We are
committed to making the right to development a reality for everyone
and to freeing the entire human race from want"* The United
Nations Millennium Declaration, 2000.

Sitting in a chilly airport lounge in Ankara Anisha emailed
to Sujit that she was on her way. She had no idea how he
would take the news and, in view of his carefree email sent on
his return, she feared he would tell her to turn round and go
straight back to London.

Last time she had arrived at Osh airport the adventure tour
company had been there to meet her in the person of Helen.
This time she would be on her own and would have to make her
own way and it was only once the plane was airborne that she
started to plan, with the help of a traveller's guide, how she
would do that. There was a railway that ran from Osh to the
town in Uzbekistan nearest to the enclave and that would be her
best bet but at this stage, as she realised the step she had taken,
Anisha's heart sank. How would she find the train station in
Osh? Decipher the signs? Explain where she wanted to go and
buy a ticket? With no friendly guide or 4-wheel drive she
would truly be an alien in a foreign land, unable to speak the
language, read the signs or explain who she was and where she
wanted to go. She did what Anisha could always do at such
times – tired out, she slept. She awoke as they were coming in
to land with the steward shaking her to prepare for landing.
The sleep had done her good and she was feeling more
optimistic. Perhaps Sujit himself might be there to meet her!

That hope was not realised, nevertheless to her enormous surprise, there was indeed a driver waiting for her with her name on a placard and with the FARIS badge concealed neatly under his lapel. She was vastly relieved and delighted to be met but in reply to her questions the driver insisted that he did not speak English and could only shrug helplessly in response. It was getting late, eight o'clock, dark and cold and she was glad that she had brought her warm coat and several layers of sweaters. They drove into the night, on roads which quickly became rough and pot-holed, and Anisha's attention was entirely taken up with coping with the swaying, bumping motion. Eventually they arrived at the check-point which was the entry point to the enclave of Shakhimardan. Here a small demonstration appeared to be taking place. Anisha tried but failed to see what it was about and the driver made vain gestures in an apparent attempt to explain. As he handed their documentation to the border police a small number of the demonstrators broke away and targeted the van deliberately, as if they had some grudge directly against them. They were quickly dealt with and bundled roughly back to where they had come from behind the perimeter fence and the van drove on. The streets of the little town were quiet enough at the late hour and they were soon crossing the bridge over the river. The gates of FARIS HQ were opened quickly with a familiar salute from the security guard. How strange to be back: what would her welcome be?

To Anisha's surprise it was Alastair, accompanied by Sujit, who came down the steps to greet her.

"Anisha, my dear!"

Alastair embraced her warmly whilst Sujit stood aside.

"I am just so sorry that this has happened!"

Anisha thought he was referring to Gregory. He must be convinced that she was deeply involved with him and had made the journey as if it could somehow help to heal her grief. But his next words stopped her in her tracks.

"If I had known it had cost you your job I would not have asked you to help. My dear, I'm sorry, but so glad that you came straight here. You must stay and I can assure you, you will not lose out."

Anisha struggled to keep up. Had she lost her job? Well, by virtue of walking out and leaving without saying a word, she probably had. But how could Alastair know that? It was not as if it was official! She had better go along with it and hope to find out more in due course. Alastair was speaking again, asking her something. Concentrate!

"I was proud when you got the job with Focus Asset Management; I know some of the people there – good sorts. And it was going to be a fine career start for you. If I had thought this could happen I would certainly not have asked you for favours on behalf of FARIS. I feel very much to blame.. I can assure you that FARIS will look after you."

Anisha's brain was working furiously. Something had happened which she did not know anything about but the only thing clear was that it appeared she had lost her job. Alastair was speaking again.

"How was your journey? You're tired out! We'll get you sorted out and comfortable and talk more in the morning. Sujit, you know where Anisha's room is. Make sure she has all she needs."

Soon they were standing by the door in the residential wing, where Anisha had stayed not long before. Sujit hesitated.

"Are you alright?"

She shook her head.

"Come in for a bit. I need to talk."

As they stepped inside she pulled Sujit to her and he put his arms round her. She breathed deeply.

"You don't know why I've come. You can't know!" she told him.

"I know." Sujit replied, holding her tight. "Alastair told me. He told me how you helped him and FARIS with some names and that you were found out and they have sacked you. So now it is clear you must be part of FARIS and you can work for us from this end. With your knowledge of the City and investments you will be invaluable."

Anisha opened her eyes wide. What was he talking about? She had done none of what he said. How had Alastair come by that story? It was beyond her.

"Sujit, I'm just too tired to think about it any more, but it's not what you think. There's something else much more important I need to talk about. Something that only concerns the two of us!"

It was Sujit's turn to look puzzled.

"Everything will be easier now you are here and now you are with FARIS. You and I can be together – at least for the time being. Unless and until I get sent somewhere: if I get a mission - if that happens."

"But that's just it. It's not clear at all that we ever can be together – at least not if you believe what my Mum believes."

"I don't follow. What does Jessica believe?"

"It's so far-fetched…."Anisha tailed off. "I must sleep. I'll tell you – if I can – tomorrow."

Anisha found herself unprepared to tell Sujit her mother's story; it seemed so absurd and surely no justification for walking out on her job and making this journey. However it was clear now that at FARIS HQ they were under the impression that she was here for an entirely different reason. Anisha unpacked the few belongings she had brought with her, demolished the plate of food that had been provided and, with her usual facility, was soon asleep.

Six hours later she awoke, refreshed and ready for the day. She lay, trying to think through and to separate out the various strands. There were two problems.

Problem number one: she was in love with Sujit – "Totally", she told me, "Body and soul". It was a new experience for her and quite different from any previous relationship. Briefly she tried to stand outside of herself and look at what was going on, acknowledging her state of excitement, elation and emotion and the sheer chemical rush of need and desire. At the same time she knew, quite simply knew that it originated from somewhere very deep inside her and that, if ever there was a time for 'follow your heart' then this, for her, was that moment. She continued to lie there, luxuriating in that certainty. Then her mind refocused and her heart sank as she contemplated the tangle of strands of a frankly unbelievable situation. If her mother was to be believed, this man could be her half brother. It was far-fetched but, if her mother knew something and was not telling, if by some remote possibility it were true, what were the dilemmas and implications which she, they, would have to unpick?

Problem number two: her commitment to the Green Team meant she now found herself on the opposite side of the fence to this odd and possibly dangerous organisation, in which her step-father clearly played a central role. By some ironic twist of fate and convolution of misunderstanding, she had become entwined with FARIS and found herself gagged by her own inability to declare her true colours. She was unable to talk frankly to Sujit and unwilling to broach the subject with her stepfather since there was no knowing what that might lead to. The result was impasse, not to mention stalemate! What could she do?

Anisha lay in bed turning these thoughts over in her mind and wondering what the day would bring.

Rob in London had called a meeting with his two decoy ducks. They met at noon to discuss how they should continue to string along with FARIS in the attempt to get to the bottom of what it was all about. Both had been on the ethical fund's advisory board for several years; Lois Fanshaw came with a background in business, Ken Severin from the healthcare sector. Both believed in the aims of the ethical fund and its commitment to its investors.

"Thanks for being here at short notice." Rob greeted them. I'd just like to be clear about this, that you really are alright with being the decoy ducks of this investigation?"

The two of them nodded and assured him of their agreement.

"It's not clear at this stage whether FARIS is simply an expensive but ultimately eccentric set-up or something more serious. My researcher stumbled over them – by a series of coincidences really and also because she's a persistent girl and a talented researcher. She likes to follow a trail and doesn't react well when people put obstacles in her way."

"Tell us how she happened upon these people"

"It was a case of pure chance initially – serendipity at work which brought the FARIS insignia to her attention. After that it seemed to keep cropping up. You know how, once you become aware of something it can reappear again and again and it makes you wonder how and why."

His listeners nodded, recognising the phenomenon.

"And because of social networking, ideas of this sort spread like a virus, as if they have a life of their own detached from human intervention!" Lois added.

"Hmm. I'm not sure if FARIS has reached that stage yet. I think they are keen to keep a much lower profile. Their dilemma is attracting the individuals they want as backers whilst at least for the time being, keeping below the radar of public awareness. That is the weakness which we can probably exploit."

"But are we sure? Are we convinced that this organisation is undesirable?" Ken put the question.

"That's certainly the first question. And how can we check it out?" Lois added.

"This is what we have to discuss," Rob replied. "Maybe all that's needed is to throw more light upon these people. But from what we know so far it does appear that the strategy for achieving their aims is to undermine much of what we regard as good work, by which I mean the whole spectrum of international bodies, NGOs and civil society."

"With the aims of....?"

"In a nutshell – with the single aim of 'starting over'" Rob told them. "Starting over on a new planet, taking the best – or what they see as the best – of human civilisation with them and leaving the rest to a slow or not so slow, inevitable decline."

"Far-fetched barely seems to touch that notion!" Ken protested.

"You're talking totalitarianism by the back door?" suggested Lois wryly.

"Yes indeed, so it would seem," Rob agreed. "Far-fetched it does indeed sound but we do agree, don't we, that we need to take a good look at these people?"

Two heads nodded in emphatic agreement.

"What next then?" Ken questioned. "Has it got to the stage where we have to commit financially if we want to get any deeper?"

"Alastair Singleton has taken the bait; he believes it was his step-daughter Anisha who sent him your names – the strategy to which you have kindly agreed. He has made his first approach, basically the soft sell, presenting FARIS as a pioneering inspiring venture, checking out if you could be onside, prepared to invest, not just your money but your influence behind the scenes. And with your encouragement he has revealed quite a lot more about the organisation and its

227

aims. What we have to do now is agree your next move, what our next steps are."

They nodded again and Ken added his comment.

"I think we have to be careful not to be seen as having any connection between the two of us at this stage."

The others agreed with this.

"To Singleton we are two entirely unconnected people who happen to invest with FAM. There's no reason why we should know each other. In fact it would be too much of a coincidence if we did. We have to be careful about this."

"Ken's right." Lois agreed. "While we can agree the content of our emails we should be careful to formulate different responses. Perhaps one of us will decide not to pursue the project any further, quite early on?"

"Good idea. Two quite different responses: different questions, different reactions."

Rob had one further point to make.

"I need to tell you about Anisha. She's the one who brought all this to my notice but I've lost her. She has gone off the radar and I'm worried about her."

"So what are you doing to get in touch with her?"

"It's rather drastic, I'm afraid, but I cannot think of any other way of making her contact me. I have 'discovered', as it were, what Anisha has done and how she has 'betrayed' FAM. Two days ago I emailed her with dismissal both on those grounds and in view of her non-appearance for work. I have made sure that this news will have reached Singleton but I don't know whether it will have reached Anisha – or, indeed, whether she has headed back to FARIS HQ. In short we have very little idea of where she is at this moment." He sat a moment in silence before rousing himself with a shake.

"Now, what we have to do today is draft your replies to Singleton – and make them as unlike each other as we can. Shall we make a start?"

Chapter 26

Green politics
Green politics is a political ideology that aims for the creation of an
ecologically sustainable society rooted in environmentalism, social
liberalism, and grassroots democracy.
The political term Green, a translation of the German Grün, was
coined by die Grünen, a Green party formed in the late 1970.
From Wikipedia, the free encyclopedia

When the end of the day came Anisha had still not found
any way to tackle the contradictions of her situation. Alastair
told her that he was hopeful of hearing from the contacts which
she, Anisha had given him. For her part she failed to compute
what ramifications were spreading out. One thing she knew for
a certainty was that she had not sent Alastair any names.
Therefore, she had to suppose, it must have been Rob: Rob,
who she had thought had scarcely taken note of her worries
about FARIS. Could he really have considered it a project to
invest in? This, in Anisha's view, went against everything that
the Green Team stood for. That Rob might be playing a deeper
or longer game did not for a moment occur to her. She quite
simply felt abandoned by her manager and betrayed by the
organisation whose aims she thought she had been committed
to. On all these counts Anisha kept quiet. The last person she
wanted to know about her disquiet was her step-father.

Sujit, however, still sleeping beside her, was another matter
altogether and she needed to talk seriously to him. But first she
would allow herself this brief interlude of peace, the two of
them side by side, as she reassured herself that what she had
known to be true, was true. Now she would sleep again. Later
would be the time to talk.

Suddenly it was later and she opened her eyes. Sujit was still asleep. Through the window she could see that the sun was high in the sky. How long had they slept?

There were robes on the back of the door and Anisha pulled one on. Taking the other she perched on the side of the bed and gave Sujit a gentle shake. He blinked sleepily and looked at his watch then pulled her towards him.

"No, now we talk," Anisha told him.

"You start!"

"Alastair knows about us?"

"Why else do you think they have left us in peace till half way through the morning?"

"Yes, I see. I had some idea that he thought it was Grego I was....."

"Oh no!" Sujit was laughing at her. "Alastair spotted right from the start."

"Spotted what? That I was....? That you were....? So what was it about Grego?" She tailed off.

"You stand high in Alastair's opinion. I could tell that from the way he talked about you that he rated you highly, even before you ever arrived here. Grego was a different matter. Alastair valued him and thought well of him but I think he also regarded him as a bit wild and possibly unreliable. Of course what happened to him was just horrible. And we still don't know the full story."

"And what about you? I mean where do you come in Alastair's ranking?"

Sujit paused before replying.

"I've known Alastair for about three years now. He's seen me at work here and I've been with him in the Gulf. I've travelled with him and spoken at the seminars he gives around the world. He knows my commitment. I think my dedication to the cause is a powerful tool for him at convincing others and raising the finance we need. And when he saw the two of us together.... Well, I think the idea seemed just perfect to him."

I can only guess at the thoughts in Anisha's head as she attempted to understand. The man she found herself in love with held views which were so entirely the opposite of her own that she did not know how to begin to unravel their strands.

"Sujit, I don't know where to start. I don't know what I'm going to do or what will happen next!"

"Nothing needs to happen right now," Sujit reassured her. "You have lost your job in London and I'm sorry for you about that. It was a good job and no-one likes being ditched like that; it's humiliating."

"It's not just humiliating, it's...."

"For now you stay here. There's work to do and Alastair can use you. Your expertise, your contacts, just what he wants."

"It's not just that, it's...."

But still she could not bring herself to explain, was unable to blurt out –as she felt she ought to – 'I'm an environmentalist! My job is working for the Green Team! And I'm your sister: half-sister: perhaps....'

She had to make a start

"There is something you should know."

"You said you had something to tell me. So; tell me now!"

"First, you should know that I'm *green*."

"Green? In what sense green?"

"I'm green in the sense that everyone knows it today!" she said, with exasperation creeping into her voice. . I'm *a* green! Doesn't that mean something to you? Green! As in ecologically, sustainably committed to the planet and to the survival of the human race!"

But Sujit failed to be disturbed.

"My darling, I can't see how that should be a problem. A lot of people feel that way today. Many of our best innovations are coming from exactly that mode of thinking and the research that comes from it. It's just that here, at FARIS, we're taking a realistic view of the future of this particular planet and the future of the human race here; and we're putting all our eggs into the one basket – so to speak – of a better future for the human race elsewhere. Not just a better future, but simply its survival. No, the fact that you adopt a green lifestyle is fine and to the good and fits well with our philosophy."

Anisha felt panic rising. She was failing to make her point.

"Sujit, you haven't understood what I'm saying or what it means. For me, being green means I am opposed to everything that your FARIS operation stands for: opposed to your philosophy and to your morality and to the whole ideology behind what you are doing. If I were interested in politics I would be a member of the Green Party."

Sujit did at last fall silent and contemplated her in silence.

"And what's more," Anisha added quietly, "My Mum thinks I'm your sister. Well, not quite that: your half-sister."

As she spoke the words she was aware of how unutterably ridiculous and unbelievable they sounded.

"......Sorry," she added in the silence that ensued. "So sorry.... About everything.   Do you think I can go home?"

And then, unusually for Anisha, sitting down on the side of the bed she buried her head in her hands and cried her heart out.

Fortunately Sujit rose to the occasion. Putting his arms around her he held her tight and rocked to and fro with her until the sobs subsided.

"Explain a bit more – please!" he told her as she sniffed and wiped her eyes. Still suppressing the sobs Anisha made an attempt.

"I thought when you came to London that I could handle the situation. That you liked me enough and that somehow we could reconcile our ideas. Or at least not allow them to keep us apart."

Sujit nodded.

"But after we'd visited my Mum, and so soon after that you had caught the plane back here, that's when she rang me in a panic, with this crazy idea and told me not to see you any more."

Sujit still looked bemused.

"But what was this crazy idea? Are you saying that she somehow thinks…. What could have put that into her head?"

"You don't know my Mum. Half the time she's unpredictable and off the wall. Usually there is some grain of reality behind the ideas she gets into her head. Do you want to know how this one came about?"

"Of course! Your mother seemed quite sane to me when I met her. We had a good long chat. In fact I think we got on rather well, which surprised me."

"Ah, well, that is not unconnected. Listen!"

And Anisha gave him, this time in more detail, a concise version of the events leading up to her own birth. The trekking across Afghanistan in the early seventies, the headlong romance as Jessica and her Indian boyfriend made their way East, the end of the affair as they got nearer to his homeland, the parting, when her pregnancy was unsuspected, and the return to England where Jessica gave birth to her daughter and called her Anisha.

"But do you know what the population of India is?" Sujit asked incredulously. "Why ever should your mother take it into her head that we are related? Is she mad?"

Anisha sighed.

"I love my Mum dearly. She brought me up alone; well not alone since my Gran was always there, my Granddad too until I was ten, and we were all very close. But Mum does get crazy ideas. You would have to ask her how she came by this one, but she did seem quite convinced of it. In fact she sounded quite panic-stricken."

"And you took this to mean….?"

"I simply told her to mind her own business; that I would make my own decision, sleep with whoever I wanted to…."

Sujit raised his eyebrows at this.

233

"Don't worry, sweetheart, I only meant you!"

Sujit smiled.

"In other words I told her I thought she was out of order, barking up the wrong tree, chasing hares – I can't remember what else! To mind her own business, I expect. But it was then that I made the decision to come back here. My visa was valid for another couple of weeks. My head was somewhat out of control in that I just walked out of my job. It's a wonder I was able to do all the necessary to get airline tickets."

Sujit hugged her. His admiration was evident. Gratification too, I am sure.

"But before all that, and what I haven't mentioned, is that I told the story to Rob."

"Sorry, Rob? Who is Rob?"

Anisha took a breath.

"Ah yes; Rob, I should have told you, is – or rather was…." she added soberly, "my line manager at Focus Asset Management. A lovely guy! He has been such a great boss; really, showing me how it's done, giving me fantastic assignments, keeping me up to the mark. I really feel I've let him down!"

"What, by walking out on him?"

"If you have to put it like that, yes, I'm afraid so, yes, that's what I did. Walked out on him."

"And he would have no idea why?"

"That's right; no idea at all."

"But you said that you told him: told him the story? What did you tell him, and what was the story?"

There was no question now but that Anisha was going to tell Sujit everything about her FARIS experiences. In other words how FARIS had come to her notice and how Grego had appeared on the scene: her trip to the Gulf, where her mother had moved to be with Alastair, and the repeated appearance of the FARIS symbol: her trek around the Gulf peninsular and the adventure, or misadventure, in the wadis of Oman. And all of this had been prompted by her research into the sustainability of water supplies, from bottled water to irrigation systems as old as the ancient kings of Persia. And wherever she went the FARIS symbol cropped up: polo matches, university campuses, Westminster receptions.

She told him how she had put it all out of her mind. She found herself in the delightful position of doing a job she loved and being well enough paid to indulge in her latest passion, seeking out the thrill of adventurous holidays and serious physical challenges. As she looked around for the next excitement, the trip to Kyrgyzstan seemed to fit the bill entirely. And so she found herself in Shakhimardan: such a convenient place for an interplanetary research station, remote and isolated as it was yet in touch with all and any of the players in the world whenever it needed to be and with access to other, similar, isolated pockets of land which it could make its base if it paid its way. And there in Shakhimardan Anisha realised how she had been manipulated and that her arrival, far from being a coincidence, was a well-laid plan.

How my grand-daughter had concealed her antipathy to everything she learned there from Alastair and his various teams, I cannot think. Perhaps they found it natural that she should be taken by surprise and interpreted her reticence as part of the shock. And all this she now related to Sujit and told him how she had come away with two overwhelming impressions: first, shock at the revelations of the FARIS project and its implications and, second, a mind in turmoil and a conviction that the man she had met, Sujit, was about to change her and change her life entirely

.

As she finished her narrative and her commentary on it, Anisha fell silent. Sujit knew now where she stood, ideologically and emotionally. But how would he take her revelations? Lovers they undoubtedly were – but siblings? Or rather half-siblings? This was far-fetched enough, though not inconceivable, but in their minds the views that they held of the world they lived in could not have been more different or more irreconcilable.

Chapter 27

Conspiracy theory
*A **conspiracy theory** explains an event as being the result of an alleged plot by a covert group or organization or, more broadly, the idea that important political, social or economic events are the products of secret plots that are largely unknown to the general public.*
From Wikipedia, the free encyclopedia

I may be guilty of criticising Jessica, my own daughter, but anyone who knows her will agree that she can be exasperating and is apt to take off on one whim or another at short notice. Being a mother had kept her grounded. Taking up the job as secretary at the golf club had been a good thing as well, but I had feared that this would soon pall and she would be off on some other improbable tack fairly soon. So it was a relief when she met Alastair and quite soon found herself, perhaps to her own surprise, a married woman for the first time. I did wonder what they saw in each other and what had brought them together but Jessica was undoubtedly still attractive. And I can say that, when I met him, Alastair Singleton did not strike me as a bad man, and I was happy that Jessica finally had someone she could call her own. She had done well to bring up her daughter and since Anisha had gone away to university and then moved to a job in the City, Jessica was very much on her own. Part of the job at the Golf Club involved looking well turned-out and being charming to the members and Jessica certainly looked after her figure and her appearance. In addition she continued to be up for an adventure; so moving out to the Gulf and setting up house – with no expenses barred – on the glamorous Palm Island development would certainly have appealed to her. If Alastair wanted something of a trophy wife I can see that she filled the bill very well, but I hoped that he felt more for her than that. As for what Jessica saw in Alastair, I hoped it was more than his obvious wealth and the life-style he offered. Sadly I saw very little of him and had scarcely any chance of getting to know him better as he was always busy flying from one part of the world to another even before they made the move out to the Gulf. I had little idea of what his work consisted of; Jessica just told me that he was 'in business' and that he had interests in companies in a number of different countries, water companies being one of them. At one stage she said he was investing in a company developing bottled water in the Middle East, the reason, I assumed, behind the move to the Palm World development. That company was Akwa, which Anisha had visited as part of the FAM ethical portfolio and I did wonder how she missed seeing Alastair's name among the list of directors. Nothing that Jessica told me about her husband had prepared me for the shock of learning about the setup which Anisha now found herself in and my reaction, naturally, was disbelief.

"You mean" I said to Rob as I heard for the first time about FARIS, "that my newly-acquired son-in-law sees himself as some twenty-first century New World interplanetary explorer?" We were sitting in his office in the City where most of the staff were getting ready to leave or had already left for home at the end of the day.

Rob nodded sombrely. "Not alone, of course. He's one of a group – and as far as I can make out he is near but not at the top of the group - who are leading this movement which they call FARIS. Its aim, as you say, is interplanetary. Now there is nothing fundamentally objectionable about that; I'm sure we all dream of the leap into new worlds at some time in the future."

"So what is it that's dangerous about the group?" I asked, "And why are they so secretive?"

"The answer to that is probably in the name. You know now what those initials stand for and the clue is in the last word, 'Survivors'. They see our planet in somewhat apocalyptic terms: on a course of self destruction in many different ways but all combining to make the outcome, in their view, the end of progress - the destruction of civilisation. Their solution is to take what they can to start afresh elsewhere."

"Their pessimistic view is probably shared by many of us if we only stop and think," I responded, "But most of us are too busy getting on with our lives to go to such lengths. Are they perhaps fairly harmless?"

"You might think so but we have learned more about their approach which makes them look a lot less than benevolent."

I waited for him to explain.

"It's not just that they think the end is nigh – to use the old expression – but that, because they see the end of our civilisation here on earth as inevitable they are not prepared to watch a slow decline. Instead their strategy is to hasten that end in order that they may be part of the vanguard of the new."

"That sounds wildly improbable," I responded. "How do they plan to hasten the end? By starting the nuclear holocaust? That's unthinkable!"

"I have not seen any mention of that, but what has become clear to me is that, in recruiting and lobbying among the powerful and well-placed, their tactic is the undermining of the organisations dedicated to progress, sabotaging, you might say, efforts to improve the human condition in all sorts of ways. All the efforts of international bodies whose ideals are the progress of the human race here on earth towards a more secure future, these efforts in the view of the FARIS movement are nothing less than a waste of resources in pursuit of a hopeless cause and would, in their view be better used in taking civilisation to…."

Rob paused.

"To…?" I echoed. "Where are they aiming to take it to?"

"That I can't tell you," Rob replied. "You've read predictions, I'm sure, of how one day man might colonise Mars but,"

"But that is way off into the future, surely?" I interrupted him

"As far as we know, yes indeed. But it seems that FARIS might have made break-throughs that we have no idea about. With the support and the resources that they have already obtained, who knows?"

"Do they really have that much support? And where do they get their funds from?" The whole idea sounded so improbable.

"It appears that a cast of leading scientists of all descriptions has been assembled over the last ten years, working in secret."

"And what about Anisha? Why has Alastair tried to draw her into this?"

"Anisha appears to fit in very neatly with Alastair's plans in that she works for an investment company and is thus in a position to pass information to him about potential FARIS investors. Plus, as she is his step daughter he thinks he should be able to count on her loyalty."

"Hmm," I responded, "He obviously doesn't know much about Anisha."

"Exactly" Rob replied. "He has no idea that Anisha is a committed environmentalist of the deepest shade of green and that she has a most determined mind of her own. Also that she regards her mother affectionately, but none-the-less as a hare-brained nut case! Excuse me for referring to your daughter in those terms: they are Anisha's not my own."

I smiled tolerantly. We both sat in silence for some minutes. I could hear the traffic faintly as the evening rush hour got under way; a steady mounting hum and the tooting of horns informed me that London was packing up for the evening and making for home or for the pubs and clubs.

"So where does that leave us?" I broke the silence. Rob nodded his head seriously but did not speak and I continued. "It seems to me that there are two problems, two main issues. One is the problem of FARIS, how seriously it has to be taken and what should be done about it; the other is the problem of

Anisha: where is she and how do we get in touch and get her home?"

I paused before adding "And you know, I am sure, which of those two problems is the more important to me."

Rob nodded sympathetically. "I appreciate that your concern is entirely about Anisha. I share that but I'm also looking at the bigger picture here."

"You surely don't think these FARIS people are a real threat do you? They sound to me more like one of these end-of-the-world religious cults than anything seriously scientific."

That was my opinion at that stage and I wanted to make it plain. Rob however was of a different view.

"I can't dismiss them in that way. Having come to hear about FARIS so recently, I begin to make sense of a chain of different events and occurrences over recent years. I am no conspiracy theorist and if I were I would have been noticing patterns long before now. But now that it is drawn to my attention – thanks to Anisha as you know – I cannot dismiss the possibility that FARIS has been behind much of these patterns."

"What kind of patterns are you talking about?" I asked, puzzled.

"Chiefly in connection with the international community's efforts to achieve all those good goals that I've mentioned already. We all know that targets are set and governments sign up to them only to find, several years down the line, that progress has been slow and targets are missed. Once you become aware of the possibility you see the hand of FARIS almost everywhere. Money is being diverted all the time. Projects that should be achievable are failing. Targets that so many countries have signed up for are missed, time and again. Far from pulling people out of poverty, the developing countries are becoming more and more polarised within themselves, the mega-wealthy and the very poor whose conditions stand still or go backwards."

241

"And you really see the hand of FARIS in this?"

"I see FARIS taking advantage of both human weaknesses and human aspirations. The community of supporters that they have created can continue to milk the system as they have always done but they can now appease their consciences by accepting FARIS's view that the future lies elsewhere and our own planet must be left to slow decline, to stew in its own juices. The idea of carrying civilisation to new worlds appeals to a natural human aspiration, for adventure, for the pioneering spirit, for a noble and dangerous cause which will salvage the best of what the human race has produced in its evolution from our cave-dwelling ancestors and to take it to fresh glories on a new planet."

"I can see that would be a heady mix of ideas," I agreed.

Rob continued. "I'm convinced that FARIS supporters see themselves in this light, as heroes, almost as a chosen few, chosen to carry the torch. It is then easy for them to regard everything they do in the light of this ideology. It is an ideology capable of harnessing not just the wealthy, although financial backing is vitally important, but can also appeal to a wider community of intelligentsia, to the scientists and engineers that it needs to attract in order to realise its ambitions, even writers and artists for they represent the softer side of our civilisation which FARIS means to take to its new world home."

"You still haven't told me why I should care more about putting a spoke in the wheels of FARIS than in getting my grand-daughter safely home," I returned tartly.

"'Putting a spoke in their wheel' as you phrase it, is something that Anisha would be keen to do. Don't you agree?"

I had to smile for he was right and Anisha would be the first to agree. But as for simply leaving her where she was, probably in a confused and emotional state, was not something I could agree to.

"We have to get in touch with her." I told Rob. "There's more to her disappearance than you might think." And I told Rob about the affair with Sujit – leaving out the far-fetched question of any possible blood relationship, which I did not believe Rob needed to know about.

Rob looked thoughtful. "If Anisha has fallen in love with this guy I can imagine that she must now be feeling torn in two. Her environmentalist self is against everything that FARIS stands for, but her emotional self wants to believe in the man she has fallen for."

"Anisha is not used to dealing with such conflicting forces" I told Rob. She will be hard pressed to know how to act.

"But the fact that she came to me and told me all about FARIS, everything she had discovered, convinces me that she will never go along with their ideas. Far more likely that she will try to persuade her man to change his own views, and we are not in a position to know if that is a possibility."

Chapter 28

Pamir Mountains

*The **Pamir Mountains** ... . are among the world's*
highest mountains and since Victorian times they have been known as
the "Roof of the World" a probable translation from the Persian.
From Wikipedia, the free encyclopedia

Sujit was at the wheel of the four-by-four with Anisha beside him in the passenger seat. They passed the gate of Shakhimardan Exploration and moved slowly through the crowded streets of the little town. At the check-point they were waved through and, leaving the enclave, found themselves, quite literally, in another country.

Alastair had agreed to Sujit's request for a vehicle and permission to be absent for a day.

"Anisha needs time to settle," he told Alastair. "We would like a day's hill-walking, time to talk and get some fresh air in our lungs."

It had not been a problem.

"Where are we going?" Anisha asked.

"Hill-walking. You'll see," Sujit replied. "I know a shepherd's hut."

And with that Anisha felt she could be content.

Two hours, up hill, down shale-covered slopes and up again, the drove on tracks, ever higher to where grass and moss gave way to snow and ice. Then they walked until walking and scrambling was all there was room for in their minds for and everything else was banished in the gasp and strain to reach the next hilltop or ridge.

"How much further?" Anisha demanded as they breasted yet another line of hills.

"Nearly; we're almost there; just down that next fold, you can almost see the spot. I promise you we are almost there!"

Sujit replied, looking anxiously at Anisha who seemed to be struggling.

"We can pause here," he told her, encouragingly. "Here, have some water; breathe!"

"I'm OK – I think!" Anisha replied, but took a swig from the plastic bottle. "It's my calf muscles. Must be different from the ones I use cycling! I ought to be fit after the extreme challenge trip. I just hope it's worth it when we get there!"

"It will be. You'll see!" Sujit assured her. "Are you alright again? Last leg – let's get there!"

Half an hour later they were sitting, collapsed in front of the entrance to the old shepherd hut. Before them stretched a panorama of mountain peaks, some already showing the first snows of autumn. Lower down tinges of scarlet and orange where the leaves on the trees were turning.

"Why here?" Anisha asked at last, after she had recovered her breathing and started to take in the vista spread below her. "How do you know about this place, and what are we here for?"

It was some time before Sujit replied. During that time, with no sense of hurry, the two of them sat, looking, drinking in the panorama, soaking up the warm sunshine and the sounds from the water flowing in the valley's creases.

Eventually Anisha prompted him.

"So? Why are we here? And how do you know this place?"

"We're here, I think, to get closer to things." Sujit began, "You and I need to talk seriously – about the things that matter to us. And also to get away from everything: if that's not too much of a contradiction?"

"Not at all!" Anisha replied, with a laugh of some relief. "It's all very intense down there, I suspect." She nodded back

245

towards the way they had come. "But I have questions; and I need answers. I mean it!"

Sujit nodded seriously, with no shadow of a smile.

"I know you do, and you deserve them. But I have questions too, don't forget."

Anisha nodded her agreement.

"Food first!" Sujit suggested and it was not until they had put paid to the supplies in his pack that they were ready to confront the serious issues uppermost in each of their minds.

At this point I confess that I have very little idea of what passed between them for Anisha told me next to nothing. But I was aware that the gulf that divided them was enormous, apparently unbridgeable even at the same time as the attraction that drew them to each other was intense. How could that be?

The answer, I think, in addition to the sheer chemistry of two young, intelligent, vibrant young people who were madly attracted to each other, was that they both had a passionate belief in – well the things that they believed in, and each was prepared to put their all into it. For Anisha it was the determination that everything she did would be to promote a sustainable future here on earth. For Sujit it was the conviction that the future of the human race lay in channelling all efforts into taking it onto the next stage and a new beginning elsewhere. Could there be any reconciling these views? It was doubtful.

Up there in the mountain hut they made love for what Anisha thought had to be the last time, and as they lay together afterwards she felt the sadness like a weight.

"You know that when I get back to London I am going to have to talk about FARIS. I shall be betraying you."

"And betraying Alastair as well," Sujit reminded her, "Which means your mother too."

"That worries me less," Anisha told him.

246

"But you have to get back first to London and I'm not sure that Alastair …. In fact I am quite sure that Alastair, when he hears about your intentions will simply not let you return."

"But he doesn't need to know; unless, that is, you plan to tell him….Do you plan to do that?" Anisha looked at him with incredulity.

"Don't be so surprised! What else do you think I would do? What choice do I have?"

Anisha was stunned.

"But you care for me, don't you?"

There was a pause, which Anisha had certainly not expected. Sujit was silent and thoughtful. Eventually he spoke, choosing his words carefully.

"I care for you, Anisha, very much, and I know that you care for me. In fact, if anything I think your feelings are the stronger. And I admire you for that and feel some shame – some shortcoming on my part."

Anisha tried to interrupt but Sujit would not let her.

You and I met… let's see, a matter of a few weeks ago. My commitment to the work I do here and to the vision it embodies took place several years ago and it wasn't something I undertook lightly. You'll understand that it is not up for renegotiation. My duty, my calling, overrides my personal inclinations. FARIS, you know, comes first."

Anisha took in the enormity of what he was saying in silence. Sujit continued.

"I know Alastair will make sure you have a very comfortable life."

"What do you mean?" Anisha exclaimed. "He can't keep me here against my will!"

"You can't be sure of that."

"But there will be searches. There will be records of the flights I have taken. I won't be abandoned!"

I know at this stage that Anisha would have been thinking of me, confident that her grandmother would never, ever, let her disappear and would move earth and heaven to discover where she had gone; and in this she was right. But Sujit apparently had other ideas and obviously knew a great deal more about Alastair and the supporters and backers of FARIS.

"He can be ruthless when necessary. And he has the power and influence beyond what you would imagine. I would not put it past him, for instance to make use of me as a hostage."

"You! How on earth could he do that?"

Easily. Suppose you threatened to walk out and spill the beans on FARIS. Well he could simply tell you that my life would be the price to pay for that. Would you be prepared to do that? Wouldn't you rather settle for going along with the organisation? And that way we could be together. The answer seems so simple!"

Anisha was now thoroughly rattled. She was up and dressed.

"It's time to go back," she said. "We've left the vehicle for too long – and it's got my laptop in it!"

Sujit looked startled.

"What on earth did you bring that for?"

"I don't know; it was just automatic," Anisha replied. "Anyway we must go. I'll drive myself if you are not ready!"

"Hold on a bit! Have you decided what you are going to do and to say?"

"I'll decide when we are on the way," Anisha told him, to which Sujit had no reply.

Scrambling and slithering downhill they covered the distance to where they had earlier left the vehicle. Then they were bumping back down the mountain track as the setting sun turned the rocks and snowy peaks to pink, fading to grey.

Chapter 29

Off Roading 4x4 Driving

It's white knuckle stuff all the way as you experience 4x4 driving to the max!

http://www.intotheblue.co.uk/driving-experiences/off-road/4x4/

Anisha's mind was racing as they rattled and bumped down and along the mountain track. Sujit's concentration, as the light faded, was entirely on the road ahead and they rode in silence. She felt she was being torn in two and, from having felt she could trust Sujit with her life her heart plummeted and she now feared that her feelings had led her totally astray and she was walking blindfold into a scenario that she could only now begin to imagine. The fact that her mother had hinted she might be involved in a taboo relationship, she realised, had worked on her in the opposite sense and had made her all the more determined that nothing should come between her and this man she had stumbled across – apparently accidentally. How could it have been possible that she, an intelligent, rational, twenty-first century independent girl, could have let her senses lead her so far against her fundamental, thought-out convictions? Not only this but that, unless she checked those senses and those feelings, she could end up spending the rest of her life in this out-of-the-way pocket of an alien land controlled by a set of fanatics determined to undermine the world she knew and cared about.

At the same time there was no lessening of those feelings. Glancing continually at Sujit's profile as he stared intently ahead negotiating the pits and potholes of the track they were descending she knew that she had embedded him deep in her psyche. From time to time she stretched out her arm and rested her hand on his leg, feeling its warmth and, as if to reassure him, pressing with the palm of her hand on his taughtened thigh.

Darkness fell and progress was slower. At one point Anisha felt that Sujit's concentration was failing: a sudden jerk and correction to the wheel startled her into the realisation that he might actually be drowsing off at the wheel.

"Let me drive for a change," Anisha demanded sharply. "It's dangerous. You need a break!" The important thing now was to get back down in one piece and the danger of slipping off this precipitous road was too awful to contemplate.

To her relief Sujit agreed. He stepped down and they exchanged places.

Clasping the wheel with one hand, with the other she felt for the handle which would jolt her driver's seat forward until she could reach the pedals and feel in control of the vehicle. She adjusted the rear-view mirror. Now – as Anisha told me with some satisfaction afterwards – she was truly 'in the driving seat'. How could she take advantage of the fact?

Sujit soon drowsed off, exhausted by a long day, some of it behind the wheel, some in full rhetorical flood on the subject dear to his heart, the FARIS project and some of it in more pleasurable activities with this glorious girl who, if anyone could persuade him away from the path he had chosen, might be the one to do it. But he would not change course. And in that knowledge, he fell asleep.

Anisha tested out her familiarity with the gear system. Four-wheel drives were unknown to her but with no time for practice she would just have to find out as she went along. Lights would be crucial on this unlit road, little more than a bumpy and at times rock-strewn track. She checked: sidelights, headlights, dipped and full: chose the setting which best illuminated the 100 metres of track ahead – at the slow speed she intended to take, this would be plenty. Tentatively at first, she eased the vehicle forwards. After ten minutes of clasping the wheel, foot on the brake and one hand ready to change to a lower gear, they were making reasonable progress and Anisha dared herself to relax – if only a notch or two. It was a mistake; the vehicle lurched into a deep and unseen crack in the already rough track. The sleeping Sujit, thrown sideways, received the full force of a sharp impact and slumped forward. To her credit Anisha kept her nerve and steered the vehicle through the deep ruts to recover the level track again. Only then could she allow herself a sideways glance and took in the fact that, knocked sideways from his sleeping position Sujit had been knocked unconscious by the ferocity of the blow. There was nothing for it but to keep going until she reached the road and could find help for him. She forced herself to breath steadily. Her lungs felt constricted as if she had been staying alive on oxygen borrowed from some other parts of her body. That could not continue and she forced herself into a breathing pattern until it became, once again, automatic.

For the next twenty minutes Anisha drove, slowly and carefully, down the mountain track. Her concentration was on the road ahead while her mind was working on the scenario that faced her.

She needed to get help for Sujit; that was obvious. But after that the choice facing her would be between staying with the man she felt deeply for and which would mean adopting his vision and abandoning her own convictions, or sticking to her own beliefs and values which would mean giving up her man and attempting to find a way to escape from this organisation which might indeed try to hold her against her will.

I cannot be sure, that these were the thoughts going through Anisha's mind as she focused intently on the rough and pot-holed track down the mountainside but, knowing from experience that abstract thoughts and concentration on immediate practical concerns can work themselves out

251

together, consciously or unconsciously, I think I understand the processes that were going on in her head as she drove back down that precipitous road. I can also believe her when she says that she did not know that she had made a decision until the moment of truth arrived. It happened soon after they reached the foot of the mountain track and had entered the relatively smooth highway and drawn up at the check-point, entry to the enclave of Shakhimardan, where FARIS had its headquarters.

When a frontier official tapped with his flashlight on the driver's window Anisha rolled down the glass plate. She was unsure still, at this stage, of what actions would be required, or what officialdom she would need to comply with in order to get help before crossing this insubstantial border post between one country and the small enclave within. All she knew was that she needed a way out of the situation before crossing the check-point and must take any chance which presented itself, with however unrealistic hope of an exit it might offer. She could only trust, as always, to her instincts. Rolling down the window she addressed the guard whilst pointing to her unconscious companion.

"Sick, sick!" she exclaimed desperately. "Hospital; must go hospital!" Hoping that those key words of 'sick' and 'hospital', coupled with her urgent gestures towards her companion, would be sufficient to indicate an emergency and prevail upon their better instincts to respond to the situation.

At this point fortune or fair weather was on her side. The border guards, eager to demonstrate their competence, had in next to no time sized up the situation – as it appeared to them – and summoned up the ambulance which waited for just such, albeit rare, emergencies.

Sujit was stretchered into the ambulance, with Anisha as passenger, and the vehicle fled into the night in the opposite direction to the enclave of Shakhimardan and FARIS HQ.

Anisha meanwhile having little idea of where they might end up kept her wits about her.

An hour or so later they were on the outskirts of a large town, Osh, where Anisha had arrived at the airport. It seemed an age ago. Ten minutes after that they drew up outside what appeared to be the accident and emergency entrance – she surmised this from the flashing blue lights and the porters who rushed to open the ambulance doors – of a substantial local hospital.

As porters and paramedics rushed to bring their patient through the welcoming automatic doors, Anisha noticed the band of taxis drawn up to one side, evidently waiting to be called on by visiting relatives of the sick.

Sujit appeared to be regaining consciousness now and Anisha watched as paramedics unloaded him from the ambulance and prepared to wheel him indoors. She delayed their movement with a gesture.

"Darling Sujit! You'll be OK. I have to go. Please let me see you in London – Please! I love you!"

And with that Anisha took the few steps needed to reach a waiting taxi.

"Airport!" she told the driver, trusting that this too was a word with international intelligibility. The driver nodded sagely, moved into gear and drew away. As Anisha looked back, the automatic doors to the hospital's accident and emergency department were closing behind the stretchered figure of the man she thought she loved

My phone rang at four am.

"Gran, it's me, Anisha!"

My head was groggy. After nights of not sleeping I had succumbed and taken a sleeping tablet: not the sort you buy over the counter but the real thing, prescribed by the doctor.

253

Anisha's voice however, dragged me to the surface, even though I hardly trusted that I was awake and not dreaming.

"I'm in Ankara!"

"What… why? How did you get there?" I struggled incoherently.

"It's a long story. I need help."

"What kind of help?" I imagined Anisha in some sort of trouble – lost passport, money, something of the sort. It turned out to be the latter, at least that seemed to be the immediate problem.

"I need to get a ticket back to London but I don't have anything left on my card. I'm maxed out – if you know the expression."

I did indeed know the expression.

"I'm so sorry! Can you help?"

She didn't need to ask and I was so relieved to hear her and relieved that it was only money that was troubling her.

"Of course. But where are you? How much do you need? "

She explained how much would get her an airline ticket to London and cover the expenses – somewhere to stay and so forth, if necessary.

"I think if you could just make a transfer to my account then I can start using my card again."

Well, I have done my banking online ever since the system was available so I had all her details in my system and it would be the work of a moment to make the transfer. But I was anxious to know more.

"Are you alright? What about Sujit? Is he with you? Are you together?"

"I'm alright Gran, but that's too many questions. I'll tell you more when I see you. I think you are probably not going to believe the half of it. Anyway, I've got to go…"

"Anisha, wait – is this about Sujit? Or is it about FARIS?"

The startled silence at the other end of the phone told me that I had surprised her.

"How do you know about FARIS Gran? What do you know about it?"

"I know what Rob has told me" I replied.

"Rob? Has he been in touch?"

"Of course, my dear. Don't you remember that you gave my name as next-of-kin?"

"Oh, heavens, yes. I did put your name down. Well I knew I could rely on you – but not on my Mum. Oh Gran, I'm sorry you have been so worried by all this!"

I could hear the remorse in her voice.

"That's by the bye," I assured her, "But I do want to know what all this FARIS business is: and where Sujit comes into it. He's important to you, isn't her?"

"He is…" She seemed to hesitate: "… or he was…"

"I can wait!" I reassured her. "Let me know as soon as you can when to expect you."

Chapter 30

The London Square
Gardens in the Midst of Town Todd Longstaffe-Gowan
*Modern-day London abounds with a multitude of gardens, enclosed
by railings and surrounded by houses, which attest to the English love
of nature. These green enclaves, known as squares, are among the
most distinctive and admired features of the metropolis and are
England's greatest contribution to the development of European town
planning and urban form.*
http://yalebooks.co.uk/

I never did discover how Anisha got herself onto a plane
and back to Ankara but as usual she had lived up to her name
and defied all obstacles in her way. Two days later I drove
with Rob in his car to Heathrow. I felt it was kind of him to
offer to pick Anisha up and that it showed how worried he had
been about her. As we speeded west with the evening traffic
along the Cromwell Road and out over the Chiswick flyover
the light was fading to a pink glow where the sun had set and
lights of all colours were beginning to shine, high-lighting the
commercial buildings along the route.

"She'll be glad to know that she hasn't lost her job," I
commented.

"But I'll be keeping a close eye on her," Rob responded.

"I'm sure she won't go *awol* again," I hastened to add.

"It's not that; I'm more worried that they'll come looking
for her." He replied seriously.

"Who do you mean by 'they'?" I was a few steps behind
Rob at this stage, I had to admit.

"FARIS of course" he replied, throwing me a surprised
glance as he negotiated the traffic, through the tunnel into the
airport complex and then up the ramp to park in one of
Heathrow's multi-storeys.

There was some time to wait until the screen showing arrivals indicated that the plane from Ankara had landed and it seemed an age until Anisha emerged. From the strength of the hug she gave me and the sob of relief I could feel as she buried her head in my arm, I knew that she had been through more than the usual outward-bound type of adventure that she normally sought. She disentangled herself from my arms and took the tissue I offered to wipe her eyes, before mustering a firmer smile.

"Thanks for being here, Gran! And for bailing me out!"

"You know you're always welcome, but if my hair hadn't been grey before it certainly would be now!"

"I know, I'm so sorry!"

"But seriously," I told her, "I shan't always be here, and who will bail you out then?"

"Don't say that!" she exclaimed then, looking round she caught sight of Rob and gasped in surprise.

"Hello Anisha," Rob said, "We've been worried about you."

"You too? But I thought you'd fired me!"

"I wanted it to look like that but, no, you still have your job – if you want it, that is!"

"Of course I want it! Oh that is so good!"

We were making our way towards the exit to retrieve the car, jostled somewhat by the crowd which was quite dense.

"Shall I take that bag?" Rob offered.

Anisha was carrying a holdall and had another black bag slung over her shoulder. As she passed the holdall to Rob and went to change the black bag to the other shoulder someone pushing a trolley seemed to miss his footing and stumble up against us. There was confusion as everyone righted themselves then Anisha gave a cry of alarm.

"Hey! He's got my bag! That's my laptop in there!"

Too quickly for anyone to stop him I saw the man disappear into the lift whose doors closed behind him, the arrow pointing down. Anisha made a dash but was too late. Rob headed for the escalator some distance from the lift but his way was blocked by any number of newly arrived passengers all intent on making their way out to cars, taxis and waiting buses as quickly as they could. Few of them were willing to give way, however much Rob and Anisha signalled the alarm. All I could do was stand and watch in dismay.

After some five minutes the two of them returned, shocked by what had happened and their failure when they reached the ground floor even to see the perpetrator.

"He could have jumped on a bus or taken a taxi, or just doubled back up to the car park. It was hopeless!" Anisha said.

Instead of the anticipated pleasant drive back into the city the next half hour was spent with the airport police who took our crime report and promised little hope of recovering the bag. Eventually we were on our way, Anisha in sombre mood now, contemplating the loss of her laptop.

"If it's just the laptop you can replace it. Surely it's not the end of the world?" I urged her.

"It's everything I've got stored on it! Not emails: I can access them from anywhere. It's the other stuff."

"And would the other stuff be FARIS stuff?" Rob asked, taking his eye off the road momentarily to look across at her gravely.

Anisha was silent and lost in thought but finally replied, quietly, "Yes, it's FARIS stuff. And I wonder….do you think that this was deliberate and not opportunistic? Do you think…." Rob nodded.

"Yes, I think you might be right. It could have been planned, which means they've got their eye on you. It may be that they just wanted to retrieve whatever you've got on the lap-top – and I hope you are going to tell me about that – or there may be more to it than that, which will mean that we need to look after you – very carefully."

The following day, Sunday, Rob joined Anisha and me for a late breakfast, to discuss the situation and to learn more from Anisha about the contents of the stolen laptop. We were in my sitting room, looking out over the London square in the autumn sunshine; it seemed a very secure environment. Anisha had slept soundly during the night and appeared refreshed but in sombre mood. She had described to me and to Rob her journey back to the enclave of Shakhimardan, where she had been determined to rejoin Sujit, tell him about her mother's preposterous fantasies and, hopefully, find themselves in agreement about making a future together. She knew that she would have to convince Sujit that he was on the wrong track but, being Anisha, she could not believe that this would present an obstacle to their love for each other. However, she soon began to realise that Sujit was never going to give up on FARIS, that indeed he saw it as his vocation, his dharma, his path in life. She saw clearly that, whatever the attraction between them, their outlooks on life were miles apart and irreconcilable. She had managed to collect plenty of evidence about FARIS, certain that she must bring this back to London and try to convince her boss, Rob, even if he had just sacked her from her job, that this was an organisation that threatened everything that the Green Team stood for.

"I was in this rather special situation," Anisha said. "Because I was Alastair's step-daughter – and Alastair made no secret of the fact: quite the reverse; so everyone knew. Because of that I could more or less go wherever I wanted in FARIS HQ and no questions asked."

"So you made the most of it and loaded stuff onto your laptop," Rob concluded.

"Right!   But I didn't have a lot of time – as you can imagine. I got a good look at some of the stuff but I also had to be unobtrusive as I did it, so no-one could see that that I was saving from their system onto my own laptop." Rob nodded.

"So, basically, I can't tell you about exactly everything that is on the laptop."

"You mean there's stuff on there which you hadn't read?" Rob asked. Anisha nodded.

"And if they think you know about it, they might feel the need, not just to recover the laptop, but to get hold of you as well and make sure you don't spill the beans."

At this Anisha fell silent, taking in the full significance of what Rob was saying.

My mind was working hard as I refilled coffee cups and indicated to help themselves to pastries and croissants, bought hot from the bakery on the corner of the square. I wondered whether I had been right to leave Anisha alone in the flat, even for that short interval. Well, no harm done this time but in future I would be more careful.

Rob and Anisha sat down together with an A4 pad of paper for a prolonged exercise in memory retrieval.

"Don't hurry; think it through," Rob told her. "I want you to remember every little detail possible, however insignificant."

Anisha nodded. "I'll try!"

"And while we're at it, see how much of the FARIS set-up you can recall, and how it might fit in."

I left them to it for an hour or more, returning only when I felt they needed a break to tell them that lunch was laid out in the kitchen.

My kitchen-diner looked out over the London square and as I tidied away the coffee cups and prepared food for a midday meal my eyes as usual followed the traffic and the pedestrians on the street below and the square beyond. Might someone out there be watching? At the same time that one man had snatched Anisha's bag, might another have been tagging us and followed us to the taxi rank, there to overhear the address, or even follow in our wake? I shook myself; it didn't do to let the imagination spin out of control. Nevertheless it was sensible to keep an eye out for unusual figures loitering, or perhaps a van or a car, parked but occupied.

In the square gardens there was the usual group of mums and buggies and toddlers. I knew many of them by sight as they came on fine days to chat and relax while older children might be in school. Nothing suspicious there. The elderly gentleman reading a newspaper was another regular and the bag-lady feeding the pigeons with slices of flat white bread – I wished she wouldn't, it made such a mess! A couple of joggers in lycra suits finished their run and flopped down on a bench, taking out flasks of water and drinking and pouring it over their faces. I hadn't seen them before: were they genuine? They looked hot enough, but that would be good cover.

Across the square a van had pulled up, the logo on its doors announcing dry-cleaning and laundry services – nothing unusual about that in a London square, even though I hadn't seen this one before. The fact that the driver did not get out of the van puzzled me: surely he must have a client here to call on? Soon after he drew up another vehicle, a green mini that had been parked nearby drew away. It too seemed to have been occupied while parked. Any coincidence here? It was impossible to know.

As I waited for Rob and Anisha to join me I lowered the roller blind at the kitchen window – just in case. There was no point in advertising Anisha's presence. In any case, the sun had gone round now and was streaming in through the window dazzling anyone sitting at the table. I usually lowered the blind on sunny days if I was eating there by myself.

There was soup and rolls, bought from the bakery earlier and we ate in silence for a while. Then as cheese and fruit followed I was anxious for an update on the contents of the stolen laptop.

"How much have you been able to remember?" I asked Anisha.

"I'm not sure how much I've missed out, but we've got quite a long list."

Rob nodded.

"Anisha's mind is in good trim. I wish my memory was as good."

"I just hope I haven't mis-remembered!" Anisha added. "It's so easy to feel sure, until perhaps you discover that some things were entirely different."

"But to be more specific," I urged them. "Is there material on the laptop that they would see as particularly dangerous? Or is it more that the whole thing is a risk to them – a risk that would split FARIS open to a public that they want to keep it concealed from?"

"That is one aspect, but there are also materials which would be dynamite if they got into the domain of the general public right now: for instance the list of financial backers and also the names of scientists who were on board."

"Obviously that would be something they would want to avoid. What else?" I asked.

"More explosive than those, I am sure," Rob began, "it's the memo on international organisations."

"Memo? That means it's written to somebody – or some bodies. Tell me!" I could not begin to think where this was leading. "Anisha, is this something you saw and read? Or just another that you copied to read later?"

"I did read this one Gran and it seemed to be about the FARIS plan over the coming months."

"Which was…?"

"Basically to organise a multi-pronged campaign to discredit and undermine those international organisations which will be taking part in the G20 summit which is scheduled for

September …. I do know enough to be aware that this is the FARIS strategy. Discredit those organisations working for development, show that their dreams are utopian and never going to work, basically that the cards are stacked against a benign future for life on this planet."

"But that's a wicked thing to do!" I exclaimed, "And I do find it hard to believe. Do you really think that is the way they see their plans working out?"

"I'm afraid so," Rob nodded.

"Then they are either insane or megalomaniacs – perhaps it means they are both."

"Unlikely though it may sound, the FARIS plan is to bring all the opinion that matters around to their view. This way resources will be poured into the project to the extent that the count-down to interplanetary colonisation and the planting of our civilisation into new worlds will be brought forward, not just by decades but maybe by a century."

"It sounds quite crazy to me," I muttered eventually. "Can these people really be a threat?"

Anisha looked at Rob. "What do you think? Can they….?"

There was a pause before Rob replied.

"I am not qualified to give the answer. I do believe that they can create a great deal of mayhem and that their efforts to sabotage the work of NGOs, international bodies, and ordinary citizens of goodwill, can seriously put back efforts for a fairer world.

But there is something of more immediate concern to us."

"Which is…?" I asked.

"The fact that Anisha has had contact with them and, in their eyes probably defected, means that they see her as a danger and will want to get her back in their control. That is a worry."

"And that is putting it very mildly!" I added with vehemence. "In fact Anisha must stay here until all this can be straightened out."

"Thank you, Gran!" Anisha replied gratefully. "It's such a relief to know that I can stay here. This is where I feel safe."

"You must stay here until it has all blown over," I told her. "You'll be safe here."

I hoped I sounded more optimistic and less dismayed than I felt.

Chapter 31

Lost Property Office
First advertising of this kind appears on papyruses in Ancient
Greece and Rome. The first modern lost and found office was
organized in Paris in 1805. Napoleon ordered his prefect of police to
establish it as a central place "to collect all objects found in the
streets of Paris", according to Jean-Michel Ingrandt, who was
appointed the office's director in 2001. from Wikipedia the free encyclopedia

The laptop was gone but it was not clear whether FARIS
agents rather than some opportunistic sneak thief had stolen it.
However we had to assume it was FARIS and that there would
be consequences and that Anisha would be targeted. At the
same time I began to fret increasingly about Jessica and wonder
what she was up to and how much she knew about all this. I
had hoped that my scatter-brained daughter had become more
responsible by now and I was sure that she would never
knowingly let her daughter be drawn into danger. When Rob
had left, towards the end of the afternoon, I tackled Anisha on
the subject.

"When did you last see Jessica, or talk to her?"

"I think it was at least three weeks ago," Anisha screwed up
her eyes trying to remember. "Oh yes, of course! It was after I
took Sujit down to see her at the house in Surrey. They got on
really well together, which pleased me." She paused… "But
then…"

"Then she changed her mind, didn't she?"

"She rang me the next day, after Sujit had left, telling me to
have nothing more to do with him. Imploring me, you might
say."

"And you worked out that she had got some idea in her
head that you might be related, is that right?"

"That's right. It sounded crazy, but then….that's Mum,
isn't it?"

"That's your Mum all over, I have to agree. On the other hand...."

"On the other hand – what?" Anisha prompted.

"On the other hand, there might have been something very strong indeed which reminded her of her own passionate romance that led to your being here at all. As your mother, she must have dreaded the idea of your taking the same route."

Anisha snorted her disdain.

"Ridiculous idea! Sujit was never going to disappear into the blue and not be heard of again. No, it was that mad idea that we were related, that an affair with Sujit would somehow be an incestuous relationship. I mean – what could have put that in her head? Apart from the fact that he is Indian, what possible connection could there be? Other than a million to one or more coincidence."

"Let's leave Sujit for a moment. How much does Jessica know about FARIS? How is she involved?"

Anisha frowned.

"Impossible to say. When I was with them in the Gulf, before I went on that oasis trip, she didn't talk about it at all. The first thing I noticed was that she had one of those jewel badges which I had seen at the polo match. When I asked about it I got the impression that she didn't know what it meant. That was early days for me and I was only just beginning to notice the insignia and registering its cropping up in a coincidental way. FARIS was never mentioned by name. If she talked about anything, other than the house and getting it the way she wanted, it was to refer to 'your step-father's business affairs'. And that was always in a detached manner, as if she was quite content to leave it to him and not get involved."

"And later on? Did you get any more of an idea later?" I asked.

Anisha thought and replied, "Alastair actually told me that she was behind him and supporting him. 'I'm very grateful for her support' he said. But I wasn't completely convinced."

"I think she most likely has no idea about FARIS HQ and what goes on there or where it's meant to be leading," I said. "I'm sure she would be frightened out of her mind if she knew of your recent activities, or if she realised you might be in danger."

Anisha smiled. "I guess you're right. Poor Mum. Best to leave it that way for the moment." She paused, thinking, then after a moment: "Perhaps I ought to give her a ring though. I mean we usually do talk every couple of weeks or so and if she has been trying my mobile she could be wondering what's up. What do you think?"

"I'm not sure. She'll want to know where you are and then, of course, if Alastair asks, they'll know where to get hold of you. On the whole I think it's best to leave it for the moment."

For the next two days Anisha was never out of my sight. If we left the flat it was to go together, to the shops to stock up on essentials and buy provisions, or to the square gardens for some fresh air and a change of scene. Anisha was quiet and it was hard to divine what was going on in her head; heaven knows there was plenty to occupy her thoughts. Eventually and one stage at a time she gave me a full account of the two trips to FARIS HQ and the two enclaves with the unpronounceable names, which I had never heard of.

Concerning Sujit she told me very little until, on the second day of our voluntary self-incarceration, as we sat on a bench in the square garden soaking up the sun, without looking at me she voiced her thoughts.

"If two people are madly attracted to each other – I mean really, body and soul attracted – and yet they hold views..." she hesitated, "…. if they hold views that are totally opposed, really, fundamentally, poles apart, irreconcilable," she was pounding her fist, gently but deliberately on the arm of the bench to emphasise her point and speaking softly, to herself as much as to me, "then what hope is there that they can ever see eye to eye or ever make a go of such a relationship?"

She looked up at me at this point as if expecting an answer, then stopped me with a gesture. "No, don't try to tell me. I have to work it out for myself."

"Your grandfather and I had our disagreements and some of them did go quite deep, but never to the extent of pulling us in different directions. I think if that is the case, then there are problems."

"Do you mean in different directions in a literal sense"

"Yes. At one time – I may not have told you about this, there's no reason why I should have: at one time when he had finished his training, he had this idea he wanted to go to Africa as a missionary. I would have found it difficult to go along with that: not the Africa bit, but the missionary idea. Fortunately he did not pursue the idea and we were able to live with our differences such as they were."

"It's not a bad comparison, Gran. What Sujit wants, above all and what he feels he is cut out for, is to take this FARIS project to its extreme conclusion. If he could be the first space coloniser, that would be the achievement of his goal. That's missionary zeal in a big way, isn't it?"

I could only nod my agreement.

"And yet why – why do I feel this way about him? Why am I so totally in the grip, dominated by my feelings for him day and night? When I know there can't be a future in it?"

Nothing I could say would make it any easier for Anisha. If I told her that time would be the healer, she wouldn't believe me and if I told her to put him out of her mind she wouldn't listen.

"What about Jessica's idea; could that be so far-fetched?" I ventured.

Anisha gave a scornful laugh.

"That is just about the craziest of my darling mother's crazy ideas!"

"But worth looking a little more closely at, don't you think?"

"No way! Do you know how many million families there are in India? Even if you narrow it down to the city Sujit comes from, and if that happens to be where Jessica's lover also came from – my father – well it may not be needle in a haystack numbers but you can see that the likelihood is so minimal as to make her idea simply an illusion which became for her an obsession."

"And yet you told me yourself that your feelings for Sujit were something like 'coming home' – wasn't that the expression you used? You seem to feel something deeper than usual in your relationship to him."

"Yes, I do." She corrected herself; "I did feel that. I seemed to recognise in him something in myself, or rather what I found in him seemed to bring to life something in myself that I had not been aware of. It's hard to define."

It was time to move. As usual I had been keeping my eyes open for anyone who might be watching us and I felt we had been sitting there for long enough.

"My dear that is enough of introspection for one afternoon. You have given yourself plenty to think about."

"Thanks for listening to me Gran," Anisha put her arm around my shoulder in a hug. "Let's go in."

I could hear the phone ringing as we mounted the stairs to my second floor flat but it stopped before I could get the door unlocked. The caller had left a message: please would I call the Police station on the number given. Nervously I rang back and explained that I had just missed a call.

"Thank you for getting back to us. It's about the laptop that you reported stolen at Heathrow. We have it here."

"Are you sure? Who…?"

"You'll have to come down and identify it of course. Can you do that today?"

"Well yes, I'm sure we can. It's my grand-daughter's in fact. We'll come straight away." I was making frantic signals to an uncomprehending Anisha. "Tell me where we have to come." I made hasty notes and put the phone down.

"That's incredible!" Anisha was as amazed as I was.

In less than five minutes we were out of the house and hailing a taxi.

An hour later, having identified the laptop to the satisfaction of the officer on duty we had returned with it to the flat where we were met by Rob who Anisha had rung to tell the news.

"Well, well," he smiled. "So it wasn't FARIS agents at all?"

"We can't be sure of that. Apparently when the thief snatched the bag and darted into the lift the whole episode was seen by this chap who was already in the lift, waiting for the doors to close. The others in the lift had their backs to the door so saw nothing. When the doors opened on the ground floor and the passengers dispersed, either to the taxi rank or to the various bus and coach stops, our good Samaritan followed the thief, tackled him and got the bag off him. He then went back upstairs looking for us but, failing to find us he decided the next best thing was to hand it in to Lost Property, where it sat for the next thirty-six hours. Meanwhile, although we had alerted the police, it took that long for the Lost Property office and the Police enquiry to put two and two together and come up with the answer, namely that our laptop was safe and intact."

"Of course, we are no nearer knowing whether the attempted theft was FARIS or an opportunistic chancer." I said.

"No, and I feel sure that we must assume it was FARIS: which means they could still be a threat to Anisha." Rob replied. "But meanwhile we can have a good look at those files and..." he smiled at Anisha, "...we'll see how good your memory was!"

Chapter 32

If the next few days passed quietly enough for Anisha and
myself, it was a different matter for Rob as he studied the
FARIS files that Anisha had saved to her laptop. The one
which interested him most was the file containing the list of
investors in his company's funds whom FARIS were hoping to
win over to their project. Back in the office of Focus Asset
Management he set about combing through them in detail. In
addition to those names which had been fed to FARIS as bait,
with their consent and connivance, there were others who had
been reached by devious means that the data protection laws
had been unable to prevent. And Focus was not the only
investment company which they had tapped into: various other
names were listed, each under the name of an investment
company immediately recognisable to Rob.

As work went on around him in the usual way Rob sifted
through one file after another. Under scientists he found names
of academics, some well-known, others new to him, and
industrial scientists attached to an array of companies on the
two sides of the Atlantic. A file labelled 'Opinion-formers'
detailed a wide selection of names from the media: press, TV
journalism and social media as well as owners and sponsors of
those institutions. By the way some of them were highlighted
or asterisked Rob surmised that this was a target list in which
some might already have been enlisted already as supporters,
others not.

He moved on to yet another file with the improbable-sounding name of 'Visionaries, Poets and Philosophers'. FARIS was certainly not missing out on any aspect of intellectual activity in its quest for support, he reflected. What he saw as he opened the file made him raise his eyebrows: 'Will the human race self-destruct before we have solved the riddle of what consciousness is all about? What a pity that would be!' and below that were listed a range of luminaries with the names of their *oeuvres* and publications ranging from the poet, William Blake, the philosopher Gurjieff, the essays of Montaigne, and the works of a contemporary neuroscientist, poet and philosopher whom Rob had heard on the car radio one morning as he drove to work. The rest were just names but he noted that the list included a number of works on Eastern philosophies.

He picked another file labelled 'multi-nationals' and clicked on it. Here he found companies with names of individuals listed below each. Judging by those highlighted FARIS had done its work and signed up a score of supporters here. The next file listed NGO's, non-governmental organisations from around the world. Beneath each organisation's name came the named individuals but only a few were highlighted: one or two all the same. He moved on to International Organisations, finding much of interest here with many organisations listed. Not many were high-lighted but those that were included some recognisable public names, representing a core of support. It was this file above all the others that Rob recognised as potentially explosive.

It was time, Rob concluded, that the FARIS organisation be exposed to the broader light of day. He took out his cell-phone and scrolled down the list of contacts till he found the one he wanted, a journalist at the Financial Times.

After that things went quiet for more than a week. Anisha was fretting, naturally, wanting to get out and about and in particular to get back to her flat south of the river and be among her own possessions instead of sheltering at my apartment. She gave Rob a ring at the office, where she would dearly like to be, back in her place in the Green Team.

"Don't you think it's safe for me to come back to work now? I'm sick of being a prisoner, even though my Gran's cooking is great!" she smiled at me in reassurance. I couldn't hear Rob's reply but, from the look on her face I could see that he didn't agree with her.

"But nothing has happened to me!" She fired back at him "No-one has got in touch, or even tried to make contact. I think they have given me up as a bad job."

After listening to Rob at some length Anisha sighed with resignation. "OK, you may be right. I hear what you say."

Next day I took a pair of curtains to the dry-cleaners and a bag of laundry to leave at the laundrette. Anisha declined to come and I popped out alone reflecting that it would only take five minutes. The sun was shining after recent rain, the pavements glittered and leaves of the trees in the square garden had perked up after the recent dry period. There was a queue at the dry-cleaners and the obligatory exchange of pleasant chat with the friendly Irish proprietor who knew his customers by sight and by name – almost by the items that they brought in for his care and attention.

"Nice to see this pair back for a freshen up!" he smiled as he pulled the curtains from the bag. "It must be a couple of years since you had us give 'em the treatment!"

"When shall I call for them?" I asked.

"Give us to the end of the week, my dear," he replied. "I'll have them ready for you to hang up for the week-end."

"That will be perfect." Out of habit I stopped and chatted before realising that I should not leave Anisha alone for too long in the flat. We still kept an eye out for any suspicious loiterers. Back at the apartment she had left a note.

'Sorry Gran, I just have to (underlined) see that my flat is OK and get some things. Promise to be careful. Will take a taxi both ways. Back by T-time! Will bring cakes!'

There was not much I could do. Anisha had been without a mobile phone since her return and, seeing as how she was staying with me we had made no effort to buy one. She didn't bother with a land line at her flat. Should I go after her? It would infuriate her. I could, and did, ring Rob.

"She said she'd be back by tea time, in the note," I told him.

"What time would she mean by that? Rob asked

"Oh, four-thirty, five-ish, I think."

"Right, if she doesn't appear then, let me know."

"I will. She has her head screwed on; I'm sure she'll be alright," I said, determined to convince myself. After all, why should anything happen to Anisha now, after more than a week?

Chapter 33

A **missing person** *is a person who has disappeared and whose status as alive or dead cannot be confirmed as their location and fate is not known.* From Wikipedia the free encyclopedia

There was no sight or sound or rumour or whisper of Anisha for more than a week. How was it possible for someone to disappear into the void like that without leaving a trace? The police were less than interested.

"The young lady has every right to go off on her own. Unless you want to post a missing persons notice we don't have a reason to go looking for her," they told me when I sat in the Police Station the next day.

I had contacted Rob again when Anisha failed to return by late afternoon and agreed that was what I should do if there was no word from her but I didn't expect much else than the reply I got.

"All the same we can take details, just in case she turns up in one of the hospitals, and you could try ringing round them yourself," the officer suggested.

I had done that already, dreading to hear both that they had no record of such a person, or that they had, indeed received her, victim of some accident, into their emergency department.

Back at the apartment I sat in front of the curtainless sitting room window, peering miserably out into the darkening evening light. I supposed that my duty now was to ring her mother. I could try her Surrey number and if that was not answering I might get hold of her at her villa on that wretched Palm Tree Island. What would the time be there, I wondered, too late for a phone call? Surely, if one's daughter had gone missing no hour would be too late? All the same, it might be needless alarm – in normal circumstances Anisha was frequently out of touch for longer periods than this. But these were not normal circumstances. How to explain that to Jessica though? Or was she already aware and in the picture? Oh, it was all too much of a muddle. Surely at my age I should be exempt form such a terrible burden of worry!

I sat with my head in my hands arguing with myself, one way and then the other about what to do: to phone or not to phone? It was on the table at my side and Jessica's numbers were programmed in. I stretched out my hand, resolved, when, anticipating me, the phone rang. It was Rob.

"I've just had a call. Someone who tells me he's from FARIS. They know that the FT is looking into FARIS and they have traced the source back to me. They have Anisha and they won't let her go until I get the newshounds called off. That's what they say. I've rung you first. I will ring the paper next. I have to tell them something; I have to decide and you have a right to be consulted."

"Yes, of course I have, but...."

I tried to think straight, reflecting again that at my age it was asking a lot.

"Where have they got her? These people must be completely mad! What will they do with her?"

"If I don't agree to what they ask they are planning to take her back to FARIS HQ and keep her there. Incommunicado. They say she'll get resigned to it and that she has a boyfriend there who'll be more than pleased to see her."

The room where I was standing spun around me. I sat down abruptly.

"I don't know, Rob. Really! And now of course I see I should have contacted her mother well before now. You must give me time to think. I will call you back in an hour."

Rob agreed. "Try not to make it longer than that."

I sat for minutes, staring vacantly down from my window to the square gardens where Anisha and I had sat in recent days. The familiar figures were there, the old gentleman with the cane, the mothers and toddlers, and, parked in the street, the usual selection of cars and vans and chained up bicycles. So someone had been watching all that time and there wasn't any way to tell who it had been but, as sure as anything, the moment Anisha left the building on her own she had been followed. Or had the watcher been at her flat, waiting, waiting until at last she did turn up? Whichever way it had been carried out Anisha had effectively been kidnapped and we had no idea where she could be. Could they, even now, have spirited her away out of the country? Did they have the ability to evade officialdom and get her away? Judging from their contacts and their resources it seemed quite possible.

The kaleidoscope of figures in the square below shifted and reformed – mothers were drifting away pushing their all-weather and off-road buggies. The bag lady appeared, sat, opened a plastic-wrapped loaf of bread and started feeding slices to a couple of pigeons: Wretched woman! I exclaimed automatically to myself and soon a flock had gathered around her scrabbling and squabbling for the food.

But what if Rob were to respond to those demands? Would those in power at FARIS HQ ever keep their side of the bargain? I doubted it for Anisha knew too much about them.

The bag lady shook out the last of the crumbs from the plastic wrapper and headed off towards the gate. The pigeons took off in a flurry of grey and pink wings, to settle quickly again, finishing the feast she had left behind.

But then I reflected that they had probably seriously underestimated Anisha's resourcefulness and her determination to let no obstacle get between her and her goals. She would find it hard to be reconciled to being bartered as the price for keeping silence over the FARIS project. With these contradictory thoughts churning around in my mind I picked up the phone to speak to Rob. I found he had been thinking along the same lines.

"Anisha would not thank us for making silence the price of ransoming her," he commented firmly, "And I'm convinced there is another way to play this."

I agreed but had no idea what the other way might be.

"We need to play it the smart way and recognise we have two separate goals in our sights. The first is negotiating with FARIS the price of our silence."

"Anisha will never agree to be silenced, not for a moment," I objected. "I know my grand-daughter and even if she has to bide a long, long time, she'll never agree to let FARIS undermine the work she has chosen, or allow herself to be part of some new version of life-on-earth in the stars."

"I'm not saying that. I'm saying that we threaten them with publicity. Now we have the files from the laptop we can do that. We tell them they have a choice: either we go ahead and blow open their mad scheme, bringing a roll-call of great and good names into discredit along with them; or they let Anisha go and agree to quietly dismantle their edifice and turn it to some other ends while we keep a close eye on them. That will be the price for us to agree that the threatened publicity will not take place."

"It sounds impossibly complicated. Do you think there's any chance of success? You've so little idea of the real extent of influence and resources they can bring to bear. They could try to discredit you, not to mention ruining the firm you work for – Focus could come off really badly if that strategy fails."

"I know," Rob replied, "But at the moment it's the best I can think of. If I go to my top management and they take it to the press we put Anisha at great risk. My way, we are attempting to finesse FARIS into dispersing quietly with minimum damage."

I reluctantly agreed and gave Rob my support.

"Oh, just before you go," I added. "What about my daughter?"

"Your daughter?"

"Jessica; Anisha's mother. What do I tell her of all this?"

"As little as possible for the moment," Rob replied. "We have no idea how much she knows of all of this. It could be that she really has little idea of what Alastair is involved with. My advice is not to ring her but to wait and, if and when she rings you, say as little as possible."

With that advice I had to agree.

Chapter 34

In criminal law, **kidnapping** *is the taking away or transportation of a person against that person's will, usually to hold the person in false, a confinement without legal authority. This may be done for ransom or in furtherance of another crime, or in connection with a child custody dispute.* From Wikipedia the free encyclopedia

The moment she opened the front door of her flat the light snapped on and Anisha realised she had fallen into a trap. Hands pinioned her against the wall. Her face was muffled by a cloth which, she said later, smelled strongly of school laboratories. It was the last thing she knew until she woke up some time later.

Blinking in surprise at the row of furry animals on a shelf opposite her, with a shock of recognition Anisha realised that she was back in her old teenage bedroom, lying on the bed where someone had considerately covered her with her duvet. She struggled to her feet feeling weak and nauseous and crossed unsteadily to the door where she realised she was locked in. She rattled and hammered at it for a while then, finding that her head was too befuddled to address the questions which were struggling for her attention, she returned to the bed, flopped down and fell asleep. When she woke again it was growing dark; someone had entered the room, re-locking the door and pocketing the key. That person now pulled up a chair beside the bed, reached for the bedside light and sat down. With the light in her eyes Anisha made an effort to lift herself onto one elbow and identify the person: impossible. It was one of those angled lamps with a narrow beam which was shining straight in Anisha's face and the woman, whoever it might be, was in the shadows. Panic rose in Anisha's throat.

"Who are you? How did I get here? Where is….?" She was going to say 'Where's Mum?' but turned it for some reason to "Where's Jessica?"

"Don't worry, Anisha", came the reply in a calming voice. "You're alright; there's nothing to worry about." There was something about the voice that rang familiar but Anisha had no time to pay attention to that.

"This is Jessica's house: what am I doing here? Who are you? How did you get me here?" Then, after a pause and as the truth sank in, "I've been kidnapped, haven't I?"

The calming voice continued.

"Not kidnapped; just brought here for your own sake."

This time Anisha made herself listen more closely; she knew the voice and she made a grab for the light, turning it to see who she was talking to.

"Ah, of course! It's you, Helen! You work for FARIS – arranging adventure holidays to faraway places! And not above a bit of kidnapping in your spare time?"

"Anisha, calm down. You have not been kidnapped!" Helen repeated, "Just…."

"Let's not argue over words," Anisha retorted. "Just tell me…."

"I'm not allowed to tell you anything until…."

"Until what ….?

The door handle turned and, taking the key from her pocket Helen went to unlock it. Anisha's heart sank as a tall figure entered the room and came to stand over her. His face was in shadow so she could not see the expression but Anisha knew that she would rather have seen anyone else in this situation than her stepfather. Her *wicked stepfather* she had once called him ironically, and this time she really did fear the power that he had over her. She twisted herself into a sitting position so that her legs were over the side of the bed and her feet were on the floor. She went to stand up and face him but Alastair

Singleton would not allow it. His hands on her shoulders forced her to sit again.

"Hey!" Anisha protested." Where's....?" She stopped herself. To say, 'Mum' or 'my mother' would make her seem frightened and vulnerable.

"Where's Jessica? And why am I here? This is her house, not yours!" She was shouting at Alastair now.

"Your mother is at the villa: on the Palm Island. No need to worry about her at all." Alastair replied grimly. "Although I'm sure she would like to hear from you. We must arrange for you to send her a reassuring email – yes. Helen will you see to that?"

"She'll be furious when she knows what you've...."

"But she won't know, Anisha, and it's better that she doesn't. She takes little interest in my business affairs: in fact no interest at all. So a friendly email about your work and your social life – Helen will see to it – will be sufficient to keep her happy."

"So this really is a kidnap!"

"It's a precaution. You have caused us some trouble. I'm keeping you safe and out of the way until the trouble is resolved."

"You can't do that!" Anisha stormed at him. "And in any case I know every inch of this house and the gardens. You won't keep me locked up here!"

Alastair sighed. "You'll be staying in your room. Helen or one of the others will supervise you to the bathroom. There are two men patrolling the garden so the windows are not an option. Those men have dogs and are well-trained - the men as well as the dogs. They know what they are doing and how to guard a house."

Anisha was silenced. I like to think that at this time she gave a thought to the warnings that Rob and I had given her, but I am not one to say 'I told you so' and it was now too late for second thoughts. I am certain however that she regretted her rash action in returning to her flat, with the promise to me that she would be 'back by tea-time'.

Alastair continued. "It may only be for a couple of days Anisha, if you agree to behave: just until we can get that manager of yours off our backs. And there, I think, you can help."

And Alastair outlined briefly what he expected Anisha to do to persuade Rob to keep the press away from FARIS.

As Rob and I had anticipated, no-one was going to persuade or coerce Anisha into going along with the FARIS plans although, from what she told me later, Alastair made a determined effort at getting her to change her mind. Anisha simply dug her heels in, ground her teeth, and was deaf to every angle of persuasion which Alastair brought to bear. He told her he could advance her career, and when that cut no ice he told her he could ruin her career. It made no impression. He told her that Jessica would feel betrayed by her daughter, to which Anisha replied that the feeling would be mutual and that although she loved her mother dearly she had no illusions about the shallowness of her understanding of Alastair's business and her complete ignorance on the subject of FARIS. If Alastair had thought Anisha would be a case of 'like mother, like daughter,' and that she could be played on and useful to him, in the end he had to accept that Anisha was not the flexible kind of card he had imagined.

With exposure in the media threatening Alastair must have decided that time was not on his side. He would have liked to head back to the Palm Island villa to co-ordinate his response from there but with Jessica in residence on the island, and the need to take Anisha along, this was not an option and the only course open was to return to Shakhimardan and FARIS HQ. The Lear Jet was at Alastair's disposal but how to get Anisha, an unwilling passenger, through customs and on board?

On the second day of Anisha's captivity Helen came into her room with breakfast and a tablet computer tucked under her arm. Somewhat grimly she addressed Anisha,

"Someone wants to speak to you."

Anisha was at a loss. The only people she wanted to speak to were myself or Rob and she knew Alastair would never allow that, given her refusal to cooperate. She took the device and, opening it, found Skype in operation. Her heart missed a beat.

"I'll leave you two to talk to each other," Helen said grimly and left the room, locking the door, as always, behind her.

Sitting on the edge of the bed Anisha contemplated Sujit – not just his image but for real: Sujit who she had last seen disappearing on a stretcher as he was wheeled into a hospital's emergency department, a scene which she would rather not be thinking about. Sujit, with a bruise still showing on one side of his forehead, evidently had something he wanted to say. She took a deep breath.

"So how are you Sujit?"

He fingered the bruise.

"I'm perfectly alright. There was no need for you to do what you did, although I know now why you did it."

She had nothing to say in response. Sujit continued,

"You and I need to have a serious talk. They want to bring you back here, you know, so we'll have that opportunity quite soon."

"I'm sorry for what I did but you're obviously alright and you know I won't go with them. They know that. They can't make me."

"They are using you as a bargaining chip and they want you back here. If you refuse I can tell you their next step and the person they have their eye on."

Anisha tried to think who he could be talking about until the truth hit her. She told me how his words chilled her and her heart sank.

"Your grandmother appears to be an easy target," Sujit told her. "You don't want them to involve her too do you? She's elderly; it could be very distressing."

Anisha was shocked and I am only thankful that I knew nothing of this threat until it was in the past.

"What do you mean? What are they planning to do to my Gran?"

"Anisha, I can't tell you because I don't know. I only know that it's why we're having this conversation. This is what I've been told to tell you: either you get on the plane willingly, or they go after your grandmother."

At this point Anisha panicked. Who knows if these were empty threats, but they were enough to convince her. Her resistance crumbled and a few hours later she found herself airborne and, a good few hours after that and at least one stop on the way, going through customs in that now quite familiar airport, where a 4-wheel drive met them for the last leg of the journey.

Anisha was not privy to the discussions and negotiations that went on over the next few days. Having got her out of the way her captors kept her more or less incommunicado. But the few crumbs of information that came her way left the strong impression that discord and disagreement had broken out among the most influential of FARIS's backers. In fact there were those who absolutely refused to see their investment go to waste. Many had pledged more than their wealth and had ideological reasons for believing that this crisis was the point at which they should go to the public, confident that they would carry a large majority of opinion with them. These people really feared that, once abandoned, the cause would take decades to re-ignite, too long for their names to be associated with it and too long to see it coming to fruition. This, it appears, was the majority view. Others, a minority, disagreed. Their view was that for the time being they should go quietly but hold themselves ready to re-group later.

Anisha could feel the strain and tension, isolated as she was. Helen and the others who supervised Anisha's restricted movements were silent and brooding and left her in no doubt of how they felt about her as the cause of the crisis. Sujit, it appeared, was also under suspicion because of his friendship with Anisha, added to which there was the continuing nightmare of Grego's death and the ongoing investigation.

From what Anisha was able to deduce it was this which brought things to a head. The investigation into Grego's death two weeks before had brought the police to FARIS's door. That meant police from the two jurisdictions, from Shakhimardan, the enclave of Uzbekistan and that of surrounding Kyrghizstan. The tensions which long existed between the ethnic groups of those two countries had, for a couple of years, been quiet but could flare up at any moment and the western company located so prominently within the enclave at this time now provided a focus. Anisha remembered the disturbing moment when a belligerent crowd had surrounded the vehicle on her return to FARIS HQ. Simmering resentment by the inhabitants of the enclave about the way that the surrounding country held them to ransom over water supplies was coupled with a suspicion about Shakhimardan Exploration and the activities of Westerners, there and in Chong Kara. Together it added up to a most dangerous situation and Grego, wandering alone – and Anisha was still unsure whether she had been the cause of that - was an easy and obvious target. While no-one was arrested for his murder it was concluded that Kyrghiz activists had abducted him across the border and taken their anger out on him.

Now the Kyrghiz authorities, always on the lookout for something to distract from their own troubles, were persuaded that Uzbekistan had stolen a march and was reaping riches by exploitation of these two enclaves. A sense of injustice was on the rise. Wires began humming between the Kyrghiz capital, Bishkek and their former Russian friends and between Bishkek and the Chinese who they were courting. Nor was the line to Washington neglected since the US airbase of Manas was another card which could be played.

Anisha, knowing nothing of this, could feel the tension in the air. She saw little of her stepfather, for which she was thankful, and had little contact with Sujit but it was he who, some four days later – she had almost lost count of the time - came to talk to her.

"What's happened? Are they letting me go? Are they giving up?" she demanded.

"I can't tell you, Anisha," Sujit replied. Most of FARIS's members have no intention of giving up, as far as I can see, but the incident with Grego has turned the spotlight on us. They seem to think that Chong Kara could become a terrorist target." He looked drawn and pale.

"Do you have any idea of what you have been responsible for?" he asked her reproachfully.

Anisha was stunned into silence and then replied angrily.

"No, I certainly do not! What are you accusing me of? I have done nothing!" After a pause she added quietly, "Sujit, I thought I could trust you. I thought there was something strong between us. How could I have been so mistaken?"

288

Chapter 35

Cooperation in Managing Water as a transboundary Resource

Water is both a source of conflict and cooperation. Transboundary water management carries with it unique challenges - as competition for water intensifies within countries the resulting pressures can traverse political borders. Neighbouring countries usually have competing water users and ecosystems that depend on different water balances for proper ecological functioning.
Waterwiki.net/index.php/transboundary_waters

A week later Rob opened up his tablet edition of The Times and noted with satisfaction an article tucked into the business pages. And at roughly the same time I was picking up my copy of the paper, which had dropped into my letter box at the foot of the stairs of my apartment building. When I got back up to the apartment the phone was ringing.

"Take a look at page 24," Rob told me. "It's better than we could have hoped."

The gist of the article was to report a 'most imaginative' deal which had been done by the British mineral water company Akwa to bring about the resolution of a long-standing conflict that had been on-going over water supplies in a place which few if any Times readers had heard of. And why should they have heard of Shakhimardan? An enclave of Uzbekistan which was a mere dot on the map, somewhere in the middle of Kyrghizstan.

'Akwa is totally committed to the sustainable use of vital water supplies and to the fair access to this vital resource by rural communities who rely on it for their livelihoods. Akwa has acquired offices to set up its subsidiary in Shakhimardan and has signed an agreement with both countries, Uzbekistan and Kyrghizstan. Access to water supplies for the enclave will be our binding obligation and the supply of bottled water to an

289

increasing market in both countries will be our core business. The communities concerned and our shareholders will both be beneficiaries.'

As I read the paragraph I found it difficult to work out how this had come about and what it really represented.

"We didn't need to go to the newspapers. Instead we used those Focus investors who had agreed to act as bait – do you remember?" Rob asked me.

I did remember.

"And they were more than happy to help us put the screws onto FARIS in no uncertain way. It hasn't been easy; FARIS was never going to give in to anything less than overwhelming odds. But, thanks to Anisha we had a roll-call of so many names that we could put pressure on."

"And is that all it has taken? Undermining investor-confidence?" I found that hard to believe.

Rob hesitated.

"There may have been something else going on. I can't be sure", he paused before continuing more decisively. "But what we did has made the difference. We have spread the word that this is an organisation with seriously bad credentials. Most of those who signed up have seen the writing on the wall. They could not wait to get to the exit! FARIS has begun to crumble and we have got our result."

"That result being?" I still didn't see what exactly had been achieved.

"The result, so far, is that Shakhimardan Exploration - or FARIS HQ to us - has become corporate HQ for Akwa East Asia – 'AEA'. And AEA has agreed not just to run a bottled water plant but to handle water resources, in an 'open and accountable' manner, for those two countries."

I was still mystified. "Who are Akwa? Why have they got involved?"

"I'm sorry, "Rob apologised. "I should have remembered. You haven't heard anything about the company. Akwa run bottling companies throughout Europe. Most of the water they sell comes under local names. They happen to be a company that my ethical fund invests in and they were on Anisha's list to do a regular health check on. She visited them in Swindon at the head offices and also at their bottling plant in Spain. What is more important, and we did not know at the time, Alastair had got himself on their board. He has some interest in that industry and some knowledge of it and he got a couple of non-execs to sign up with him. They did it in a personal capacity but, if it comes out into the open the company could well be vulnerable. In short, Akwa have come on board to do this deal. Henceforward FARIS HQ becomes the head office of Akwa East Asia.

"And can they be trusted to carry that out? And how is it in the interests of those two countries?" I asked. "It seems to me they would be handing over a great deal of power and control?"

"It would appear so at first glance. But that's the deal for keeping quiet about FARIS. We know that many companies, including Akwa have been potentially compromised by that FARIS venture; the price of keeping their names out of the public sphere will be their cooperation in implementing and keeping oversight of the undertaking."

"Hmm…" I was still doubtful.

"Rivers flow across national boundaries; aquifers run beneath them. Control of water cannot be left to be dominated by any one of these. It must be truly international. Internationally monitored, controlled and accountable water supplies; that would take one cause of conflict between states out of the equation I think what we have here is a step in that direction, an instance of a system that can, with political will-power, be made to happen. And it is a prize worth having."

He was right. Anisha, I reflected, would be the first to applaud.

And the other enclave? What's it called…Chan Kara?" I asked.

"Ah indeed," Rob replied thoughtfully. "The installations at Chong Kara. What is happening to that is still not clear."

Two days later I received a call from my daughter.

"Well, my dear," I adopted my most comfortably motherly tone. "How are things with you? And where are you ringing from?"

"Back home in Surrey, darling!" she bubbled excitedly sounding, I thought, rather relieved.

"Are you tired of luxury Gulf living?" I enquired..

Not usually sensitive to nuances of tone she replied, "It's too hot for my taste at this time of year, and staying indoors to keep cool was becoming just ever so slightly boring. The swimming pool is, of course cooled,"

"Of course," I echoed her as she chattered on.

"But there's a limit to the number of times one wants to swim and even going over to the mainland becomes a chore, and most people…."

I cut her short to enquire, casually because I didn't know if I was treading on ground she knew,   "Has Anisha been out to see you recently?"

"She's used up all her holiday time. She's been working away over most of the summer. Haven't you heard from her?"

"Not recently, no."

"She sends me emails; I gather the office is keeping her pretty busy. Maybe she's got a new boyfriend. I'll give her a nudge and remind her not to neglect her Gran!"

"Thank you dear, that will be nice. I expect I'll be seeing you soon, now that you are back?"

"Well, yes, soon-ish. I'm actually going up to Scotland for a couple of weeks tomorrow. Alastair has a place, if you remember me telling you?"

"Ah yes, of course." I replied. "And will he be there too?"

"Sadly not – isn't it a shame? He's got meetings here and there for the next month at least."

After a few more exchanges of inconsequential chat Jessica promised to ring and let me know when she was back from Scotland.

I had no way of knowing whether Jessica really was in the picture as far as FARIS was concerned and therefore was covering up for her husband, or whether he had kept her pretty much in the dark with broad-brush descriptions of 'business affairs' which kept him busy flying here and there. Whichever was the case it was too early to challenge her until I was sure that Anisha was safe and would be returning soon to London.

"Take care of yourself, Mummy,' Jessica began to end the conversation but interrupted herself with a further thought. "You ought to think of taking a holiday yourself, you know. It's not good to stay the whole summer without a change of scenery."

"Thank you dear, you know I do get away – at least once a year. Don't worry about me in that respect."

"Oh well, don't leave it too long."

A thought struck me.

"Perhaps I should come out and see the two of you and your Palm Island. How would that be?"

There was a pause. I heard perhaps a note of alarm in Jessica's voice as she replied.

"Alastair's going to be terribly busy when he gets back from all those meetings and the house isn't ready to make you comfortable yet. Best to leave it until after Christmas: January or February perhaps: the weather's lovely just then."

"All right dear; it was just a thought. Now, off you go and get ready for Scotland and thank you for ringing. Give my love to Anisha when you next email to her."

I rang off, not very much the wiser on what Jessica knew or didn't know or how far she was involved with FARIS. I

293

couldn't even work out if she had genuinely heard recently from Anisha. For Anisha as far as we knew was still in Shakhimardan, at least up until the finalising of the Akwa deal. If she had been in touch with her mother, was she pretending it was from the London office? Or did Jessica know where she was and why?

I was soon to find out when she rang my doorbell two days later.

"I wanted to surprise you Gran!" Anisha exclaimed, her face drooping slightly as she registered my shock. "Let me in and let's both sit down."

"Yes indeed!" I replied faintly, I think. "You must remember that people at my age can't take shocks in the way you can."

"Sorry, sorry! Here, I'll make some tea."

"Certainly not! But do you realise that I haven't seen you since you sneaked out of here two weeks ago - against my strict instructions and Rob's?"

For the next hour Anisha brought me up to date with all that had happened from the moment of her abduction outside the front door of her block of flats in South London.

"They must have used old-fashioned chloroform or something because I hardly knew what happened until I woke up in my old bedroom."

"But they had to get you through customs; how did they persuade you to go along with them?"

I could not believe that Anisha would have gone quietly and was shocked and dismayed when she told me how they had blackmailed her.

"You did that for me, my darling!"

I was shocked and lost for words, unable to take in the pressure she had been under and how she had reacted. I let her continue.

"I found myself back in the surroundings which were becoming too familiar to me, FARIS HQ. Then nobody let on to me what was happening for several days. I could feel the tension in the air but I was kept separated for the most part from other staff. Although I ate in the refectory I was always supervised and anyway, none of the staff wanted to speak to me"

"What about Alastair? Did you see him? What did he have to say to you?"

"Alastair was angry and very threatening. Mainly he was angry with himself, for having mistaken where my interests lay. Also I think with Mum, for not telling him: poor Mum!"

"Your mother would have wanted simply to impress him by having a daughter in a City investment firm. She wouldn't have wanted to spoil the story by telling him you were in the Green Team. That would have been 'batting for the opposition' in Alastair's eyes."

"To be fair, I don't believe that Mum understood, or understands even now, what FARIS was all about," Anisha replied in an unusual show of loyalty to her mother. "Anyway he was angry with me because I had helped myself to all those files which I put on my laptop and took back to London."

"Of course! That is what threatened to give the whole FARIS show away," I reminded her. "And led in fact to your being abducted and taken back. Did they tell you what their plans were for you?"

"At first Alastair told me that I would be staying indefinitely. He assured me that FARIS would not be blown off track and that I could either join and work with them, or spend the rest of my days in a life of luxurious confinement. In fact I really don't think he had thought it through further than the next months or year at the most. Sujit was there but we were not allowed to see each other for long and in any case he was blaming me for what was happening. Then, as the days passed the atmosphere seemed to be getting more tense and confused until, once again I was put on a plane and told I was coming home. And I still am totally in the dark about what has actually been worked out and why I'm here."

I was, in spite of my hazy understanding of it, able to give Anisha an account of the agreement that Rob had told me about, by which FARIS would quietly disperse and much of its funds would go into the AEA, or Akwa East Asia, deal.

"That's so surprising!" Anisha exclaimed. "You know how I began to be fascinated by water companies, water systems, the whole question of water."

"In fact this result is not something you have worked on or in any way brought about by your efforts, but I do think that unwittingly you have been the pivot around which it has all come together."

"Nonsense Gran! You're exaggerating!" was Anisha's response. "But it has given me a hell of a lot to think about."

Chapter 36

Street Markets

Greater London is home to a wealth of covered, outdoor and street markets. Many specialise in a particular type of goods or sell different things on different days. Most open very early in the morning and close early or late afternoon. From Wikipedia the free encyclopedia

They walked together, Sujit and Anisha, through Borough Market, not far from Anisha's flat in Southwark. The area buzzed with life with stall-holders displaying wares from every part of the globe.

Sujit had flown to London, his world turned upside down by the dispersal of FARIS and determined to confront Anisha again about the part she had played. Anisha found him depressed and diminished by the turn of events. She felt obliged to justify herself for what she had done, to explain herself and the way she had betrayed him in order to make her escape from Shakhimardan. He walked beside her, oblivious of the noise and colour that surrounded them and listened in silence. She got no response.

"FARIS was your world," Anisha admitted quietly. "I do know that: your vocation, even. What will you do now?"

The heady and intense days of their early romance seemed a long time ago, and both were shaken, shocked, by the realisation that their fierce sexual attraction was entirely at odds with their opposing but equally passionately held outlooks on life. The tension between the opposing forces was unsustainable and had cracked, back there on the mountainside, when Anisha made the move and, in effect betrayed Sujit, in order to make her escape.

But now, strolling between the market stalls, picking and choosing from the expensively-priced exotic fruit and

297

vegetables, they found they could at least hold hands, in surprising companionship.

Anisha gestured around her and tugged at her listless companion's arm.

"Look at this! Don't you find it exciting?" she asked urgently. "This is real life, buzzing and teeming. How can it ever be taken to another planet? How can this ever be replicated?"

"Replicating is not what it is about," Sujit replied darkly. "This is exceptional, untypical of most of the world. Why would we want to replicate the squalor, the dirt, the poverty? That's just what we don't want to replicate! The FARIS vision was to take only the best."

"And what sort of a world would you create with only the best?" Anisha demanded. "If you leave behind the muddle and confusion to create a brave new world where everything is gleaming and sanitised, what room would there be for creativity? You eliminate the resources that produce anything new. I think your new world would wither and die in a short space of time."

"We can only agree to disagree." Sujit responded. This world is on the route to self-destruction. You don't need me to repeat the evidence: FARIS was the bid to take action before it is too late."

Anisha sighed. "You are a glass-half-empty person while I represent the glass-half-full," she said. "You want to cut and run and start somewhere else. I want to hang on in and shore things up."

They had stopped in front of a stall selling mangoes and other tropical fruit.

"We'll have some of these and then some spices. I'm cooking Indian for us and you can tell me how well I do it."

Back at the flat Anisha placed the mangoes in a fruit bowl and tipped the spices into their jars: haldi, dhaniya, jeera and chakra phool into jars she had labelled turmeric, coriander, cumin and star anise. She loved the names and she especially loved the small, exquisitely-shaped star anise.

"So is this something you would miss in your brave new world?" she asked as she chopped garlic and onions and stirred spices into the contents of the pan.

"Of course I would miss it!" Sujit replied. "But you have to be prepared to make sacrifices. We can't take everything. But," he went on after a pause, "With digital resources we can take a heck of a lot more than the Pilgrim Fathers were able to take to their New World. We can take everything that has ever been published. And that includes recipes too, don't forget! We would be able to take the entire digital culture of this world. Think about that!"

"I do," Anisha replied, "I do; and I wonder what you could do with it? I mean, could you ever create the richness, the inventiveness, the creativity of our present world?"

"Ah, but would you want to when you could create something so very different?" Sujit replied.

And all the while as they ate, in Anisha's mind was the question how did she want the evening to end? An affectionate embrace and an agreement to keep in touch? Or would they sleep together, here again, back in the place where they had first made love? She leant across the table to touch Sujit's hand and stroked it thoughtfully then withdrew as she registered the same old electrical reaction and their eyes met.

"And would you miss this too?" she asked seriously.

They had moved to the bedroom.

"Hey, what have we here?" Anisha asked, discovering a thin chain around Sujit's neck, which she was sure he had not worn before. She fished it out from beneath his shirt. "The FARIS symbol, on a chain!" she exclaimed. "I thought every FARIS brooch and pendant had been collected in? That the

299

whole image was consigned to history, gold brooches to be melted down and re-fashioned! How come you kept one?"

"I managed it, somehow. I'd like you to have it. Will you keep it?"

"Do you really think you could trust me? After all, I betrayed you once already."

"This time I don't have much to lose. I'm willing to give it a try."

They spent the night together and, Anisha told me, it was as good as it always had been, but this time underlain by the knowledge that they knew they were going to part. As they ate breakfast the next morning Anisha confessed, "You know, I feel so comfortable with you and as if I had known you for ages – almost as if I had grown up with you."

"Like 'family'?" Sujit asked smiling. "Are you thinking of your slightly crazy mother's notion that we might be related?"

"I think of that, among other things, when I'm wondering why I feel so good with you," Anisha admitted.

"Why don't you find out?" Sujit asked. "While I'm in America you could get a DNA test done. I'll leave you a sample of something – what would you like? A toe-nail clipping? A snippet of my hair?" He teased her.

"I might just do that," Anisha replied. "I'll go for some of the hair off your chest – a nice curl. I'll get the scissors right now!"

It turned into a tussle which ended with Anisha folding a curl of hair from Sujit's chest into a tissue and sealing it carefully in an envelope. Sujit was happy to let her do it.

"What's this about going to America? Anisha asked when the task was completed. "Have you got a plan?"

"I need to get my CV in order and present myself with the right FARIS-free credentials but I should have a good chance of a crack at NASA or, failing that the European Space Agency."

"You are determined to stay in the space industry then?"

"Of course!" Sujit replied and, struggling to express himself he continued, "I,
I may, just may have been trying to rush things by joining the FARIS movement, but one day I know it is going to happen. Man – and woman of course – will go out and set up home on new worlds."

Anisha watched his face.

"Unfortunately I won't be one of them but I know it will happen. Even though we cannot hurry it, I still want to be part of the making of this history."

"That's fair enough," Anisha replied, "And I'll carry on trying to improve life on earth for the rest of us who want to remain here."

Later that day the two of them carried out the difficult task they had set themselves of visiting Gregory's parents at their home in Hertfordshire. They found them still desolate from the loss of their son, photographs of whom stood on the table of the room where they sat, and unable to understand how or why he had been taken from them. Answers to the parents' questions about the organisation that Gregory had gone off to work for were unsatisfactory. Offers of compensation were rejected as offensive and insulting. They were determined to get to the bottom of it but were at a loss to know where to begin. They had been told officially that records would not be made public and that, for some reason, they came under the thirty year rule.

"And we may not live to see the records released," Grego's father admitted.

Anisha, convinced that FARIS was best left buried and never heard of again nonetheless felt deeply for the grieving parents.

"I feel sure that more will become known about FARIS, but it will take a lot of determination to make that happen." Anisha agreed. "I suppose some good has come of the affair, at least to that part of the world. You heard that the company taking over is to manage water supplies, under internationally agreed supervision?"

"We did hear that."

"It could lead to the setting up of a new agency, like the FAO and the ILO, for water management globally. Right now to the people of that region it means a lot – it will really affect their ability to make a living and live in peace with their neighbours."

"I'm sure that is a good thing," Gregory's mother nodded, her eyes fixed on the photograph of their smiling son. "It is just so very far removed from us, and nothing that can ever compensate for losing our son, our Gregory."

Anisha and Sujit walked to the tube station in silence, deeply affected by the grief of that house.

"It was senseless, what happened to Grego," Anisha spoke at last. "It was an accident, or at least an incident that happened accidentally but happened in a part of the world and under the responsibility of a project which cannot be made known. And because of that those parents are never going to find peace of mind. Unless, of course, they find some way of pursuing the truth."

"And how responsible should we, as individuals, feel for what happened to Gregory?" Sujit added. "Is that what you are asking yourself?"

"Yes," Anisha responded sombrely. "And I'm not at all sure. In some ways I feel as if I've got off very lightly."

Sujit looked at her enquiringly and she continued by way of explanation.

"Looking back, a lot of what I did was acting on impulse. I plan to be a lot more careful in future."

"And does that also have some significance where we are concerned? Do I take it that you will not give way to the impulse to jump on a plane to the USA any time soon?" He was more than half serious. Anisha thought carefully before replying.

"If you were to issue an invitation, and if I were to accept, it would have to be planned in advance and not the response to some spur-of-the-moment impulse."

Sujit smiled and took her hand.

"Let's wait and see, shall we?"

They both spoke the thought together, then, surprised by themselves, found themselves laughing quietly and walked on.

Chapter 37

Genealogical DNA test

A genealogical DNA test looks at a person's genetic code at specific locations. Results give information about genealogy or personal ancestry. Generally, these tests compare the results of an individual to others from the same lineage or to current and historic ethnic groups.
From Wikipedia, the free encyclopedia

Sujit left for America and Anisha rang me to ask if she could come round for a chat.

"Come for supper, dear," I urged her. "And stay the night if you feel like it."

She was round in half an hour and, tucking her feet under her on the sofa, remarked gratefully, "Thanks, Gran, you are a star – always there when I need you!"

"But I won't always be; you know that," I reminded her, "So make the most of me while you can!"

"I hope you'll be here for a long time," she told me, adding seriously, "You listen to me, you take me seriously and you give me wise counsel."

"Thank you, dear. I try to do just that, but my counsel may not always be very up to date. And when I don't have any sensible advice – well I just keep quiet and leave you to make up your own mind."

Anisha smiled at this adding "When I have to make up my mind quickly I don't always stop to think too hard. I suppose I just follow my heart. That's why some people call me impetuous; but I'm going to change all that."

I was not sure how successful she would be at that, but not wanting to discourage her I simply said, "But you have a good heart, and that is fundamentally important. Judgement is something that grows with experience but I trust you and I trust your judgement."

Over the course of the evening, as we ate supper and talked well into the night, Anisha filled the gaps in the story of the last few weeks. And I was able to complete the picture for her by recounting how Rob had worked on her behalf. The following day we took the train together to visit Jessica, back from Scotland. On the way we speculated on how much my daughter was aware of the activities of FARIS.

"Darlings!" Jessica exclaimed in joy. "Fantastic to see you. I've been so excited ever since you phoned."

She embraced me warmly. "Mummy darling, it's been such ages since you were here. When are you coming to stay on Palm Island? Alastair says he's dying to show it off to you and you can come any time."

She chattered on in an ecstasy of excitement and anticipation

"We'll take you to the desert, and to the polo matches! Anisha, you just loved that didn't you? Alastair has had to sell some of his ponies. I'm not sure what happened there, and the boat might have to go too," she looked worried. "I'm not sure how we will manage without it, but the water taxis are quite reliable."

Anisha and I were feeling our way as we probed for snippets of information.

"So Alastair's business has suffered a bit recently?" I suggested? "Have you any idea how much?"

"Oh I keep well out of the business side of things. Alastair likes to get on with it by himself. I'm sure it will be fine. There are always ups and downs in business, aren't there? What do they call it? The business cycle or something? I'm sure this is just part of the business cycle. Swings and roundabouts, don't you think?"

I nodded.

"I expect so" Anisha replied. "He's a clever man. I'm sure everything will be fine. And if not," she added, "Well, you've always got the house here!"

Jessica nodded doubtfully. "I was thinking of putting it on the market...."

"Oh Mum, don't do it! You know we talked about it before. I'm very fond of this house and one day you might need it!"

"Well, in fact Alastair said last night on the phone that he thinks I should hang on to it for a bit. Anyway," she smiled happily, "That will save me a lot of trouble with estate agents, won't it?" then she turned to address Anisha seriously. "What about that boy-friend of yours now? I hope you've moved on from him?"

"He's gone to America, "she replied.

"Well that's a good thing, I must say." Jessica's relief was quite plain to see. "A delightful boy, but not suitable for you. No need to talk about that now, seeing that he's out of the way."

Anisha bit her lip. "You had some crazy idea, Mum, about how we might be related. With absolutely no base for the notion! I think you just took it into your head and let it become an obsession!"

Jessica looked obstinate. "If I do get ideas from time to time I don't always know where they come from. But I can't dismiss them! But since he's out of your life we don't need to discuss it anymore."

Anisha made no comment, either to confirm or deny to her mother that Sujit was out of her life.

"Since you raised the parentage issue, Mum, I want to take it further. I've lived long enough without knowing who my father is and I've decided to find out."

"Oh, you'll never manage to do that!" Jessica retorted crossly. "Don't imagine I haven't thought about it many, many times."

"If you don't mind me saying, Mum, you don't know how to go about it," Anisha told her.

"Oh, and I suppose you do know, is that right, Miss Oh-so-clever?" Jessica returned sarcastically.

I thought it was time to intervene. "If Anisha thinks she can kind find some kind of lead, don't you think we should let her try?" I suggested.

"Not if she's going to throw up a perfectly good job in the City to do it," was Jessica's reply.

"I'm not going to do that." Anisha assured her, "But in my spare time I will do what I can from London and then, who knows, I may take a trip and visit India. You know I love travelling."

Jessica still looked doubtful so Anisha pushed home her message. "Actually, Mum, there's not much you can do about it. I'm determined and I won't let anyone's objections get in the way."

Jessica shrugged her shoulders helplessly. "Well darling if you really must; let's not quarrel over a small thing like that!"

At this Anisha and I exchanged incredulous glances – I really did despair of my air-headed and inconsequential daughter. It would indeed be interesting to find out who Anisha's father was, if only to find out where his daughter got her own good sense from.

After a pleasant tea Jessica drove us to the train station. At Waterloo Station Anisha and I parted, she to make her way to Southwark and I took the underground and was soon letting myself into my apartment.

I sat in the square garden the next day, watching the usual kaleidoscope of people coming and going, children playing, the bag lady feeding the birds, office workers stretched on the grass eating lunch-time sandwiches in the warm sunshine. Jessica was a puzzle; it seemed as if she had had no knowledge of the FARIS project beyond their pretty badge, receptions and glamorous events like polo matches. How could anyone be so unaware of what was going on around her and what her husband's affairs consisted of? How could she be content to live in such blissful ignorance? And how could she have brought such a clever and switched-on daughter into the world? But then, what had got into her head to take so violently against the boyfriend that Anisha brought to visit? I sighed inwardly and shook my head. Some people just seemed content to live their lives unconscious of what was going on around them

The sun had slipped behind some trees and my seat was in shadow. I would soon have to move, but it was peaceful now that the office workers had gone back to their desks and most of the Mums had loaded their toddlers into buggies and left for home. The square garden was unusually quiet for a week-day. In the hush my senses were freed to catch the scent of the flowers from the lime trees in bloom. As I sat back to enjoy the moment a flock of pigeons swooped over head in tight formation, swooped and, altogether as if by telepathy, turned and stooped in downwards flight before, changing direction, they soared up again, the sunlight catching their wings as they switched from right to left, from low to high. The sound of their wings reached me like a sigh and, several seconds after they had vanished from sight my head was fanned by the down-draft create by those synchronous wings. What telepathy was at work there?

EPILOGUE

The air in the palm gardens trembled with the heat of noon. The Arif had finished his rounds, moving the tiny dams to divert the rivulet of water from one garden to another as the timetable of allotted hours dictated for each plot of land. The water was running slowly. The small frogs which lived on the edges of the falaj in and out of the water's edge were breeding less copiously. The palm trees on the fringes of the village were ragged and brown under the stressful conditions. The Arif sighed, consulted his watch and prepared for two hours of sleep before his next round was due. The upright stick which he had used to check that his watch was keeping good time had fallen into disuse. Systems of sun, moon and stars were forgotten as quartz and atomic time-keeping rendered them redundant: why keep a dog and bark yourself? Why strain your eyes to look at the stars when you can glance down at the illuminated dial of a quartz watch, keeping atomic time.

In the 14th floor boardroom of Al Zuwaidi enterprises the air was pleasantly cool. The group of board members was standing by the plate glass window looking out towards the sea, which today was choppy with a wind blowing white tips off the waves. For the most part they were dressed in the white robes of the Gulf States, overlaid with a finely spun loose black coat, braided with gold around the edges. Their head-dresses were variations on the theme of the Arab turban and at their waist many wore the traditional silver *khunja* or ceremonial dagger. Alastair Singleton stood in their midst, the only suited figure in the group. The atmosphere was cordial.

"Gentlemen! Let us sit to start the business." They took their seats around the carved and gleaming table and the hum of conversation subsided. The chairman, whose eagle eyes

309

glittered like those of a desert bird surveying its territory for prey, swept around the table with a look which commanded attention. All eyes were on him, expectantly.

"Gentlemen! My friends; and…" he turned to address the Englishman, "and especially my friend Mr Alastair. In recent weeks we have seen much turmoil." No one stirred. "Some members of this board had put their trust and their funds into a venture which others - myself included – felt was ill-advised, implausible and unconvincing. The ramifications of this enterprise extended into boardrooms and committees across the globe, and were intended to subvert many of those international organisations which our states have signed up to and support." One or two of the figures around the table shifted uneasily in their seats.

The Chairman continued. "Certain members of our group, absent today, were involved to a significant extent. Others to a lesser extent and some of us avoided the project – a project which was never, I repeat, was *never* sanctioned by Al Zuwaidi Enterprises." He glared around the room as if daring anyone to challenge him on this score before continuing. "If hints of its existence had reached the public ears it would have 'gone viral', as they say, in less time than it takes for me to address these words to you. We know all too well the speed and power of social networks and the word would have been round the world quicker than it takes a hawk to dive on its prey, or a flock of starlings in their thousands to fill the sky, flinging their message in all directions as if possessed of one single brain."

His listeners struggled to take in this flow of rhetoric but felt the force of his warning.

"What could have been a major international scandal has, I am glad to say, been averted and the misguided enterprise has been quietly dismantled without reaching the front pages of the press or the invisible virtual airwaves. Nothing more will be heard of FARIS!"

At the uttering of the word a frisson of shock reverberated around the room.

"After today that name will not be spoken: either here or in any other place. I hope that is understood."

A murmur of assent and nods of agreement travelled around the table and the chairman sat back in his seat, apparently satisfied. After some moments of reflective silence he leaned forward again, grasping the gilded arm-rests of his chair. Now he was all smiles and cordiality.

"Mr Alastair Singleton! With that business all firmly behind us, we welcome you back to Al Zuwaidi Enterprises to discuss the future, the bright future, of Akwa, this addition to our family of businesses."

Alastair acknowledged the welcome with a smile and received the nods and smiles from the rest of the table with evident pleasure. The Chairman continued. "We have heard of your success in a part of East Asia where we have, as yet, little business and I and my colleagues here, would like to learn more about it."

"Thank you indeed for your warm welcome," Alastair responded smoothly. "And it's a pleasure for me on behalf of Pure Spring Akwa – or Akwa, as it is known in the United Kingdom - to let you into the secret of our success in the 'Stan' countries, Uzbekistan, Kyrghizstan and others, where we have recently made an excellent start. We are establishing bottling factories catering to the growing demand for bottled water. We have been given the task of managing water supplies and distribution in an area where water is a matter of potential conflict among the various neighbouring states and small enclaves which exist within them."

The members of the board listened with polite interest.

Alastair continued, "As someone who has always supported the role of intergovernmental agencies in the resolution of conflict and the improvement of access by rural populations to all the means which will improve their livelihoods and, as is

311

eminently the case with access to water supplies, to their health and well-being…" He paused and glanced down, as if trying to remember a script. Hesitating a moment more he consulted a page of neat notes on the table in front of him. He gulped, like someone swallowing an unpalatable morsel, before continuing.

"….As someone who has always supported the rolling out of international law I am very happy that our efforts in those new areas of Akwa's endeavours may, indeed I feel sure, will lead to the establishment of an international organisation for water just as one exists for food and Agriculture, for World Health and so forth. That would be reward indeed."

Appreciative comments were heard from his listeners and especially from the Chair.

"Mr Chairman, our plans on paper for the Gulf water bottling plant, which you commissioned last time I was here, are ready for your inspection. Perhaps after the formal part of the meeting you will allow me to present them?"

"Certainly. I have reserved the first part of the afternoon for exactly that," responded the Chairman.

"Meanwhile," Alastair continued, "We at Akwa need to know the current state of the application for extraction of water from the pure springs that run under your desert states."

"Of course, that is indeed the key to the success, indeed to the first beginning of the enterprise," the Chairman acknowledged.

"To put it bluntly, Sir, and I know that some opposition has been voiced. Can I take away with me today your assurance that extraction of underground spring water will have permission to go ahead – here and in the neighbouring states?"

The occupants of the table looked expectantly to their Chairman.

"Such opposition as exists has not been well-informed. The requirement to modernise is overwhelming. Desalinated water is the future of agriculture as well as of our urban populations. Groundwater supplies will feed the demand for pure mineral water and the word from our leading Councils is that, yes indeed, you can have our assurance that your bottling plant will receive all necessary authorisation and support and the future of the industry is assured."

Satisfaction, but no sign of relief crossed Alastair Singleton's face. He packed up his papers, patting them into a neat pile and slotting them into his briefcase, before standing up, straightening his tie and striding towards the next room and the awaiting buffet lunch.

Acknowledgements
The author gratefully acknowledges permission from the following to quote from their websites:-

Water Footprint Network, from their glossary, for 'Blue water footprint' and 'sustainability criteria'. Chapter 4.
http://www.waterfootprint.org/

Cambridge University Press: Cambridge Advanced Learner's Dictionary & Thesaurus for 'aquifer' (Chapter 5) and 'the great and the good - UK – definition' (Chapter 32)

Time Outdoors (www.timeoutdoors.com) for 'Extreme Charity Challenges' (Chapter 14)

OCA Magazine and Discovery Central Asia for descriptions of Kyrgyzstan and the Fergana Valley (Chapter 14 and 16)
http://www.discovery-central-asia.com

Dennis O'Neil, Professor of Anthropology, Palomar College, San Marcos, CA 92069 for 'What is Culture?'
http://anthro.palomar.edu/culture/culture_1.htm (Chapter 21)

The UN Millennium Development Goals are quoted from the United Nations Millennium Declaration. (Chapter 25)

'Intotheblue.co.uk' for 'Off Roading 4x4 Driving' (Chapter 29)

Yale Books, Yale University Press, for 'The London Square' (Chapter 30)

All other webquotes are from Wikipedia, the free encyclopedia, with just one from Waterwiki.

www.ingramcontent.com/pod-product-compliance
Lightning Source LLC
Chambersburg PA
CBHW022135170626
46807CB00005B/1954